ALSO BY MICKEY SPILLANE

I, the Jury

Vengeance Is Mine

My Gun Is Quick

One Lonely Night

The Long Wait

The Big Kill

Kiss Me, Deadly

The Deep

The Girl Hunters

The Snake

Day of the Guns

Bloody Sunrise

The Twisted Thing

The By-Pass Control

The Delta Factor

The Body Lovers

Survival . . . Zero!

The Erection Set

The Last Cop Out

The Day the Sea Rolled Back

The Ship That Never Was

Tomorrow I Die

The Killing Man

Black Alley

SOMETHING'S DOWN THERE

A Novel

MICKEY SPILLANE

POCKET **STAR** BOOKS

NEW YORK   LONDON   TORONTO   SYDNEY

This book is a work of fiction. Names, characters, places and incidents
are products of the author's imagination or are used fictitiously. Any
resemblance to actual events or locales or persons living or dead is
entirely coincidental.

 A Pocket Star Book published by
POCKET BOOKS, a division of Simon & Schuster, Inc.
1230 Avenue of the Americas, New York, NY 10020

Copyright © 2003 by Mickey Spillane

Originally published in hardcover in 2003 by Simon & Schuster, Inc.

ISBN: 0-7434-7891-6

First Pocket Books printing November 2004

10 9 8 7 6 5 4 3 2 1

POCKET STAR BOOKS and colophon are registered
trademarks of Simon & Schuster, Inc.

Cover design by Tony Greco

Manufactured in the United States of America

For information regarding special discounts for bulk purchases,
please contact Simon & Schuster Special Sales at
1-800-456-6798 or business@simonandschuster.com.

To my daughter,
Caroline,
a real product of the beach

SOMETHING'S
DOWN
THERE

Chapter One

It was hot, the way it gets in the Gulf Stream during mid-July. Since sunup, Hooker had been stretched out in the ancient canvas deck chair, letting the sun bake him even darker, enjoying the strange feeling that the intense solar radiation was squeezing out all the aches and pains he had ever had in his life.

For the past hour he had been going through his ritual of forgetting, letting the present take hold. It was another nice day, almost too hot for people. Every so often the birds would circle overhead and squawk, but they didn't dive, so he knew there were no baitfish surfacing yet.

He was totally awake, even though his eyes were closed, and he could sense Billy Bright looking at him. Old Billy was one of the few real Caribs left around the islands, and even though his skin was a bare two shades darker than Hooker's, white men were white men and damn well were supposed to stay that way, and when nature turned them toward his color something was very funny indeed.

Hooker felt a grin pull at his mouth and let his

eyes come open. For a second they met Billy's, then the Carib jerked his head away. Self-consciously he straightened the captain's hat his new boss had given him and lifted the lid on the bait box to check the dozen blue runners swimming around inside.

"When you going to catch me a fish, Billy?"

Not looking up, Billy said, "We do not catch the fish, Mr. Hooker sar, the fish, she catch us."

"Better be soon, then," Hooker told him. "We got nothing on the table tonight."

Billy let the cover slam down and turned around, a puzzled scowl on his face. "Mr. Hooker, sar, in my life, many men I have taken to the fish. Some want them for the excitement, some want them for the wall, some want them for the money. But you want them for the stomach."

"I like fish."

"All the time?"

Hooker nodded. "Know anything better?"

"Perhaps the wife . . ."

"I like women too, but not when I'm fishing."

For a moment Billy looked thoughtful, then he said, "On the other side of Peolle Island, sar . . . a very pretty lady, she lives there. Once I worked for her and . . ."

"Come on, don't line me up any dolls. Catch me a fish."

Idly, Billy Bright looked up at the sky. "It will not be too long, sar."

The breeze freshened then and the beat-up old forty-footer rolled gently. Hooker grinned and reached for another beer, wiped the ice off the sides, then dropped it in the Styrofoam cup and popped the top. Yeah, it was another nice day. He was the owner of a boat he had paid cash for, two thousand gallons of high octane in a buried storage tank on shore, and now he could enjoy his retirement.

Back on the mainland they could go scratch themselves, except everybody hated each other too much to bother. Good luck to them all. Hooker had retired and had gone fishing. He had never fished for a living before and he had never expected to do it now, but by golly, here he was.

The reel only made a few fast clicks, but Billy looked over quickly. So did Hooker. In a few weeks he had learned what the sound could mean. There was a heavy drag on the eighty-pound test line and anything that could move it had to be big. Hooker got up slowly and pulled the rod out of the socket, getting ready to set the hook when the time came.

Once again the line ran out, but Hooker didn't move. "It's playing with me, Billy."

"They do that, sar."

"How deep is the planer?"

"Fifty, maybe sixty feet down."

Hooker nodded and reset the drag a fraction. "Hand me my beer, will ya?"

Billy reached for the can just as the fish hit. The initial strike was hard and Hooker set the hook in without waiting for any further action. Billy was about to tell him he was nothing but a hell-to-gone dumb mainlander even if he was a white man and his boss to boot, then he saw the line tighten and run and kept his mouth shut, because even hell-to-gone dumb mainlanders can get lucky once in a while.

Hooker read the expression on Billy's face. "He's on there, buddy. I can feel his mouth lapping right over the bait. That baby is on there right up to his nostrils."

With a shrug, Billy stepped back and watched his new friend handle the line. He has lost weight, he thought. There was little fat left and it was easy to see that he was a powerful man. In a short time the sun had made him almost black until he took his shorts off, but while his skin had turned darker, his hair had bleached almost white. Even his eyebrows and the hair on his arms were an odd yellow color. For a moment he wondered why it didn't happen to him that way, losing himself in an age-old problem of genetics, then he saw that Hooker was winning the fight against their supper and he picked up the gaff to drag it aboard.

Hooker staggered and almost fell on his tail. He said, "Damn!" and winched in his line furiously.

"You didn't loose he, sar," Billy said.

"He sure went someplace," Hooker said. "I hope you like eating blue runners for supper."

"They are not so bad, sar." He grinned at his friend, watching him closely as the leader cleared the water.

"Damn," Hooker said again. On the end of the line, the blue runner bait still sticking out of its mouth, was only the head of what would have been a fifty-pound wahoo.

"Mr. Shark got you, sar. He like to eat your fish supper too."

"That baby I'd like to eat."

Billy shook his head. "He be too big, sar. Look down," he pointed, "see, thar he go and what a big mister he is."

It looked more like a shadow than a real thing, but there was no mistaking what it was. For a moment it circled out of sight, then came back and rose slowly until the full length was visible, turning on its side so the enormous black eye seemed to be looking straight into Hooker's.

"I'd like to catch that sucker," he said.

"But why for, sar? Mr. Shark, he must eat too."

"Not my fish, Billy."

"There is still plenty for all of us. Tonight I take the head of your fish and make a fine stew."

"You must be kidding!"

Billy's face looked hurt. "My cooking is no good for you?"

"Hey . . . your cooking's great. You hear me yell about it yet?"

"Then you will like my stew."

"Billy . . ."

"What, sar?"

"Take out the eyes first, okay?"

"Sar . . . that is the best part."

"Do it for me, please?" Hooker asked.

"For you, sar," Billy told him reluctantly.

It was a good deckside supper, he had to admit, even if Billy wouldn't let him look in the old chipped enamel pot. He wiped up the last of the gravy with the sourdough bread and wondered if the crazy Carib had really taken the eyes out of the wahoo head or not. When he thought about it again it hardly bothered him at all. When he first got to the islands he'd no more eat out of a native pot when he saw what they were cooking than dive into a septic tank. Now he could handle almost anything. Except the eyes. Somehow that just plain got him. Eyes were not for eating.

Billy took his plate and handed him a fresh beer just as the raucous blare of a carrier wave erupted over the radio speaker. The talk came on fast, a rapid staccato of garbled tones that sounded like nothing more than human static. Hooker knew what it was even if he couldn't understand. It was some islander, probably in a frenzy offshore because he ran out of gas. He looked at his watch. It was an hour and a half from dark.

Superstition alley, Hooker thought. No way you were going to get a native to be out on the sea after sundown, no way at all. Two hours ago Billy had turned the *Clamdip* on a heading toward Peolle; they were only forty-five minutes out now and Billy was happy. Tonight he wouldn't get "et" by the thing that "et" boats.

The radio ceased for a moment and Hooker asked, "Who was it, Billy?"

"Peter-from-the-market, sar."

An odd tone was in Billy's voice. The subtle expression on his face was plain. His mouth was drawn tight and inwardly he was thinking about other boats and people dying in them and a terrifying eater in the ocean.

"Trouble?"

"His boat, the *Soucan*, has just been hit."

Hooker stood up quickly. "Where is he?"

Billy pointed to the northwest. "Twelve miles . . . there."

"How bad is he?"

"He is taking water fast, sar."

"What hit him?"

"Something came up from the bottom, Peter said."

"Billy, he's in over four thousand feet of water out there . . . no reefs, no nothing!"

"Something hit him, sar. He thinks his bottom has been bitten out."

"Billy, damn it . . ."

But the Carib had turned around and pushed the throttles forward. His face was a subtle mask of concern for his friend out there, yet touched by the anxiety of time itself. Billy didn't own a watch, but he could compute hours and minutes nearly to the seconds themselves, and now he was hoping they could make contact with the *Soucan* and get out of the area before the darkness owned the ocean.

Hooker could only shrug and get the binoculars out of the locker. For all he cared they could stay out here all night and he'd see what he could drag up on a deep line, but Billy would be a raving lunatic by sunup, so he'd just have to play by local rules. It really didn't matter anyway. There was nothing else to do.

Billy spotted the dot on the horizon before he did and said, "There's the *Soucan,* Mr. Hooker, sar."

Following his direction, Hooker zeroed in on the boat. It was another one of the oldies, a Matthews made back in the thirties. Probably about thirty-five feet, he figured. It was listing badly to port, its bow headed for home and a thin tendril of smoke from one exhaust tube showing that it still had some power.

Even as he watched, the *Soucan* seemed to lurch and the exhaust smoke stopped. A figure came out of the cabin, waved in their direction, then disappeared back into the wheelhouse again. Once more the radio blared on and the staccato rattle lasted for a full minute.

Billy half turned and said, "He is going down, sar. All power lost."

"How long has he got?"

"Ten minutes, sar. There is a mattress stuffed in the hole, but it will not last."

"We going to make it?"

"Yes, we will make it, sar."

Hooker grinned and glanced up at the sky. "But we'll never make it back before dark, will we?"

Billy Bright wanted to hate his boss man right then. He wanted to hate him very hard for that easy way he had when death could be only moments away. He wanted to hate him for not respecting the strange wild things that lived in the vast waters of the world, for not fearing them at all. But he really couldn't hate him because Hooker was a good man. On the mainland he could have been a tough man, for the scars he carried showed he had met others in the deadly way and won because he was here. Yet he was good. An islander could tell if he was not good, and he was not so very bad.

"We will not make it back before dark," Billy said.

"You scared of getting 'et'?"

"I do not look forward to it," Billy said, hoping Hooker would change the subject.

"What's going to eat a boat, Billy?"

"Something 'et' five, sar. Peter will be the number six."

Hooker could see the *Soucan* plainly now and put the glasses away. "He probably blew an engine rod right through his bottom."

"Peter would have said."

"Would he know?"

Billy nodded. "He is an engine builder. Not good, but he makes them go. He said something hit him. It bit a hole in his bottom."

They closed in on the old Matthews, throttled back and headed into the breeze. The boat was going down fast, keeling far over on its port side. A tall, skinny native with a chubby kid beside him was braced against the rail that was nearly awash, and when the *Clamdip* edged in they both jumped; Hooker took them in over the rails, one in each arm, and deposited them on the deck. Almost formally, Peter-from-the-market bowed, shook Hooker's hand and went to stand beside Billy.

Very slowly, the *Clamdip* circled the *Soucan* until

they were looking at the bottom. Something inside the sinking boat made a loud, screeching noise, ripping at wood and metal, then the hulk turned completely over and exposed her barnacled underside for three long seconds before dropping into the total oblivion of the gulf, almost as if it were being sucked down a giant straw.

Hooker had seen it.

He wished he hadn't seen it at all.

There, sure as the sun sets, was a big hunk taken out of the bottom of the boat, and where it looked like it was regurgitating steel springs and cotton out of its maw, Peter had jammed the mattress. But it wasn't the mess of garbage that was sliding into the water that made the impact on Hooker.

It was those beautifully regular six-inch sawtooth marks on the top break of the wood that were clearly visible in those few instants that made Hooker feel as though a cold wind had just blown down on him from some northern ice field.

Quickly, he turned to see if any of the others had spotted it, but their eyes were studying the setting sun and the distant horizon. Under his breath Hooker muttered his disbelief, then opened another beer. He looked at the chart and saw that they were coming into the two-thousand-foot level.

It could have been his imagination, he thought, or the way old, water-soaked boards broke off around their supports. He tried to reconstruct his short visual sighting but found the image getting obscure. He took a sip of the cold beer and shook his head.

Man, he was getting as creepy as these crazy islanders.

Luckily, Hooker got the old tires over the side before Billy hit the dock. Usually, he was pretty adept at sliding the *Clamdip* into its berth, but this time he came in too fast, the reverse didn't engage quickly enough in the ancient gearbox and when it did the boat was all out of position. The old hull slammed into the pilings with one hell of a jolt that could have been disastrous if the Firestone fenders hadn't cushioned the shock.

Hooker saw it coming, sat on the beer box to keep it from spilling and let everything else go to pot. Tomorrow Billy would see what kind of mess he had made and would clean up without a word, the way he made everybody else do who pulled something stupid.

Crazy, he thought. Everybody was afraid of getting "et," as they said here. He looked at the boats on each side of the *Clamdip* and finished the rest of the beer. They were all rotted hulks, held together with driftwood and rusty nails. Some of them sunk right there at their moorings in calm weather and sometimes they just plain came apart out at sea like a woolen sweater in a washing machine. And these people thought because they lost *six* of them there was something out there eating them up.

He threw the can in the trash box and reached for a fresh one.

Those damn tooth marks in the *Soucan* were still there in his mind like a bad dream.

The first half hour on the beach was a solemn

time. There was the loss of a boat and a near loss of a friend, but most solemn of all was the story that had to be told, retold and embellished with every telling. The fifth time around, the solemnity was gone and the excitement had crept in, and if Hooker hadn't made inroads into the cold beer, he would have sworn it was all a dull dream.

Somebody poked at the driftwood fire and it flared up enough to show the anxiety on the faces of the listeners. They looked like wooden statues.

Before, it had been bad enough. The eater had come always at night, and by simply sailing during the daylight hours they could be sure of safety. Now all that had changed. The hunger of the thing had forced it to select a meal in broad daylight.

Under questioning, Peter-from-the-market gave his answers as honestly as he could, being deliberate about every word. They were on the way home, the day fair, the sea calm. There was no activity at all to indicate that the eater was there below. Yes, the birds were squealing and dipping overhead but that was because the *Soucan* had a good catch of fish and the boy was emptying the dead bait in the wake of the boat.

There had been little warning at all, no ruffling of the sea's surface, no sound like the others had heard during the night attacks, a strange, foul smell, then that one powerful grab at the bottom, making the *Soucan* heel violently, and the eater was gone. One quick look below told him he had been badly holed; he dragged a mattress on deck, tied a line to the rail and the other end to the mattress, and got it under the stern and pulled it into position to cover the gaping rent in the bottom. At first it stymied the water's onslaught, but the bedding was too old and began fraying, spitting its entrails into the hull. Peter tied the other end of the line to the opposite rail, then stood in the stern with his son. All he could do was radio for help and hope somebody would hear. Luckily, the *Clamdip* was not too far off.

Hooker squashed the empty can in his hand and tossed it into the fire, then got up off his haunches and nodded for Billy to follow him. He was getting that edgy feeling again, the kind he had known for too many years in the past when something was happening and all you knew about it was the bits and pieces. No doubt about it, there were six local boats down in the area, all sunk in the last few months. There was no insurance scam involved because nobody could afford it anyway, and there wasn't one islander about to scuttle his only means of livelihood.

"What is it you wish to ask me, sar?"

"I think you know, Billy."

He felt, rather than saw, Billy shrug.

"Why didn't you tell me what everybody else seems to know about those sinkings?"

"They were 'et,' sar. There is an eater in the sea . . ."

"Come off it, Billy."

"On the mainland, the white men call it the Bermuda Triangle," Billy finally said. "They say there are many, many more ships than our poor six."

They had reached the glow of the kerosene lamps hanging from the porch roof of their cottage and Hooker stopped and looked at his friend. "Let me tell you something, buddy. That ocean out there is a very busy place with traffic going by day and night and in good weather or bad, so you're going to get a lot more accidents than you would in some inland lake. You understand that?"

Billy looked skeptical, but he nodded.

"A few unexplained things have happened, all right, then some story-hungry reporter came up with that Bermuda Triangle deal and it was good enough to start all kinds of yarns going. You think we believe it?"

"Your papers and the radio . . ."

"Baloney. You see all that ship traffic out there? You see the planes go overhead? You think Esso and Shell and all the banana boats and thousands of sports fishermen are going to risk their hulls if that story was real?"

This time Billy frowned uncertainly. His boss did make sense, for sure, for real sure. Even now he could see the lights of five ships on the horizon, not one of them worried at all about the eater. But his mind went back to his first question. "You were going to ask me something, sar."

"Yeah. Why didn't you tell me about the sound your friends heard when their boats were hit?"

"You would not have been to believe."

"Why?"

"Because it was the breathing they hear. It

breathed on them and the smell was foul with rotten-
ness like the dead fish on the shore from the red
tide."

"Everybody heard this?"

Billy shook his head slowly. "There were four who
did." He paused and his face went tight. "My friends
Poca and Lule both . . . saw it."

"What did 'it' look like?"

Again, he shook his head. "It was . . . just a darkness. A very big darkness. Much darker than the
night. It made the stars wink out."

Sure, Hooker thought, there's always got to be
some romancing of the unexplainable and nothing
could beat foul breathing and big darkness. But six
hulls were gone, two people were missing and he
had seen that toothlike rent in the bottom of the
Soucan.

Damn it, there had to be a *why*. He said, "Come
on inside, Billy. Let's get out the maps."

Two hours later Hooker had studied every detail of
Peolle and Ara, the island to their north, his attention
riveted on everything Billy told him. There was not
one cove or inlet, not even a hill or rock outcropping
Billy wasn't intimately familiar with, and now he
rolled up the charts and stuffed them back into their
plastic tubes.

"What was it we were looking for, Mr. Hooker,
sar."

"You know what sabotage is, Billy?"

"I know."

"If any of those boat captains could have known

something . . . even something they weren't aware of . . . and someone wanted them eliminated . . ."

"Sar," Billy broke in, "we have thought of that. No pirate ships have ever made this their landing. There is no buried treasure. Even now, every summer the students from Miami come with their funny machines to search for metal. They find beer cans, an old wrench, maybe, but no treasure."

"You know, friend, you're one hell of a lot smarter than I gave you credit for."

"I still will not sail at night."

"How about daytimes?"

"That I must do, sar. Starving is not my pleasure." A faint smile touched his weathered face. "And there was no sabotage, sar."

Hooker grinned back and nodded. "Saboteurs don't put on an act with breathing and big black shapes, do they?"

"Never."

"You really believe that stuff, Billy?"

Seriously, he said, "My friends said it, therefore I do believe it, sar."

"Uh-huh." Hooker looked at his watch. It was almost midnight. "How about doing me a favor, Billy."

With a big grin making his teeth flash in the lamplight, Billy said happily, "Yes, sar. Anything you ask, sar."

"Quit calling me sar, will you?"

For a moment, Billy studied his boss. White mainlanders' ways were very perplexing, he thought. "Mr. Hooker, sa . . . Mr. Hooker, I . . ."

"And forget the Mr. too. We're friends."

"That would not be polite. And I do not know your front name."

Hooker felt the laugh rumble out of him. "Believe it or not, my front name is Mako."

"But . . . that is the name for Mr. Shark, the wild one the boats from Miami come to catch . . ."

"Billy, it was my mother's last name before she got married and she liked it so much she gave it to me up front, like you say. Here it can belong to Mr. Shark, but in the old country it was a plain old Irish name. So take your pick . . . Hooker or Mako, just don't . . ."

Billy held up his hand. "I know, call you late to eat."

"Sharp, kiddo."

"Sure. Now I sleep."

Hooker nodded and went to the radio. All of the clocks on the island were hand-wound, and if you didn't set yours with a time hack from Miami every night, you'd never know what the hour was. Not that it mattered much. He flipped the switch, waited a moment, then dialed to his frequency. When he got the time he set his watch ahead eight minutes, then went through his ritual of turning the channel selector just to see what was happening on the night traffic.

When he hit the emergency channel he felt the icy-cold chill of sudden dread blow down his back again, because the voice he was listening to was cool and professional, but so quietly urgent he knew it was happening again. The *Arico Queen* was giving its position at fourteen miles off Peolle Island and was going down fast. Something had reached up out of the sea with a terrible vengeance and shook the ship like a dog does a bone, ripping the bottom right out of it. The crew was taking to the boats and the operator was signing off.

On the ship-to-ship channel he caught the interchange between the nearest vessels. Both would be at the site within thirty minutes. The United States Coast Guard ship *Ponteroy* was an hour away, heading toward the scene at flank speed.

Hooker closed the set down and went outside and stared toward the darkness of the ocean. The waters were so calm he could hear no surf sounds at all. The rescue should be routine, he thought. For a change nature was on the side of the stricken.

Momentarily, he wondered what it would be like sitting out there in a small boat, knowing that you weren't really alone at all, that you were just on top and underneath you was a vast wildness . . . and something was down there.

He didn't realize he was holding his breath and let it hiss out between his clenched teeth. He was getting more like Billy every day. Almost silently he whispered something unintelligible again, and shook his head.

Chapter Two

From the bridge of the converted minesweeper, Chana Sterling scanned the shoreline of Ara Island through the 7 X 35 sporting binoculars. She panned down the dockside with its rickety slips until she came to the southern end where the *Tellig* would moor.

It was the deepwater area, the only place a ship drawing eight-plus feet could tie up, and even though the Company had a ninety-nine-year lease on the spot, it wasn't unusual for the islanders to stick some old hulk in there just to get it out of the way. The last two times they had worked in this section they had had to drag out sunken ketches before they could berth.

"All clear for a change," she said.

At the wheel, Lee Colbert squinted across the water and nodded. The sun had cracked his lips again and he fished in his pocket for the tube of Chap Stick and wetted them down. Many months on the ocean had tanned him deeply, but an exposure after a week away tinged him with a new, subtle redness, a color that shadowed well on his taut frame. The past three days he hadn't said much to anyone, not that his long silences were unusual, but this was one trip he never had expected to take. The Company had promised him retirement the end of last month, then Monroe had come down with pneumonia, this damn trip had come up and the Company exercised their recall clause in his contract, and here he was back in the Caribbean instead of on his new farm in Vermont.

"Take another look at the channel," he said. "They had one wild blow here two weeks ago."

Once again, Chana searched the deep water marked out by the buoys, following the cut all the way to dockside. "Nothing sticking out this time." She leaned over and checked the depth recorder. There was thirty feet under them and it would diminish to twelve feet at low tide when they were at the dock. Eight years ago the Company had blasted this entry out of the solid coral and hoped the Ara natives would think enough of it to keep it clear, but to them it was just another sign of mainland intrusion and they used the cut as a dumping ground for anything that could sink.

Colbert eased the *Tellig* into the channel and brought her against the pier so gently that the pelican on the piling didn't even stir. Chana was first off, fastening the bowline around the iron cleat, then going to the stern to help the crew off-load some of the equipment.

This time it wasn't much. Their assignment was to make an information contact with the *Sentilla* and complete an undercover search-and-report analysis of the latest missing boats and ships in the sector IV area. The strange stories that the islanders were telling about the destruction of the vessels in that area had been a bonus for the media when everything had gone quiet on the political scene. Everything that had ever happened in the Devil's Triangle had been rehashed, two TV networks had flown camera ships over the area and one taped a wild account from a survivor of a charter boat.

Ordinarily, little would have been done about the situation, but the president of a cruise ship line and the captains of some of the longer-ranging charter boats out of Miami had feared a sudden loss of revenue and made their feelings known in political circles where it counted, and Washington began to move in its usual mysterious ways.

For the past three months the government scientific research ship *Sentilla* had been doing an intricate study of the ocean bottom for reasons not disclosed, but it would be natural for another ship to be sent in to make contact and resupply her; the *Tellig* drew the assignment.

What nobody realized, however, was that the *Tellig* was only camouflage for the highly sophisticated scientific machinery on the *Sentilla*, run by a bunch of Ph.D.'s equipped to do maritime detection work of almost any nature.

When everything was secure, Colbert left Joe and Billy Haines in charge of the ship and joined Chana on the pier. He took the pipe out of his mouth and pointed it toward the shoreline. "Berger gets fatter every year. Look at him."

They watched a rotund middle-aged man scan the boats from the safety of the pier.

"He doesn't have to pass any physicals," Chana said. "They told me he looked like that when they recruited him." She waved and the fat man waved back. "I wonder why he doesn't come down to meet us?"

Colbert grinned and shook his head. "He gets seasick, that's why. No way he's going to come down those steps to dockside. Let's go get a drink."

Charlie Berger greeted them with a handshake and his famous smile. As hot as it was, he wore a seersucker suit and a stained necktie because he thought it made him look like Sydney Greenstreet in *Casablanca*. "Hope you had a good trip," he said.

"No trouble," Chana told him, "the usual dull journey."

Berger glanced toward the horizon and gave a small shudder. "You heard about the *Arico Queen*?"

Chana nodded. "The *Ponteroy* had just reached them. They picked up all hands out of the lifeboats. Anything new on it?"

"Nothing came in here. They'll probably interrogate them in Miami and we'll read all about it in the papers. That flash the radio operator put out about something grabbing them from the bottom had to be a lot of garbage. They were in water five thousand feet deep."

"Something sunk them," Colbert said sourly.

"Sure," Berger admitted, "but it was more likely

something that blew up in their hold. The *Queen* has been making regular trips down to all those hot spots in South America, and if they were carrying munitions that went off suddenly, that could be your answer."

"You know something the Company doesn't?" Chana asked.

Berger felt a sudden chill and wiped the sweat from his face. The crazy tide of politics had squeezed a lot of the lifeblood out of the Company, but it still was a powerful force that could be felt anywhere in the world. And Chana was his immediate superior. "I guess I've been in the tropics too damned long," he said. "I'm getting the Sydney Greenstreet feeling again." He grimaced at the thought and harrumphed the way the actor did when he played in *The Maltese Falcon* with Humphrey Bogart. It was a damn good imitation, he thought.

They turned into the ramshackle building that had BAR painted over the porch and went inside to unexpected coolness. The concrete slab floor was kept constantly wet from a ten-foot length of half-inch well pipe drilled every two inches or so, and an ocean-fresh breeze blew right across it.

"Didn't anybody ever hear of water conservation?" Chana asked Berger.

"They don't need it here," he added. "That's artesian water. Been flowing from the ground since the island was formed, I guess." He led them to a table that had to be his personal spot, considering the size of the chair in the corner. It was evidently handmade, being oversize and extra well braced. He grinned when he lowered himself into it and relaxed with satisfaction. "A man needs a few small comforts," he said. A wave of his hand brought the bartender over with a pitcher of cold beer and three glasses, and when they were filled he toasted their arrival and said, "Now, where do we begin?"

Chana reached into her pocketbook and took out her compact, laying it beside her glass. It didn't look like a miniature recorder at all.

"Nice equipment," Berger said. "How long does it run?"

"An hour fifteen minutes."

"Won't take nearly that long," Berger told her. "You want to ask questions or for me to just tell it?"

"Since we have all your initial reports, suppose you just update them and then we can do the question bit."

"Sure, but I wish I knew what to tell you. One thing is certain . . . those boats were sunk. Ain't no way these islanders would do that to themselves or anybody else either. Trouble is, the stories we get are ridiculous. Each one gets worse than the last one."

"How?"

Berger spread his hands and shrugged. "Well, these people are . . . islanders, you know? They believe in a lot of funny things and when it comes to superstition ain't nobody got them beat. So whatever one says or thinks he sees, then the next one's got to double it, and believe me, don't try to change their mind none or say they're lying. Do that and you're out, and I do mean out."

Chana nodded, frowning. "Is there any common point in their stories?"

"Yeah. Something is trying to eat them. Doing a damn good job too."

"That's nonsense and you know it."

"But they don't know it. The thing has been seen . . ."

"Your report said 'not actually.'"

"True," Berger agreed. "It was something there in the night. It was seen against the stars. It breathed and smelled bad."

"Could that be imagination?"

Berger finished his beer and refilled his glass from the pitcher. "Absolutely. I've seen them imagine a lot worse. Thing is, you can't tell. Put them on a polygraph and there wouldn't be a single indication of them lying. What they tell you they absolutely believe in."

"What do you think about it, Charlie?"

After a moment's pause, Berger looked at her seriously. "I'm only contracted to work at a local level, Chana."

"Fine, we'll regard it as educated guessing. You've been here nearly twenty years, so your opinions could mean something."

"Okay," he said. He took out a section of map from his pocket and spread it out on the table.

"Where's the rest of it?" Colbert asked.

"This is all we need." He had circled an area to the east of Ara and Peolle Islands and tapped it with his forefinger. "What we're interested in is here, not the whole supposed Triangle. Now a few accidents have happened recently outside this area, but they were fully explained. All the crazies are right in here."

"What do the numbers mean?" Chana asked him.

"Those indicate the order they were sunk. Notice that there's no set pattern except that the early ones weren't too far off the islands. Then one goes out a hundred miles, the next eighty miles south, then in close, south again, then a hundred fifty miles north, then right up to the *Arico Queen*, who went down a hundred ten miles due east of here."

Chana turned the map around and studied it, then passed it to Colbert. When he finished he looked across the table and said, "What's it mean to you, Charlie?"

"Well," Berger said deliberately, "whatever's getting them doesn't stand still. It goes looking."

"Nonsense," Chana almost hissed. Then she stopped and looked at Colbert. The captain's face had the same expression Berger's had, as though they were talking about something they couldn't quite believe but had no choice because the evidence was right there in front of them.

With a laugh, Chana broke the tension. "All right, enough jokes. Let's just drop the monster theory and zero in on other possibilities. What have you got that's political, Charlie?"

"Only what I hear from the fishermen. They make observations, never conclusions."

"That's our job anyway," Chana told him.

"Uh-huh. Well, they got a lot of Cubans out there on the water."

"There have always been a lot of Cubans out there."

"I know. Number five on the map there was a Cubie and he got it just like the others and was just as shook up as they were too."

"That isn't political."

"No, well, the way another Cubie boat got in and took the two survivors off the rescue craft before they could reach shore could be. The trawler that went down was low in the water as if they had a full hold, but one of the boats that had seen them headed south said they couldn't have had fish aboard because their nets were just junk, all rotted and kind of hanging there, the same as they was the last time he saw them a month before."

"What are you thinking, Charlie?"

"They don't import narcotics into South America. They do import guns."

"So they had a cargo of Russian armament on board. If that was the case the Company will have a record of it."

Colbert let out a noncommittal grunt and said, "Maybe that's why she sunk. The Company likes to let the Cubies know they're being watched."

"Possibly," Berger said. He sipped at his beer again, then put the glass down and leaned forward. "Does the Company know about the three mines that drifted up on the south end of Scara Island?"

Chana and Colbert looked at each other. This was something they weren't briefed on, so the Company didn't have any knowledge of it at all. "When did this happen?"

Berger shrugged. "I can't pinpoint it, but they appeared at different times, maybe four weeks between each sighting, and are still there."

"Why didn't you report this?" Chana demanded.

"Because I just heard of it yesterday. Scara isn't much of an island . . . no water, little vegetation, some trees . . . nobody lives there and the only reason the mines were spotted was because the boats pick up a few sea turtles in the area."

"Did they know what they were?"

"Sure. They saw plenty of them during the war."

"They should have said something!"

"What for? Those mines weren't going to damage anything. Whatever grounds itself on Scara stays there. It's a collect-all around here. The existing currents seem to bring all kinds of crap to that place. What I'm getting at is an old rumor about a ship that went down out there about 1942. Supposedly, a couple of the old hard-hat divers went down on her but there was nothing to salvage. The rumor says the deck was loaded with crated mines."

Colbert tapped the table impatiently, a new look of concern on his face. "That wasn't a rumor. That was the *Alberta*. She took a torpedo in the bow, tried to beach on one of the islands but couldn't make it and went down in three hundred feet of water."

"How would you know that?" Chana asked him.

"I was on a ship back then too, young lady. On a U.S. destroyer."

Chana felt her face redden and she had to compose herself. "Make your point, Charlie."

This time Berger didn't address her. He looked directly at Colbert and said, "Could time and natural deterioration finally eat out the metal holding those mines down?"

Colbert frowned, his mouth tight. "There would be one hell of a coral formation around them."

"Those mines had quite a positive flotation, Captain. That constant strain could conceivably crack the coral."

"No," Colbert finally said. "The flotation just isn't that great. The coral would be too much for it."

"Supposing it was given a little help from outside?"

"What are you getting to?" Chana asked him.

"The *Sentilla* has been making seismographic recordings of the area where that ship . . . the *Alberta* was supposed to have gone down. They touch off two-hundred-pound charges of high explosives in various areas and record the echoes that bounce off the bottom."

Chana saw what Berger was hinting at and said, "Damn!"

Colbert needed more convincing. "They don't use explosives now. It's all done electronically."

"Their equipment went out and they didn't want to interrupt their schedule while the repairs were being made and went back to the old method for two days."

"Well?" Chana asked.

Colbert nodded. "It could happen."

"Oh boy," Chana said, "the year of the mines. Let's hope they all wind up on Scara."

"It could be that they didn't," Berger said. He looked at Colbert again and wiped the sweat off his brow. "I'm no explosives expert, but I picked up something in a technical journal a long time ago that said the United States was making mines with a built-in attrition. After a certain period of time the explosive would have no force to damage. You know about that?"

Colbert nodded. "I heard it, not that I believed it, though. It sounded like propaganda to me."

"Not necessarily," Berger argued. "After a war no one wants live mines floating around, not the winners, not the losers, so it could make sense."

"So," Chana added, "these loose mines, now still active, but at low power, could be responsible for wiping out those boats. No big blast, just a nice low thud, enough to take them down."

Berger bobbed his head. "Something like that."

"You sure do get political, all right. If that theory ever proved out everything would get dropped in Uncle Sam's lap with a roar heard 'round the world. Look, all we have right now are three things tentatively identified as mines on the shore of a barren island. Let's keep it that way until we see what it's all about. To date, the official position is that these sinkings are a remarkable coincidence." Chana knew that the skepticism showed in her voice, but she went on doggedly. "As far as anybody is concerned, we are independent shipping resupplying the *Sentilla*."

"Good luck, lady. You're going to need it." Berger's eyes were laughing at her.

"Why?"

"Because in a couple of days another ship will be laying off here ready to get in on all the action they can." Berger grinned then and added, "It's a motion picture company. They're doing a movie on the Devil's Triangle with a sea monster angle."

"We have nothing to do with them," Chana snapped. "This is a fairly innocuous mission that hasn't even been discussed publicly."

Berger let out a deep-throated rumble again and said, "A Hollywood publicity crew doesn't wait for public discussions. They make up what they want. They can smell out details like our brunch here. They can put two and two together."

"Nothing's been said about our mission," Chana reminded him.

Berger twisted his lips into a sardonic smile. "You're going to provide great background for them. They've already got shots of the *Ponteroy* picking up the crew of the *Arico Queen*. Give them half a chance and they'll put all the bits and pieces together, and even if they don't fit they'll make something up that does."

"The Company know about this?"

"Right," Berger said. "They called me an hour before you docked. The admonition given was to keep a very, repeat very, low profile and don't let any official position rear its ugly head in this case. Or else."

The way Berger said it made Chana's skin crawl. She knew how the Company could work under special conditions. "Or else?" She made it sound unconcerned.

"Yeah. The Company scares me sometimes, the way they think ahead so damn far. They've had a man over on Peolle for a couple months already."

"What!"

"Ever hear of a guy named Hooker? Mako Hooker? He's one of their big heavies. Took out those two Russian rascals right in the subway station in New York. We were still in the Cold War then."

"Hooker's retired," Chana said quietly.

"I thought in his department you had to get killed to get retired."

"Sorry, but I'm not familiar with his department."

Berger watched her skeptically. "Well, he's retired right next door, only twelve miles away. He bought into a damn good boat with a native captain who knows these waters like the back of his hand, and the way he cruises in it he's going to be as familiar with it himself before long."

"Hooker retired," Chana insisted. "State practically forced the issue."

Berger snorted and went back to his old island-gruff manner. "State is a bunch of dummies. Fat-assed, pantywaist slobs who can only mess things up. If they let the Company handle it we'd never be jammed the way we are now. Damn jerks." His eyes raised and caught hers in an unguarded moment. "I didn't know you knew Hooker."

"We met," she said.

Her tone was convincing enough and it was only Colbert who saw the tautness in her hand that was lying on the table.

The tip of an orange-red sun was hovering on the edge of the horizon, taking a last look at the sea for the day. It was another calm time, the water's surface rolling gently under soft two-foot swells. A large school of menhaden suddenly blackened an area the size of a football field, made it roll and sparkle in the fading sunlight, then disappeared as suddenly as they came. A loose group of birds cruised behind them, disinterested because their feeding was complete and they were racing toward home grounds. Their flight course was exact and unwavering.

When the first bird uttered a raucous, piercing scream the small flight twisted and split up in sudden terror, evading the area where the menhaden had been only a second before. The birds were not hatchlings. They had made these flights hundreds of times and instinctively recognized the workings of a nature they were a part of.

But apparently they were seeing something too foreign to be natural. It was not something they could even identify and be sure of, but it meant danger, the presence of a predator. It was only a dark thing, huge and deadly, and it was lurking, that they could sense. They were around it in seconds, then regrouped again on their course line home. A moment later they had no memory of the incident, but on subsequent flights instinct would trigger them into circumnavigating that particular area.

For a moment the shadow became substance, rippling the water with the tip of its forward parts. It had direction and motion, heading south-southeast fast enough to just barely make the water bubble. Then, as though it had seen or smelled enough to satisfy it, the shadow left the surface and dropped deeper and deeper until it was no longer visible from above.

It was likely that Joe Turkey was the oldest man on either Peolle or Ara. At least none of the natives doubted it. He knew the history of everyone and everything as far as anyone's memory could reach. Some said he could remember as far back as the Great White Fleet, the United States Navy ships that had made the famous world tour at the turn of the century.

But Old Joe Turkey was not a man who stayed on the beach. Twice weekly he put to sea alone in his hand-built sailing dory, made sure the forty-year-old two-cylinder Johnson outboard would start, then shut it down and hoisted his single sail. The antique outboard motor was really not for general use. It was Joe's sign of prestige, like his friend Lula's electric washing machine in a house that had no power hookup. But it was there also because Joe was a careful man.

This night they sat around him at the fire to hear the story told again. It had been a good day, a very good day, and he was two hours away from his island with enough fish to make many weeks happy. Oh, there had been some boats missing and the stories had started, but Joe knew the ways of the people and had only nodded at the accounts without putting any belief in them at all. Twice, he himself had been nearly wrecked by migrating whales and some years ago something had torn the rudder right off the steel pins on the transom. On the night in question he had taken a big swig of beer from the last bottle in the ice chest and had set back with his arm around the tiller bar, watching the night close in. Ahead of him he could see the little yellow dots of light as the lamps were lit in the houses on Peolle.

He must have dozed. It had been a good day and a tiring one and he was old. But the tide was right and the wind was behind him and he knew any change of condition would awaken him. And he was right about that. He came awake with a start, his nose sniffing the air, suddenly alert because now there was no wind at all and he was sitting there behind a sail that hung totally limp in absolutely still air. Even the water seemed dead, with not enough swell to make the boat rock. The tidal drift had turned him sideways, still taking him toward Peolle, but so slowly it was hardly noticeable.

Still, there was nothing to worry about, was there? He could still see the lights of the island; the stars overhead were bright sparkles in a dense black sky and surely the wind had to start blowing again. Or, at the very least, he could always start his engine and be able to tell everyone how it took him safely home from such a great distance offshore.

So he lay back and watched the stars. He could smell the sea too. Whenever the wind stopped, the water gave off its heat and smelled different, as if the smells were coming from the very bottom, where it guarded all its secrets. Here and there he picked up the odor of a dead fish, its flotation bladder keeping it on the surface.

One by one, he picked out his favorite constellations, always amazed at their absolute steadiness in the universe. A faint rank odor made his nose twitch, a pungent fish smell like the red tide brings, but even that was not a new thing to him, so he went back to watching the stars again and felt the dory bob gently. Good, he thought, the wind must be picking up. But he looked at the sail and frowned. It was still limp, the silk streamer at the tip of the mast lying against it, unmoving.

The dory bobbed again and that smell seemed to be coming from the port side. Then Joe Turkey looked up and saw that his favorite star cluster that lay low on the horizon wasn't there anymore. Oh, it was there, but he just couldn't see it. Something was in the way, something blacker than black that was shielding the stars, and even while he looked it rose still further to blot out another segment of the night sky, and whatever it was began to breathe the horrible death smell down on him. All Joe Turkey could do was push the Johnson off its chock and try to get the cord wrapped around the flywheel—with hands that fumbled until sheer habit got everything set and he yanked the starter rope with all the strength he had. The Johnson spit, coughed and snapped into life and old Joe swung the dory toward Peolle and never even looked back until the self-contained gas tank went dry a quarter mile offshore.

But by then the wind had picked up and he

docked, unloaded his fish and knew he had a story to end all stories on the island. Later, he would embellish it, but right now it was pretty good just as it was.

The islanders sat up close to Joe Turkey. Not only did they not want to miss any of his words, but his tone of voice, his inflections were as descriptive as his narration. No one spoke, not even a slight movement interrupted the moment.

Behind them Berger and Colbert were listening intently, their expressions bland. Only Chana showed any emotion at all, her face reflecting what she thought of native beliefs and their acceptance of strange stories.

Charlie Berger squashed his cigar butt out under his heel and glanced over at Chana. "Now that's a firsthand account. What do you think?"

She tried to repress a smile. "Well, they haven't got television." She watched the small group, each one now adding something he had heard, seen or suspected, and they reminded her of when she was a child, listening to the stories someone told her on rainy days.

"You're wrong," Colbert told her abruptly.

"What?"

"Five years ago I would have turned you in for a retraining program, girl. Everything is showing in your face now. Quit that stupid simpering. Those are people there, maybe not as educated as you are, but they have their own ways and own knowledge that lets them survive in places that would wipe you out."

Chana felt the fury eat her up and her mouth went

dry. Colbert's status was at least equal to hers and there was no way she could take him down for being so insufferable. But she knew he was right and said, "You don't believe this bull, do you?"

"Why not?"

Deliberately, she took a deep breath, waited a moment until her composure was back and said, "Keep it on a scientific level, Col . . . sea monsters are figments of the imagination. Nothing, repeat nothing, eats boats."

"What sinks them, then?" He was taunting her and she knew it, but she had to answer.

"There is a reason. There has to be a reason."

"They get hit from the bottom in water nearly a mile deep, there is eyewitness evidence of something, so I guess there damn well has to be a reason, all right." Colbert took his pouch out, refilled his pipe and lit it. "You have any answers?"

"I'm not guessing."

"Then speculate."

"Balls," she said.

"Well, at least you're beginning to sound like a sailor."

Charlie Berger let out a muffled laugh and said, "Welcome back to the islands. It's gonna do you good to get away from the political scene and live where the monsters do."

"Listen, Charlie . . ."

"Oh, come on, young lady, take a little kidding. You can't be serious every minute of your life."

"The hell she can't," Colbert muttered.

The fat man gave them one of his best Sydney Greenstreet smiles. "Oh, really?"

"Yeah, really," Chana told him nastily. She didn't like being the only woman caught between two overbearing males.

"Then let's go have a beer," Berger said. "You can get serious again. Your friend Hooker came over an hour ago and you guys can have a reunion."

Chapter Three

Hooker wondered why the hell he had bothered to take a bath. He was sweaty all over again and even though they had cleaned the boat out he still could smell something fishy. My shoes, he thought, damn canvas shoes always smell like fish.

"Hey, Alley . . ."

The bartender looked around.

"Fill me up, okay?"

A full stein slid down the bar at him and stopped right in his palm.

"Why do you always have to show off?"

"Because you're the only one who appreciates it."

"Hell, nobody does that anymore."

"I do, buddy. A guy just got to exploit his talents, small as they are. By the way, is it true your front name is Mako?" He smiled. "Billy was on the horn before. You know how they pass info around this place. So?"

"Yeah, that's my front name. Damn, you're as much native as they are."

"Ten years here, man. Beats being a New York fireman. Pension check every month, most of it in the bank."

"How about the rest?"

"Man, you don't catch the scam around here, do you?"

"Buddy, I'm not interested."

"Baloney. All that sweet money is going into the project on Corin Island. You know what I got?"

"Tell me."

"A down payment on a dockside saloon," he said. "Not a lounge, but a good old-fashioned pirate-style saloon the tourists expect to see in the Caribbean."

"You sure there's going to be tourists there at all?"

"Man, don't you ever read nothin'? That Midnight Cruise company's already got eleven shore points working for 'em. They're even putting down golf courses for the people who get tired of shuffleboard. They're playing it smart too, keeping 'em small and cozy. A guy like me with just one operation can get soaking rich in no time."

"What about liquor laws?"

"You kiddin'? Midnight Cruise own those island stops and if they're on the mainland you can bet they own the local constabulary too. Hell, you ought to know about those things."

"How would I know that?"

"I got a boat, broads and a clientele who likes to rent both items. Good money, I pay my taxes and when I feel like it I can partake of my own damn good fortune, like a boat ride with a beautiful blonde."

"What a way to live."

"Don't con me, old shark man. You got that pension check coming in too."

"Who says, pal?"

"It figures," Alley told him. "You busted loose from the big town, you got a spot and you damn well grin all the time. Now . . . if you're still doing that next year this time, I know I got you tagged. Am I right?"

"My friend, you are absolutely right," Hooker told him. "Now get me another beer and bring it to me like it was New York."

This time Alley came down with an iced stein in his hand. He set it down and flipped the foam from his fingers and leaned on the bar. "Can I ask you something?"

"Sure."

"I saw you with your shirt off. How'd you get the scars?"

"We had some wars, remember?"

"Yeah, buddy, I remember, I was just wondering what you were gonna tell me."

"Why?"

"Because I was in the interrogation room on the Gorman deal when those terrorists collapsed the Arby-Bennet building. I was on the arson squad then and they brought in a specialist who had just squandered a half dozen unfriendlies and was pretty shot up himself. I had a quick look at the big heavy before they hustled us out and he sure as hell looked a lot like you."

"The Gorman deal was a long time ago."

"I didn't think you'd forget. It was you, wasn't it?"

"Hey, I read about it in the papers."

"Horse manure." Alley gave him a big grin and said, "Man, you can tell me anything. I'm just a lousy bartender on pension in a crazy island in the Caribbean. We're both has-beens anyway. Maybe I'll even think you're lying."

Hooker let out a grunt and put down half the stein. It was cold, the way he liked it, and he wiped the froth off his mouth. "It was me," he said.

"You was a cop?"

"Not New York."

"Oh boy," Alley said. "Should I go further?"

"I wouldn't advise it."

"Good, pal, we keep it that way. You know Berger, like how he always wants to be the Sydney Greenstreet type? Well, figure me like Hoagy Carmichael, off in a corner playing a piano or waiting on a bar. You be Bogart if you want to."

"Come off it, Alley."

"Hooker, I got to ask it. I just got to."

"So ask."

"Federal?"

"Of a sort."

"Oh hell, I did have to ask, didn't I?"

"Don't matter, pal. Like you said, we're all retired."

"In the pig's tail you're retired." For a long moment Alley studied him and his face was troubled. "You're here to kill somebody, ain't you?"

Hooker put his stein down and looked at the bartender. Alley was tall and skinny, a guy in his late fifties who had never had a home except a hook-and-ladder station in lower Manhattan. Somehow, life had passed him by, but now he was in his own dream world and was trying to sop up all the details of a world he had left behind.

"I don't want to kill anybody," Hooker said.

"You came at a funny time."

"What makes you say that?"

"Twenty-four years with the fire department. Head of the arson squad. Lots of time in bars and scenes with the cops. All one big family so you get to know how to tell our people from the civilians." He glanced up at the door. "Suddenly the feds are crawling up on us."

"What the hell are you talking about, Alley?"

The bartender pulled another beer, set it in front of Hooker and said, "Look what Berger just brought in."

Hooker didn't turn around. He simply let his eyes slide up to the dirty old back bar mirror and he saw Chana at the same time she saw him and their eyes met and for a second he wished he had been packing his .45 and the piece was in his hand with the hammer back so he could turn and shoot her guts right out of her beautiful belly and it would finally be all over with for all time.

She came up to him and said, "Hello, Mako."

He put the beer down and stood up. He knew how she hated to have to look up at him, but now it was his turn to lay it on. "Hello, doll," he said. "This is a real surprise."

"Like hell it is." She was smiling at him and said it quietly. "I didn't think the Company was that sharp."

Hooker put his hand under her chin and tilted her head up. "They're not, kid. No way. They ever put you with me after the last time, I would stretch your hide out from here to there. Even when you're on my side, you only shoot me once and get away with it."

"I wasn't briefed," she said.

"You didn't think, you stupid broad," he said.

She felt the muscles tighten in her back and she was almost ready to move before she remembered there was no way she could take him the way she could almost anybody else. "I'd sure like to do it again," she told him.

"I'd sure like to see you try," he said.

"The next time I won't try. I'll do it."

"Kid, you're a loser. Don't go after the men that way or your tail will burn. Right now I'd love to rap you right in the chops, but that wouldn't be the American way, would it?" He gave her a small grin, his teeth flashing in the light. "How about a beer?"

"Drop dead."

"After the beer." He held his hand up and signaled Alley over. When the steins were there in front of them Hooker said, "The next time you talk to me like that I'm going to knock you right on your beautiful *tukhes*." He grinned again, bigger than the last time. "Understand?"

She picked up the stein, wondering if she could swing it fast enough to lay his head open, then decided she couldn't and sipped the foam off it. "Sure," she said.

"Just like old times now," he told her.

"Not quite," Chana reminded him. "I heard you were retired."

Hooker hoisted his stein and drained most of it before he put it down. "You heard right."

She turned her head slowly and stared at him with an expression that said he was a damned liar and an idiot for even trying to con her. Five years with the Company made you a veteran and she had had twelve of them. Maybe the Company wasn't much now, but the political ax had only lopped off the heads that didn't count; the heavy hands were right where they always were and the codes hadn't changed a bit.

"Good for you," she said. "I understand you're living on Peolle."

"Berger's a smart little fat boy. I didn't think he knew me."

"He had memory training."

Hooker nodded slowly. "I must be slipping. I forgot the Company keeps those outpost types in all the potential hot spots."

"Yes," she said meaningfully, "they do that."

He got her intent and shrugged. He couldn't give a damn what she thought anymore. Once, maybe, but not now. "How long you going to be around?" he asked her.

"Who knows? It's only a minimum assignment anyway, and if I'm lucky I'll get a week in the sun."

"Try swimming off the side of your boat. There are some fish out there who would like to meet you."

Chana finished her beer and put the stein down

gently. She smiled up at Hooker and said softly, "Slob," then turned and went back to Colbert and Berger looking as though she had just had a charming conversation, and sat down at their table.

Alley came up, his eyes going between Hooker and the table. "Who's she?"

"Old friend."

"Ho ho ho."

He finished the beer off and handed the stein out for a refill. "I knew her back in the old days."

"Like knew her how?"

"Quit being so nosy."

"What else I got to do? Nothin' goes on fire around here and if it does they piss it out. I can't even use my expertise, like they say. So I'm nosy." He handed a beer to Hooker and waited.

Finally Hooker said, "We had some business together."

"Beddin' down a broad is some business." Alley grinned.

The look Hooker gave him turned the grin right off. "I don't think they taught you much in the firehouse, pal, but if I was bedding her, as you say, I wouldn't talk about it. But I will tell you this: one of those marks on my frame you find so fascinating, she put there."

"Damn. Sorry, buddy."

"Don't sweat it."

"What're you gonna do with her?"

"Let her be, Alley. I just let her do her thing, whatever it is, and watch her sail away into the sunset.

Maybe my luck will hold and she'll get 'et' by that thing out there, though I doubt she could stay down in anything's stomach."

A small frown puckered Alley's forehead. "You don't believe that crap, do you?"

Hooker shrugged. "They made a movie once about a spider that ate Pittsburgh, didn't they? Of course it's crap."

Alley snapped his fingers. "Hey . . . maybe that's what they're gonna do here?"

"Who?"

"That movie bunch that's coming in and . . ." He stopped and squinted again, annoyed at himself.

"What are you talking about?"

Alley put Hooker between the table and himself, leaned forward on the bar and said, "Keep this quiet, but old fat boy got a call in here today and he took it on the wall phone at the end of the bar. What he didn't know was that I was in the can. What I could hear on his end was something about a movie company coming in who was out taking pictures of the *Arico Queen* wreck."

"Why would he care?"

"Hell, man, maybe he needs to stock up some trade goods in that general store of his. I don't suppose a movie company hides what they do. Anyway, we could use some off-season money around here."

Hooker shook his head. "Pal, you're a one-man news broadcast."

"Trying to be helpful. Not much to talk about these days."

"And frankly, kiddo, I don't give a hoot. That's what I'm here for. Like they say, no news is good news." He put his empty stein down and threw some change on the bar.

"Want another?"

"Nope."

"Maybe you ought to send one back to the broad."

"Order some." He burped, slid his hand over his hair, picked up his cap and left.

When he was outside he walked up the walkway, turned left and followed it down to the dock. It had started off to be a good day, but it turned lousy real fast.

He let his mind drift back over the easy weeks of not knowing and not caring what was happening, then all of a sudden everything got spicy with boats gettin' hit by something strange, then Chana Sterling turns up on the beach right next to his own personal island.

Silently, he cursed. The easy days were gone and he knew he was right back in the mess again whether he wanted it or not. Something was happening and the Company was in the game with their top personnel, and there he was, supposedly out of everything but knowing he was in up to his ears.

He said, "Sheeeit."

"Man who talk to himself say much, sar."

Hooker almost jerked around, feeling his hand go for a gun that wasn't there anymore. "Damn, Billy, you are a sneaky Pete."

"You say I have sand in my foots, sar."

"I thought you were going to call me by my front name."

"Yes, I think on it vary hard, but something tell me Mr. Shark out there want me only to know him by that name. That okay, sar?"

"Sure, Billy, but you don't think a fish cares what you call him, do you?"

"Them fish, he think. Oh, he sure think, all right. He think how he chop off the one you catch right behind the head. He think how he sees a foot dangle in the water and how he pinch him right off by the ankle."

"He think about you, Billy?"

The big Carib grinned. The only way Hooker knew was because his teeth showed in the darkness. "All the time we think about each other, sar. I wait, he wait."

"What for?"

"For when one of us does not think, sar."

"Great," Hooker said. He nodded toward the shadow at the dock. "You know that ship, Billy?"

"She named *Tellig*. Come here five, six times before you come. She U.S. ship."

"How do you know?"

"We know."

"What do they do?"

For a moment Billy Bright said nothing, then, with an invisible shrug that ended the discussion he said, "Funny things."

Later he would ask him again. Later, he would get an answer. Hooker felt a twitch of irritation touch his shoulders. Too often the governments and bureaucracies got wrapped up in their own superiority. Because you lived in a state of seminudity and had a hooch on a sandy beach, you didn't exist and could be totally ignored. Stupid. These islanders had their own ways, their own thoughts and could get their own answers.

"You ready to go home, Billy?"

"Yes, for sure, sar. This night has been very good to me."

Hooker gave him a little meaningful grin.

"She still love you?"

His teeth flashed again. "Oh, yes."

"How about you?"

"I love that girl hard and long, sar."

"Is that a double entendre?"

"A what, sar?"

"Forget it."

Chapter Four

An hour before sunup Billy shook Hooker awake from a dream that had him clawing at an invisible something, and when his eyes opened there was a fine bead of sweat across his upper lip. This was another thing Billy found hard to understand: the mainlanders' inability to sleep peacefully. All too often he had seen the movement in Hooker's hands and he knew his boss was off in the night world, his fingers around a gun.

"Mr. Hooker, sar, it is time."

Abruptly awake, Hooker said, "It's still dark."

"The sun, she will soon be seeing you."

With a nod, Hooker sat up and rubbed his face. He could smell the coffee brewing and heard fat sizzling in the pan, so he knew he could shower and shave before breakfast. A good man, that Billy Bright, he thought. Each day he was bringing him closer into the native ways until there would come a time when he would almost be the equal of Billy himself. Hooker let a small grin crease his face. Wouldn't be too bad at that, he reflected.

On the way down to the boat Hooker asked, "What did you pack for lunch, Billy?"

"I don't think you'd be pleased to know, sar."

"Then why did you make it?"

"Because, sar, you will be pleased with the taste."

"Gonna be one of those days," Hooker said under his breath.

"What was that, sar?"

"A nice day," he told him.

"Yes, a very nice day." There was that lilt in the Carib's voice and Hooker knew that Billy had heard what he said.

Guy's got ears like a deer, he mused, silently this time.

An hour after they left the dock the cooler box at the transom was packed with fish, carefully iced down. Their catch would hold them for a full week, including a few cookouts for the friends in the area.

Times like this Billy fully appreciated his boss. He was not one to waste a resource like some of the other city people did. No fish would be hung on nails to be photographed, then discarded to the crabs under the pier. It wasn't just sport. What they caught, they would eat.

"How'd you know these fish would run today, Billy?"

"It is something they do the same day every year, sar."

"Since when do you own a calendar?"

Billy simply shrugged. "I can tell," he said.

"Native intuition," Hooker said, smiling.

Somehow, Billy grasped the meaning and smiled back. "Something like that, sar."

"Then how about the others? We're out here all alone." He saw the little scowl of consternation on Billy's face and let out a laugh. "Okay," he told him, "I get it. These are fish for us city types. You only eat them when you douse them in that crazy sauce."

"But they make good bait too, sar."

"For what?"

"The great bill fish."

"And what would you do if you caught one?"

"We would have a mighty feast, sar. All the village would come. We could invite the lady from the other side of the island . . ."

"Billy . . ."

"Okay, sar, I knock it up."

"Knock it off, Billy."

"There is a difference?"

"Yes. A very big difference."

For a full thirty seconds Billy had been scanning the horizon, now his eyes were fixed on one area. Hooker squinted, trying to see what he was looking at, then finally spotted a pinpoint of a dot where the ocean met the sky. He was reaching for the binoculars when Billy said, "She be the *Tellig,* Mr. Hooker, sar."

When he had focused the glasses, Hooker nodded. "How'd you know that?"

"Her name is on the stern, sar," Billy said jokingly.

Hooker didn't know whether to believe him or not.

"Know where she's heading?"

"Scara Island. Only place in that direction." He walked to the wheel, made a twelve-degree correction to the east and locked it in place. "You want to go see," he stated.

"Why?"

Billy shrugged again and simply said, "Lady on board. You know her."

So, anything that went on in the bar was now public knowledge whether anyone was there or not. He wondered whether they had ESP or were all mind readers. He hoped it wasn't the latter.

There were eight of them in all, four-foot-high spheres with equally spaced protrusions over their surfaces, completely covered with a coral formation from long years under the water. They nestled in soft beds of sand where the tides had deposited them, as far beachward as nature could move them. All around were pieces of wreckage and odd flotsam that had followed the sea drift to this one place. Palm trees, ripped from their islands by storms, lay like matchsticks the full length of the beach, and higher up wooden hatch covers from old sailing ships lay like white, feathery skeletons on the sand.

Chana finished photographing the last of the relics and put the camera back in the case. Talbot had carefully chipped away the coral in an area Lee Colbert had indicated until the identifying numbers were exposed. "They're ours," he said.

"I wonder how long they've been here," Chana said.

"Considering how they're sitting on top of other wreckage, they seem to be the latest stuff to arrive. There's not much sand buildup around them at all." He paused, thought a moment, then, "There was a full moon two weeks ago. If they came in on a flood tide, then it would account for their position. They were just set down nice and gently."

"Not hard enough to jar those fuses?"

"That coral formation was heavy enough to stop that. Besides, there's probably a good rust seizure around the base of those spurs where they enter the main body."

"Maybe," Chana said.

"Yes. Maybe."

"You think they're capable of detonation?"

"I wouldn't want to be sitting on one if you hit it with a sledgehammer."

"What about Berger's theory of blast attrition?"

Lee gave her a curious stare and got right to the point. "If you want to set one off, let's do it. We haven't got the equipment to fire at one from the ship, but we do have the makings for our own detonator."

Chana tapped the large camera bag she was carrying. "I've already brought the plastic and fuses."

"I thought you would," Lee said. "C-4?"

"A low-intensity variant. The activator is on the ship. We can blow it from there."

"Then let's get on with it. That one at the south

end is the farthest away, so there shouldn't be a concussion effect on the others."

"Suppose a hunk of shrapnel hits one?" Talbot asked.

"That would answer the other question. Do the fuses still work."

It was a full hour before they were satisfied with the placement of the plastic explosive. Sand had been carefully piled up around the aged mine to constrict any outward force, and all debris pulled as far back from the charge as they could get it. When the fuse was finally set and the tiny antenna checked, the three of them got back on the dinghy, started up the fifteen-horsepower Johnson outboard and headed back to the *Tellig*.

From a mile offshore they watched the beach while Chana went up to the bow, held out the electronic activator and flicked the switch to on.

All they saw was a small puff of sand onshore as the mine reacted with a miniature explosion whose noise, coming seconds later, was little more than a dull plop.

"Looks like Berger was right," Chana told them.

Lee Colbert switched off the power to the long-lensed video camera and pulled out the tape. "Want to see it close-up?" He slid the tape into the viewer and turned it on.

Distance meant nothing to modern technology. The camera put the viewer directly in front of the sand-packed mine so that every detail was visible. They could see the plastic with its fuse and antenna plastered to the coral, the scattered wreckage around the area and a lone fiddler crab that had wandered too far from its shoreline burrow.

And then it went off. There was no startling explosion, just a silent eruption of sand and metal, with the big steel ball seeming to break apart into dozens of chunks in the middle of a rain of sand. It all settled down quickly, lay there a moment, then the screen went blank.

"I guess Berger was right," Lee said. "It'll make an interesting report."

"Run it again," Chana told him.

"What's to see?"

"Maybe that fiddler crab escaped," Talbot snickered.

"Just do it," Chana stated.

With a shrug Lee rewound the tape, pushed the button and the scene came alive again. When it got to the end Lee asked quizzically, "So?"

"Once more," Chana stated.

Lee went through the procedure again. This time Chana held up her hand right after the detonation and just as the picture cleared she said, "Stop."

Lee hit the pause button.

The mine lay there like something long dead, ugly hunks of metal in a blown-out sand hole. "What do you see?" Chana asked.

After a few seconds Talbot said, "Beats me."

"You, Lee?"

He shook his head.

"Don't look at the mine."

Again they started, but saw nothing at all. Chana picked up a pencil and pointed to a dot in the background at the crest of a sand hill. Lee and Talbot looked at each other, perplexed.

"Tap it up a half second further, Lee."

He hit the start and off buttons quickly and they looked back at the screen. There was another dot beside the first one.

"Do it once more," Chana told Lee.

A half second later the two dots were still there, but farther to the right this time. Another time increment and the dots were almost off the screen.

"We had visitors," Chana said.

"Could have been animals," Lee added. "Or birds."

"Let's keep it as a worst-scenario viewpoint," Chana said quietly. "They were people."

"Supposedly, this island is deserted," Talbot said. "If anyone came here, it would be by boat. In that case, they would have had to land on the far side to keep us from seeing them." He looked at his watch and frowned. "It would be an hour by the time we sailed around there, so they could be long gone."

"Why don't we check while we still have some light?" Chana suggested.

They all agreed, even though they weren't hopeful about results. As Talbot had said, it was an hour before they made their way around the island and by then the tide was almost full again. They beached the dinghy and looked for signs of other boats having landed, but there were none. The incoming water had totally blocked out any traces of evidence, so they motored back to the *Tellig*, put the dinghy in the chocks on deck and headed back to their base.

Overhead the stars were beginning to show and there was a dull, ominous rumble of thunder in the west. All around them, the sea was empty of boats. Lee Colbert said wryly, "I wonder if that thing has had its supper tonight."

Talbot grunted and glanced at the scope on the side scanner. "Well, if modern electronics can pick it up, we'll see it before it takes a bite out of us."

"What if one of those mines is floating on the surface directly ahead of us?" Lee said.

"That would make someone I know real happy," Chana told him.

Hooker had outguessed the crew of the *Tellig*. It was only by accident that he had picked up the flash of light from the lens of the TV camera and realized that the detonation was being photographed. He knew that they were in a partially exposed position and started to scurry out of sight after the blast; and taking no chances, he boarded the *Clamdip*, ran for the other end of Scara Island and was out of sight when the *Tellig* dropped anchor.

The pair was sitting on the side of the inflatable, watching the night close in around them, Billy's eyes darting toward Hooker every so often. Finally, the big man stood up, stretched, grinned at his buddy and said, "Billy, me boy, don't get all bent out of shape. We'll spend the night here on the beach."

"Oh, mon, I do thank you, sar!"

"Come on, I couldn't stand your moaning and groaning all the way home. How come you act like some superstitious old lady?"

Billy grinned good-naturedly, now that he knew they could be safe on the sand that night. "That's why that lady got so old, sar."

"Okay. Now, tell me something. How long do you think those mines were on Scara?"

"Not long."

"How many days?"

"Sar, I do not know that, but two months ago I was here and there was nothing on the shore."

Hooker stretched his legs out and dug holes in the sand with his heels. Seven mines left. The tide brought them in, all bearing signs of deepwater submergence for a long time, most likely since the wartime years of the forties. There were no known minefields in this area that anyone remembered, but here they were, and, most likely, all from the same source.

"Billy . . . your people tell stories about the old days?"

"That they do, Mr. Hooker, sar."

"Any that tell about mines like these around here before?"

For a few minutes, Billy let himself get lost in thought. "A very long time ago, yes. Two fishing boats from Ara caught one in a net. One boat wanted to tow it in. The other said it was a bad thing and wouldn't touch it. They watched while that first boat went very close and saw it touch, then there was a great explosion and the boat was no more."

"How old were you then, Billy?"

"Maybe eight, maybe ten." He paused, made a grimace and added, "There was a sinking. Many life jackets floated by. Tins of food."

"Whose ship was it?"

"I remember . . . American flag on the jackets. Small, up here on the collar part."

"Any attempt at recovery?"

"No divers, no cranes. The water is deep there." He looked at Hooker, a frown crease between his eyes. "What is it you are thinking, sar?"

"If those mines broke loose from a U.S. vessel, the publicity can be pretty bad and right now that wouldn't be good at all."

"That one they blew up, sar, it hardly even made a hole in the sand."

Hooker nodded, toying with an idea. "If a real one, a big fat live one, blew under some important foreign ship, who would know the difference? What a beautiful terrorist operation and all the heat would go right on the U.S. of A."

"Who would do a thing like that, sar?"

"Nobody you would know, pal, but it's something to think about."

"I think about all the work on Corin Island, Mr. Hooker, sar. Many of our people will make more money there than by fishing."

Hooker shook his head in amazement. "How long have you known about that project, Billy?"

"Six months, maybe, when the lumber ship put in

for water. They asked how many men would move there."

"And . . . ?"

"None of the old men would leave. The young men, they want the money, see new things. They like the new ways." Billy saw Hooker's expression and smiled sadly. "Our people, they don't talk much."

"You mean to outsiders like me."

"Yes."

"Why not?"

"If I say, you will not get mad?"

"No, I wouldn't think of it."

"Because to outsiders we are not really people. We only live here. Our language is like for children. Do you know we have words for everything you have?"

A laugh started deep in Hooker's throat. "Billy, you amaze me. Your insight and intuition are absolutely phenomenal. Can I tell you something now?"

"But certainly, sar."

"You will not get mad?"

"Never."

"Okay, buddy." He let the grin get bigger and said, "You think the same way about us, don't you?"

"How did you know, sar?"

"Hell, it just figures. Good thing we like each other, though, isn't it?"

"A very good thing, that, sar."

"Quit calling me 'sar.' My front name is Mako."

"I do not wish to make Mr. Shark mad, sar."

"Come on, Billy, he'll only be mad at me, not at you."

Billy thought about it for a moment, letting the logic of it sink in. "That may be so. I will give it a try, sar."

"Let's forget it, buddy."

Chana had wanted the meeting held on board the *Tellig*, but Berger was insistent upon not going aboard any ship at any time, regardless of the consequences. Finally Chana relented and they met again in the same setting as before.

When Berger absorbed the information the team gave him, he nodded solemnly and folded his hands together. "Could be you solved the big mystery."

"You don't sound convinced," Chana stated.

"I don't like answers that come real fast, lady."

"Then give us your objections."

"Look, you people are the brains. I just sit here and watch the world go by. Maybe I've been here too long, but I'm thinking more like these islanders do than the crowd in D.C. or Langley."

"That's not an objection."

Berger's interlaced fingers did a little dance, then he looked at them, each in turn. "If those mines all came from the same source and wound up on Scara, then why didn't the rest of them do the same?"

Quickly Chana answered, "Because they weren't all released at the same time. Different tidal effects got them and swept them in another direction. Not everything winds up on Scara."

"True. If these mines were floating, then why

weren't they spotted? I can see a ship like the *Arico Queen* missing them, but the fishermen in the small boats see anything—and I mean anything—on the surface when they're working their lines."

Lee Colbert broke in with, "We discussed that and came up with a probability. Those mines had minimal flotation. At best, the tops would barely crack the surface, and any wave action at all could make them submerge, then reappear at great intervals. If they were below waterline levels they could make contact without being seen."

"There was never any blast noise heard."

"What little noise there was got muffled by the water."

Berger said, "Ummm," and twiddled his fingers again. "There was a sighting. Two natives, Poca and Lule Malli, brothers, you know . . . they saw something enormous. Everyone on the islands knows about that."

"And everybody in the United States knows about Santa Claus too, only they don't necessarily believe it. Except for the children, of course."

Berger pulled his fingers apart and took a deep breath. He was starting to get annoyed again. At one time he thought a life in the States had given him all the answers, and here in the island he would be a man of supreme intelligence and wisdom among a population of inferiors. It didn't take long for that idea to change. Now, he realized, he was simply tolerated with a good-natured humor, and sometimes pitied because he was deathly afraid of the sea around him. Yet, with all that, he realized how lucky he was and how much he liked it here.

With a deep sigh for their ignorance, Berger said, "I believe it."

Chana's eyes narrowed as she starred at him. "You know, Berger, it's very possible that you've outlived your usefulness here. A reorientation program at Langley might be what you need."

There was a hint of laughter behind Berger's eyes. He knew it and realized that it was something he had held back too long. He let the smile show on his mouth, and what was in his expression made Colbert and Chana frown somewhat. Softly, Berger said, "Don't hand me that crap, lady. I may be nothing much as a field hand out here, but I don't take kindly to threats from you or the president of the U.S.A. or Castro or whoever's running Russia at this point either. To keep you up to date, my paycheck's gone into buying this place out along with several other pieces of property in the neighborhood. When Uncle Sam's lease ran out the owners decided to sell to me rather than renew. I guess that piece of paperwork hasn't caught up with your department yet. So, if you want an instant resignation from the spook work, just try that reorientation bit on me again."

The quiet outburst was something neither of them had expected from Berger and they exchanged a quick look. "You surprise me," Lee Colbert said. "Does the Company know about your attitude?"

"I don't give a damn if they do or not. Now, do you want to get back to the business at hand?"

Lee Colbert saw the anger rising in Chana's face and spoke before she could. "All right, forget the islanders. What other proof have we?"

"Mr. Hooker saw tooth marks on the bottom of the *Soucan* . . ."

"He thought he saw what *looked* like teeth marks," Lee corrected. "That is hardly proof. There were other witnesses and they saw nothing."

"Only Hooker was watching at the moment."

"That's not enough."

Berger looked at Chana curiously. "Do you believe him?"

Right then she was almost furious enough to call Hooker a bloody liar and an idiot to boot, but she knew she would be wrong and that was one thing she hated most of all to be. She said, "I believe he saw something. How accurate his statement was, I don't know."

"What do you believe?" Berger asked her.

"That there was a hole in the bottom. It was big enough to be the result of a low-yield explosive. I don't believe in teeth marks."

Berger chuckled again. "That doesn't leave you much of an option, does it?"

"What do you mean?"

"Until you find the source of those mines and learn how many are floating around, you are going to be on one hell of a fishing expedition. There's a lot of water out there."

Rather than answer him, Chana shut the miniature tape recorder off and stood up. Berger's security clearance was at a level that didn't require him to know certain facts, and she'd be hanged if she would give him any unnecessary information at all. "We'll meet again later," she said.

"I'm sure we will," Berger told her.

"I trust this place hasn't gotten into you too far. You did sign certain documents at Langley."

"Of course, Chana, of course. I really don't enjoy the thought of being targeted for extermination on account of a silly indiscretion. Such a waste of a bullet."

"Regulations call for a minimum of two," she said nastily.

As they left, Berger called to her, "I hope they're head shots. Or large-caliber to penetrate all my fat."

"Oh, they'll be both," Chana told him over her shoulder.

When the door closed Lee shook his head. "You're a pisser, Chana, a real pisser." When she looked at him with a smirk he added, "You never mentioned the blast tape to him."

"No need to know. Why alert anybody? We should be able to learn which boats were out and where they were working."

"It was a good day. They all were out and working. And nobody is going to tell us anything that isn't vague and uncertain, so get with it. Look in a different direction."

Over at the main dock the *Clamdip* was tied to a piling fore and aft while Billy Bright filled the main tanks with the new unleaded gas. Hooker was seated on the transom, one leg up on the footrest of the fighting chair. He had a can of Miller Lite beer in his hand and when he saw her watching him, he raised it in a mock toast.

"Maybe I will," Chana told Lee. "Later."

Chapter Five

Billy Bright's eyes had been watching the gas gauge for the past five minutes. A rag in his hand was ready to mop down any overflow that might splash on the console and a small grin made his mouth twitch.

Hooker couldn't see anything really pleasurable or very funny about filling a gas tank and was about to ask him what he was daydreaming about, but a soft, low voice behind him said, "Good morning, Mr. Hooker."

He had had too much training to let surprise show and when he turned and said hello to a tall, lovely brunette, he knew what Billy was grinning about and wanted to kick that cat-eared Carib right in the britches. She was wearing topsiders that made walking silent to him, but Billy had not only picked up the sound, he knew who was making it.

Billy said, "This be Missy Durant, sar. She the lady from the other side of the island." He still hadn't turned around to verify his words.

"Judy," the brunette said.

"Mako," he told her. "Mako Hooker."

"Ah, yes, the Mr. Shark man. Billy has told me." She caught the sudden consternation on his face. "Billy brings me fish to eat."

The beer can in his fingers suddenly felt out of place and he didn't know what to do with it. You don't sit on a transom and toss beer empties around with a gorgeous woman in khaki shorts and a beautifully filled out short-sleeved shirt watching you.

He laughed and said, "Care for a cold one?"

She stepped from the dock to the deck like an old pro and laughed right back at him. "I'd love one. I've been pedaling a bike for two hours to get over here."

He popped the top on a pair of iced Miller Lite beers and handed her one. "You made my day, Judy. I didn't expect company."

She took the beer, chugged down half of it gratefully and let out a ladylike burp without excusing herself. "Ah, that was good. Am I interfering with anything?"

"Are you kidding?"

"Well . . . I really came to see Billy."

He heard Billy chuckle and said, "I think I'll kill him. He's already got a girl."

"Sar, I think Missy Durant wants the fish."

Judy's teeth flashed under the smile and she pushed her hair back with a deeply tanned, short-nailed hand. "For a cookout," she explained. "I'll be feeding about thirty people. Think you can handle that, Billy?"

"Oh yes, missy. Mr. Hooker and I get you all you need. Conchs too and the crabs. We take good care of you."

"Where are the thirty people coming from, if you don't mind me asking?"

"Hollywood, Mr. Hooker. That motion picture production company will be landing here tomorrow to shoot a few segments and I want to treat them to some island hospitality."

"Well, you certainly look better than any Hollywood actress I've ever seen," Hooker told her. "You really in the business?"

Another low laugh trickled from her chest. "Not quite," she explained. "I own half the corporation." She saw the question in his expression and added, "I inherited it from my father. That was one of his toys."

"Toys?"

"He was really a banker. He could afford toys like that."

"What happened to him?"

It was a casually innocent question, but it caught her off guard momentarily. She finished the beer in the can and handed the empty back to him. "He was shot, Mr. Hooker. A lousy street robbery. They took his wallet and his watch and killed him." Her eyes suddenly filled with tears.

"Sorry," Hooker told her. "That was a pretty dumb question."

Judy blinked the tears away and smiled. "No . . . I understand. Usually I don't get bothered by someone asking, but all morning long I've been thinking about him." She paused, then explained, "I never really saw much of him. But we had an entire week together before . . . it happened."

"Time will take care of that, ma'am," Hooker said, shifting uncomfortably.

"Please . . . Judy." She held out her hand.

"I'm getting as bad as Billy. He's 'sar'd' me so long I almost forgot my front name. It's Mako."

"Well, I won't. And I like Mako. Will you and Billy join us at the cookout?"

Before Billy could voice an objection Hooker said, "You can bet on it. Black tie?"

"Sneakers, shorts and T-shirt."

"Ah, really dress up. Limousine ordered?"

"Since you're bringing the fish early, boat is the best bet. The others are coming in Willie Pender's launch."

"Who's doing the cooking?"

"I wouldn't have anybody else but your friend Billy there. And his lady, of course."

"Naturally."

Judy Durant stepped on the rail, then jumped to the dock. Her motion was gracefully fluid, like that of a trained athlete. She waved good-bye, then half ran up the planked walkway, mounted a man's three-speed bicycle and pedaled toward the packed co-quina path that traversed the island.

"You like she?"

"Billy, you are a sneaky slob, if ever I saw one."

"I did not invite she, sar."

"You made sure she'd have to come here to get you to fish for her."

"But I did not invite she." He wiped the rag over the face of the console again and grinned. "So . . . you like?"

"Beautiful, Billy."

"Indeed yes, sar. But do you like?"

"Kiddo, she's an anatomical dream with the most kissable mouth I ever saw."

"The last part I understand, sar."

"Someday I'll explain the rest to you." Hooker laughed.

Billy smiled back. "I think I know, sar." He turned his back and began to tighten down the cap on the gas tank.

Grinning to himself, Hooker said, "How'd you know when that movie bunch would be here, Billy?"

"Sar?"

"You heard me."

"I think it, sar."

"You're thinking of how not to tell me anything. Now don't give me any Carib jive, old buddy."

Billy made a gesture of defeat with a jerk of his head. He wouldn't lie and deviousness wasn't part of his makeup. "Sar, the radio."

"It's been on the weather station?"

With a bob of his head, Billy said, "To a ship outside it tells good sky for movie shooting. The ship can come in."

"That broadcast was in French, pal."

"Yes, sar."

"You understand French, Billy?"

"Yes, sar."

"How come?"

"Me one smart Carib like you say, sar."

"You're a real smart-ass, all right. How long have you known Judy?"

Moving his shoulders with an inscrutable shrug, Billy said, "Long time, sar."

"Uh-huh." Hooker waited, knowing he was annoying Billy by not prodding for a more explicit answer.

"Her father, I knew him too. Very nice man."

Hooker still waited.

"She come every year since a little girl. Most times her father not here. Much business in faraway countries."

"Banking," Hooker acknowledged. "He handled your finances too?"

Billy finished with the gas cap and wiped his hands on a rag. He caught Hooker's eyes and grinned a little. "I take him fishing. He was very good on boat. His friends"—he wrinkled his mouth—"bad city people. They do not know the fishing at all and get very sick." A small smile touched his lips.

"But they all pay very well," he added. "Big tips."

"Didn't you take her out too?"

"No. For the missy it was to look at. Sometimes I would take her for the crabs. Sometimes for the conchs." He paused, a look of reflection on his dark face. "She did not like to see any of those great fish killed."

"I can understand that," Hooker told him.

"But she would fish with me. For the eating. We catch just enough for the table. Everything goes. Nothing left. Guts and cleanups from the plates go into chopper, then into big pile that goes to garden when it is rotten."

"That's a compost pile, Billy"

"Smells funny."

"She is taking care of the environment, pal."

He looked at Mako, not understanding what he meant. Hooker waved his hands at the ground and the sky and then Billy knew what he meant. He nodded with a very positive movement and said, "Good girl, she."

"Very good girl," Hooker added, with a grin. "What was her father like?"

"Much money," Billy told him. Then he frowned. "He never have pocket money. Sometime he sign his name or little funny man who worked for him would pay."

"Howard Hughes was like that," Hooker said.

"I don't know he."

"Howard wasn't into fishing. He liked to fly airplanes and make money."

Billy nodded sagely. "You think that's why Mr. Durant was killed?"

"They took his wallet," Hooker reminded him.

"But if it had no money . . . ?"

"I suppose it could make the muggers mad," Hooker suggested. "Where did it happen? You know?"

Billy bobbed his head and pointed north. "He be in Miami, that day."

"Alone?"

This time Billy shrugged. The ways of a city were not his ways and he didn't dwell on trying to understand them. He changed the subject abruptly. "We go get conchs now." He made a rough oval with his hands. "About so big. Okay?"

"Right on, pal. We'll make a party she'll never forget."

Judy didn't have to make any special preparations for rain. Here any downpour was written in advance on the calendar, with occasional squalls penciled in. In this latitude the seasons dictated the weather, with the exception of the occasional hurricane.

The Durant estate had been carefully selected to accommodate a rich man's preference for solitude. The main house was nestled in the dunes, almost invisible at first because of its shell-covered facade. The broad leaves of the native palms shaded the area gracefully, planted in clusters and looking well tended. No brown fronds were among the green ones and there was a decorator's touch to their placement.

A natural channel cut an entrance to the grounds, going in a good hundred feet, then breaking sharply to the right around a natural outcropping of barnacle-studded rock. The pier with the floating dock could handle three good-sized yachts or a dozen native crafts. Unlike most boating facilities on the island, this one wasn't haphazard. All the pilings and bulkheadings were sea wood imported from Miami, guaranteed to last many years longer than local products. On one end a tall pole carried an anemometer and a box evidently laden with weather information instruments. At the far end was a shack built like the cabin of a small ship with three antennas rising from its roof. One would be the VHF for contact with boats at sea, another could be a single sideband rig for long-distance transmitting and the other could be almost anything.

Hooker scanned the docking area and nodded his approval. "Your friend Judy has a nice place here."

Billy grinned slightly. He knew Mako's approval was more than just a passing remark. "She do the big house long time ago. Her father like the boat parts."

Idly, Hooker asked, "He have a license?"

"Why for, sar? He own he boat. He do what he wants without papers."

"Well, was he a good sailor?"

"Ha."

"What's that mean?"

"He go out with somebody. Not alone. Sometimes I go for to fish. Mr. Sar Durant, he didn't like to catch the fish anyway. He liked to watch somebody else catch them. He take pictures all the time."

"Of what?"

"Other boats sometime. Getting conchs for chowder, sometimes just fishing. Nothing special."

"What kind of camera did he have?"

"Mr. Sar Durant, he have many for picture taking. He use the little one like the tourist."

"Thirty-five millimeter?"

"Yes. I save the little round boxes he get with the film."

"Why, Billy?"

"I don't know. Keep good things, maybe. You tell me good things come in little package boxes. Someday I get good things to keep." Mako gave him a sidewise glance and Billy added, "I know. I am one crazy Carib."

"I didn't say that."

"Sar, you think very loud."

Mako had come in gently, the rub rail squeaking against the plastic bumpers around the pier. He tied off the stern line while Billy threw a hitch around the bow bollard, then the both of them began unloading the baskets of choice seafood for the garden party. By the time they had everything off-loaded, two young islanders came up pushing an empty cart, stored the load on the bed, and then wheeled it up to the big house.

"Mako . . ." The light from behind silhouetted her body under the yellow silk sarong, and when Hooker turned to look at her he felt as if he had been punched in the gut. It had happened before, so he realized what it was and let the old armor plate settle over the part of his mind that was being targeted.

"Hello, Judy." He grinned at her and felt that armor plate getting thinner, making him more vulnerable than he wanted to be. He knew that somehow he had been manipulated into this situation by Billy, but he couldn't figure out just how it had happened. "Your party here yet?"

"One more hour. This occasion does not work on native time."

"Don't knock it, lady. These islanders can split a second in half if they want to. Luckily, not wanting to is part of their charm. And I'm beginning to get that way too."

Her laugh was soft and enticing. She said, "Whether you want to or not, you do have a certain charm yourself."

"And I clean up pretty nice too, right?"

"Right," she told him.

"So where do we go to work?"

"Billy will show you. I'll go change clothes and help you clean the fish."

Before he could say not to, she headed back into the house while he followed his friend's tracks in the sand to the outdoor picnic area, where a huge charcoal burning pit was already smoldering. There were cleaning tables for opening shellfish, and scaling tools and knives for filleting or steaking, and curious partygoers could watch the delicate machinations that go into preparing a genuine native seafood dinner from the seats around a tiki bar made from the wreckage of old sailing ships.

Gentle native music flowed out of the hidden speakers, occasionally turning staccato with the thumping of drums. Fine original music, Hooker thought. The only trouble was, it originated in Hawaii.

"Nobody will care," Judy said from behind him.

Hooker put his basket of clams down and said, "You know, you're as cat-footed as Billy and he can sneak up on a seagull."

"So I dress barefoots," she said, mimicking Billy. "He tell you I talk good Carib too?"

"No, but I wouldn't doubt it."

Billy had made himself busy twenty-five feet away cleaning fish, hearing everything, but giving no indication of paying any attention.

"Would you like to come up to the main house and meet my guests? Some you already know."

"Thanks, but I've got too much to do . . ."

"Mr. Hooker, sar," Billy called over, "it is better I work alone. You go talk stateside stuff to the people."

"See?" Judy smiled.

Mako shook his head in mock defeat, washed at the tap, then took Judy's hand and led her to the house. It was a gesture he'd use on little kids to help them cross a ditch, but when he felt her fingers tighten around his, the armor plate turned into tinfoil. There were things going on in his mind he thought had been safely put away.

But emotion was not new and could be handled. He had handled it before. Sometimes he wondered if it was worth it, when it had interfered with his work and could have affected his finely tuned reactions. Now there was no need to watch his back or any reason to practice with the weaponry of his former trade.

It was still something to be handled, though.

Coming over the sand dune, he saw the two ships behind the *Clamdip*. The first one was an eighty-foot yacht gleaming with polished metalwork and burnished mahogany and teak. The nameplate on the bow read *Lotusland*, and from the displayed bunting in the rigging to the camera stands clipped to the rail, it spelled Hollywood, U.S.A.

The third ship was the *Tellig*, freshly washed down and sparkled up as much as a phony supply ship could be.

Judy caught his studying the dock and said, "*Lotusland* is my company ship . . . sort of like a second unit. It's completely equipped for filming and film processing if necessary."

"Fancy."

"You know Hollywood."

"Do you?"

She smiled coyly. "Enough to stay away from it. However, the company has made three very successful pictures in the past two years where the boat has been a necessity. Have you seen them?"

"Judy, I haven't been to a movie in five years."

She thought about that for a few seconds and said, "Mako Hooker . . . what do you really do?"

"I fish."

Her eyes were doubting him.

"Ask Billy, he'll tell you."

"No, Billy doesn't tell things about people he likes. He intimates."

"Like what?"

"Oh, he says you are a very good person. You do nice things for people."

"I'm merely being polite."

"He says you have no fear."

"He's wrong there. A lot of things scare me."

"Are you afraid of them?"

"Certainly, that's how I stay alive. I don't play with rattlesnakes or keep scorpions in my pocket."

"But you go out on the ocean and don't fear the eater."

A little laugh jerked out of him. "Do you believe there's an eater?"

There was a very small pause, then, "Something's doing it."

"Something is something that I'm not afraid of.

I'm afraid of what I know that can get to me if I'm not careful."

Judy paused thoughtfully. "Mako, I asked my first question in the wrong tense."

"Oh?" He waited, curiosity in his eyes.

"What *did* you do?"

He knew then that she had queried Billy and had been told nothing at all. He had not even intimated. "I stayed alive," he told her.

She poked at him gently, then stood back while he opened the door of the big house.

They were all there, everyone not born on the island, with the mark of the city on their gently tanned faces and the inescapable touch of acute civilization in the style of their dress.

He didn't look too much out of place. His shorts were clean, but one back pocket had been sewn repeatedly and he had forgotten to take his small Schrade Old Timer knife and leather holster off his belt. His dark shirt was as native as they come and his Topsiders had many months of deck time on them; he could have been one of the crew from the yacht, but the sun had ground in a quality of wet mahogany colorization that only his features saved from being taken as that of a proper native.

Chana Sterling was standing in a patch of sunlight cooled by double-paned windows, a well-built man wearing a captain's shirt talking to her intently. Berger was watching them both from a big chair, sipping a tall drink. The bunch from the *Lotusland* all wore the latest in Hollywood fashion and were busy talking movies. Hooker located the bar and went over and got a cold Miller beer in a mug.

He had barely sipped the foam off the top when Judy walked up on the arm of a distinguished-looking man who looked like he had stepped out of the pages of *Esquire* magazine. The blue blazer, with a gold embroidered emblem on the left pocket, had a military cut to it and the white trousers were knife-creased and wrinkle free. He was fully as tall as Mako, about the same age, and although he had a slim look, the way he moved said that there was strength and speed under his stylish garb.

"Anthony Pell, this is my neighbor, Mako Hooker," Judy said when she introduced them. "Mr. Pell has a business interest in our production company."

Mako shook Pell's hand, not changing his expression. He said, "I've never met a movie mogul before."

Pell gave a self-deprecating laugh. "I'm hardly that, Mr. Hooker. Judy's father and I made a joint investment in the business years ago and it turned successful despite us."

"Are you in investments?"

"Here and there," Pell told him casually. "My principal interest is in taking care of Judy's interest in Hollywood. What line of work are you in, Mr. Hooker?"

"Would you believe it, I'm a fisherman."

Pell's mouth creased into another smile. "Yes, I can see that. I was wondering why you carry that strange knife at your side."

Just as casually, Mako said, "That's in case I'm

snatched over the rail by one of the denizens of the deep. I'd just cut myself loose from the line."

"Don't tell me you wind a high test line around your arm?"

"Sometimes I forget," Hooker said. "So you like to deep-sea troll too, eh?"

"On occasions," Pell answered.

"Enough fish talk," Judy cut in.

Mako lifted his beer can in a mock toast. A new expression pulled at the corners of his eyes and he felt a faint twitch in his shoulders.

Anthony Pell, he thought. No wonder you're in the movie business, you must have taken acting lessons. And you're good, Anthony. It's a long way from being Tony Pallatzo, a little soldier in the old Bruno Bunch out of Brooklyn, New York. How the hell did you beat the contract Bruno put on you for fingering his two best men to the Feds? You must have made a great offer, so good they took it, and here you are strutting around like a character out of an old novel.

A sudden hello snapped him around and he said, "Hi, Alley. Who's minding the bar?"

"Got old Doc-Doc there. That geezer doesn't drink, doesn't steal and works cheap, so I can't lose."

"Thought you didn't like stateside parties?"

"Hell, man, this ain't stateside. You think I'd pass up anything different that happens around here?" He answered his own question. "No way. This is an event. You see all those pretty girls on that movie boat?"

"Come on, Alley, you're too old for that."

"Sure, but not too smart."

"So go catch a bloodcurdling disease," Mako said.

"I'm *that* smart," Alley said with a smirk before he walked away.

Something was happening inside of Hooker. It wasn't what he liked, because it was something coming out of the past. Back when he walked the deadly roads he had had the same feeling, knowing that his training was warning him that normal wasn't the name of this game at all; and past experience was kicking up the adrenaline, because right within reach he was being challenged and he didn't know who the enemy was.

Tony Pallatzo? Was his appearance accidental or coincidental? What was he now, a heavyweight or a misplaced featherweight? A phone call to Miami would answer that one.

Chana Sterling? Female shooters he never did like. They couldn't be trusted. They acted emotionally instead of rationally. What the hell was she doing here?

"Strange person," Pallatzo murmured. "He a fisherman too?"

"He owns a bar," Mako told him.

Tony's eyes washed over him casually. "But you are a fisherman," he stated.

"It's a living."

"You must eat very well." A touch of derision was in Tony's voice.

"I still don't like the eyes," Mako told him.

"Pardon?" He had never heard him at all.

"Just an inside observation, Mr. Pell."

"Oh." He smiled again and turned toward Judy. "Excuse me, my dear. I have to speak to one of our people."

When he was out of earshot Mako said, "Who's the majority stockholder in your movie company?"

Judy frowned, puzzled at the question. "It's a public corporation."

"But somebody has to call the shots. Who's got the votes that count?"

"Well . . . I think my father had."

"And he left them to you?"

She nodded again, still puzzled.

"Who is the chairman of the board?"

That one she knew right away. "Mr. Pell acts in my behalf. Daddy always told me to do it that way when he was alive." He got that frown again, then, "Why do you ask?"

He picked up one of the canapés from the table and tasted it. "Because he acts like the big boss."

Her chuckle had a sincere note to it. "Oh, Mako, that's just his way. He has a very big job and the movie company has made oodles of money, so I have nothing to complain about at all. Whatever he wants to do with Lotus Productions has my full approval."

"You don't veto anything?"

"Really, there's nothing to veto. After *The Lost King* and *Mineshaft* were top Hollywood productions, then our own Anthony Pell produced *Escarpment New York,* and Lotus was one big, bustling company. I have good accountants and good lawyers," she added.

"And you're wondering why you're telling me all this personal stuff, right?"

"As a matter of fact . . . yes," she admitted.

Mako grinned again and threw her a fastball.

"How come you're not married? I know you've been asked."

"I've been begged," she smiled back. "On bended knee. Many times. Some were rich, some were poor, but I had to turn them down."

"Why?"

"I didn't like them that much."

"How much money did the poorest one have?"

"He was practically poverty-stricken," she told me. "A couple of million was all he had in the world."

"Tough."

"Quite." She let a little pause come in, then flicked her eyes at Hooker. "How much money do you have, Mako-the-shark-man?"

"That depends on what you pay us for our fish," he said.

"Now, before they start talking about us, do you mind if I go speak to my guests?" She smiled.

He nodded his head in a regal gesture. "By all means, go, my dear."

She said "Idiot" very quietly, masking it with a small grin.

Watching her walk away gave him the same sensation as when he lost a nine-hundred-pound marlin in the tournament out of Miami. He had lost the fish, not because he had made any errors in getting him to the boat, or because the great marlin was smarter or even more experienced in breaking loose from a deadly situation, but simply because it wasn't to be. One day that fish would be caught, but the person on the end of the rod would be somebody else and all he would have would be the memory of that sleek, wet body arcing sensuously in the air, beauty and power rippling in the morning light. It stayed with the boat and played with the line until it was ready to go. It was in close, the leader was almost within reach and everybody was watching.

Suddenly everyone in the room got hungry at the same time. Outside, the delicious smells coming from the fire pits drew everybody to the table to pick up a stainless steel tray that had seen military service during World War II. The lines formed on either side of the table and the island boys dished up the delicacies Billy had cooked up; from the satisfied sounds everyone made, you would think they were eating at a five-star restaurant.

Hooker caught Billy's eye and gave him a "well-done" wink, but he didn't need it at all. Give him a fish and a fire and he was in culinary heaven.

Without realizing it, Hooker had gotten edged in line right behind Chana Sterling. She was so engrossed with a soft-shelled crab that she didn't notice him until he said, "Beats the fast-food places in Miami, doesn't it?"

But she recognized his voice and turned so he could catch all the cold in her eyes and the smile that wasn't a smile. "It did," she said. Her voice had a hiss to it, making sure it emphasized the past tense.

"Don't tell me I'm spoiling your fun."

"You certainly don't improve it."

"Well," he said, "don't take any guilt trip for that bullet you put in me, kiddo. Sometimes I get teed off when I think of it, but it bought me a ticket back to civilian life."

This time there was a small light in her eyes. "I radioed Washington about your status, Mako. Nobody seemed to agree on just what happened to you. The head office won't talk, of course, but the scuttlebutt seems to be that you are simply on a hiatus of some sort."

"And what do you think, Chana?"

"I think the agency is smarter than I gave them credit for. They saw something coming up and assigned you a deep cover to wait it out."

"So, what's wrong with that . . . if your supposition is correct?"

"It's crap, that's what!" Her voice went low, tinged with suppressed violence. "You're a slob, Mako. You've been in the field too damn long. You're washed up and you know it. All you do is stand in the way of more competent personnel and make it harder for all of us!"

"Not you, Chana. I wouldn't stand in your way. You shoot people."

"I sure wanted to shoot you when you poked around Scara Island!"

This time he didn't answer her. He gave a tight-lipped grin and took another bite of his fish sandwich.

"Don't pull that on me, Mako. You know damn well it was you on the other side of that island. Just let me tell you something . . . you keep away from that place. There are American munitions washed up there and that place is strictly off-limits."

Mako's face changed. A new hardness creased his eyes, and his lips hardly moved when he spoke. "You listen hard, Chana. That island is not a piece of the good old U.S.A. It was formally assigned to the native government of Peolle on March 9, 1949. If you forget the date, remember that it was the anniversary of the battle of the *Monitor* and the *Merrimack* in Hampton Roads, Virginia, 1862. It's just a collection place for all the junk in the ocean, but it's a junkyard that belongs to the people of Peolle, and believe me, they can boot you out of here anytime they want."

"We have an agreement . . ."

"To tie up at the dock you built, that's all."

She sensed the implied threat but let it roll off her. Chana was a woman totally devoted to her job and what she couldn't conquer immediately she put in abeyance for later. Her voice took on a degree of stability and she said, "Whose side are you on, Mako?"

"I didn't know we had a game going."

"It's no game."

"You mean something is really eating those boats?"

"What's happening, Hooker?"

"What are your orders, Sterling?"

For a moment they just stood there looking at each other, then realized the foolishness of their attitudes. Finally, giving away nothing, Chana said, "We were taken off a routine patrol to look into all the excitement here. The media in the States have been playing it up harder with every incident."

"The incidents have no proofs so far."

"Some powerful forces can influence the government to investigate any action, you know that."

"No names, of course," Hooker said.

"Of course."

"Then what you ought to do, Chana, is enjoy your assignment. Look at the great weather, all the good food and the exciting company you have around here. And nobody's even shooting at you."

"No," she said, "all they want to do is eat me."

Mako looked at her and grinned, and when her face got red he grinned and walked away.

The island help was starting to clean up, so they'd be leaving soon, and Hooker didn't feel like doing any boat-handling with even a mild high. There was one other man at the bar rail nursing a drink, and without turning around the guy said, "How's it going, Mako?"

"Still on patrol," Hooker answered. "Who am I talking to?"

The guy turned around, his face immobile. "I was your contact once in Madrid."

"Lee Colbert," Mako stated.

"You got a good memory."

"We were trained that way."

"Not really. You had to be that way to start with," Colbert said. "We only had a two-minute exchange. That was twenty years ago."

"I thought you'd be retired by now."

"So did I, then this boat-eating business turned up and here I am."

"Tough."

"Damn right. I have a farm I want to go to." Colbert took another sip of his drink and put the glass down on the bar. "How'd you get pulled into this thing?"

"I didn't. It just happened around me."

"Sure, and the Company doesn't have any contingency plans." Colbert lifted an eyebrow.

"I'm out of it, Colbert."

"Cut the garbage, Mako. I've been in the business too long to fool."

"What will it take to convince you?" Hooker asked.

"You can't do it."

"Call the office. I'm wiped off their roster. Personal decision. No chance of reinstatement. I've been kissed off with prejudice. No authority, no contacts . . . absolutely nothing."

A barely concealed smile flitted across Colbert's face and he said, "And just by accident you wound up in a strange place like this where something wild has gotten started that nobody can understand. Is that it?"

Mako nodded. "Something like that."

"Something like that," Colbert repeated sourly.

"I've been here two years, Lee."

He studied Mako for a moment. "I think events got a little ahead of us. We weren't given any advance information except to explore the situation. It doesn't take too much thought to figure out that we were to contact you somehow. Okay, we made the contact. What's happening, Mako?"

Disgusted, Mako shook his head. "If I were you, Lee, I wouldn't go any further until you've called the office."

"It's that big, huh?" Colbert said.

"Lee . . ."

"Okay, okay. I got the picture. I'll let the office clue me in. Just one question. What is this party all about?"

"I thought it was just a Hollywood bash," Mako told him. "All the ingredients are there . . . the *Lotus-land* crew, your bunch, and the short guy over there with Judy."

"Know who he is?" Colbert asked.

They both turned and watched the pair. The pudgy guy was in his fifties, nicely tailored into classic yachting garb. He wore a toupee and had a stylized mustache, and Mako knew that he had seen him before but not at a party like this. "He's with the Midnight Cruise lines. Name is Marcus Grey."

"Right," Colbert agreed. "Two years ago he was indicted on a stock fraud charge but was cleared. Something to do with international money laundering."

"Are those Swiss bankers still uptight?"

"One of their main money sources is drying up, which makes them pretty darn nervous, but that hasn't got anything to do with us. How did you know him?"

"File copy stuff. There's another heavy hitter here too."

"Who's that?"

"Anthony Pell. He's one of the biggies in Judy's movie company. He used to be Tony Pallatzo, a minor capo in one of the smaller mob families."

"I was never detailed to that scene."

"No big deal. Looks like he went legit and wound up in show business with Judy's father, Arthur Durant. These days a lot of the Made Men have got something square going for them. Crime is so high tech you have to be a university grad to keep up with it."

"Mako, for a guy supposedly out of the action, you seem to have kept up with current affairs."

A little laugh escaped Hooker. "It's all old stuff, Lee. You should know that."

Colbert's expression grew suddenly serious. "What about the new stuff, then?"

"Like what?"

"Like what eats ships and why."

Annoyed at the thought, Mako said, "I wish I knew, Lee."

"Have you got any ideas?"

"Nope. No ideas, no answers and I don't intend to look for any."

Lee Colbert swore under his breath and made a gesture of impatience. "Well, we'll probably be getting orders at the same time, pal. No sense rushing things. Incidentally, you got old Chana all bent out of shape. She never expected to see you on top of this deal."

"I told you . . ."

"Yeah," Lee said, "you never were on it."

From the end of the dock Hooker and Billy watched Judy wave off her guests as the boats pulled away into the channel. Willie Pender's launch took Marcus Grey and four of his friends back to the new motel on the south end of Peolle Island, the *Tellig* close behind her; *Lotusland,* waiting until all was clear, pulled out slowly, the bunch on deck still partying.

The quiet was noticeable and a pleasant relief from the festive noise of flatland foreigners let loose on a Caribbean island. Judy came up to the *Clamdip,* still looking fresh as she did at the beginning of the day, and handed Hooker an envelope. "For your seafood delicacies. They were fabulous."

Mako took the envelope and grinned. "It was a pleasure to work for you, ma'am."

"Stow that ma'am bit, my friend," Judy said. "You and Billy could make a fortune catering. Do you know that?"

"But you'd be the only customer," Hooker mentioned.

"Yes." Judy smiled. "Wouldn't that be wonderful?"

Hooker saw Billy grinning at him and frowned. Once again, he was getting that feeling of being manipulated. "I wish I were younger," he told her.

"I don't," she said impishly, her eyes meeting his with a directness he felt go right through him.

Hooker and Billy got aboard the *Clamdip* and Hooker fired up the engines while Judy threw off the lines on the cleats and Billy coiled them on the deck. She watched them and waved as they rounded the point and were blocked from view.

Only then did Billy say, "The missy likes you ver' much. You like she back?"

"Why are you so nosy, Billy?"

"I ask questions to get smart. So . . . do you like she?"

"Yes," Mako said to him. "I like she. I like she very much. Now, does that satisfy you?"

"Maybe you marry up with she?"

"Billy, you are a pisser," Hooker told him.

Fifteen minutes out the strain was beginning to get to Billy, he kept watching the decline of the sun and made sure the *Clamdip* ran at full throttle and all the dials were in the green. Mako knew fear of the unknown was touching his partner, even if he was silent about it, but in another hour they would be pulling into the harbor and there would still be light, so there was nothing at all to worry about. He cranked the wheel for a small turn to port, straightened up and saw the lights of home low on the horizon.

Mako knew the run so well that he never checked his position, but just before he called to Billy to take over the wheel he looked at the compass and his eyes tightened into a scowl.

The *Clamdip* was twenty-five degrees off course and there was nothing to account for it. He let out a muttered "Damn!" but it was loud enough to draw Billy to his side.

"There is something, sar?"

Hooker pointed to the compass, Billy took it in quickly, checked with the light ahead, then just looked puzzled at Hooker's strained expression. "We had that instrument lined up two days ago."

"Yes, sar. That we did."

"Get the handheld compass, Billy."

He found the small tackle box, rummaged in it and came up with an ancient brass Boy Scout compass and read off the direction. "Says we go right, sar. We on course."

"Let me see that."

Hooker took it from his fingers and laid it on the console beside the *Clamdip*'s main compass. They both read the same. Both were twenty-five degrees off course. He took the small unit, stepped back away from the wheel and looked at the dial. The twenty-five-degree difference wasn't there any longer.

This time he moved quickly, but very deliberately. He told Billy to take the wheel, and after scanning the immediate area, he pushed open the doors to the lower cabin, flipped on the overhead lights and went down the steps. He knew what he was looking for and he knew where to look. The old Matthews was a solidly built wooden boat, made before there was a need or desire for fancy accoutrements. Directly against the bulkhead below the wheel was a door that opened to access the instrument panel, and when he pulled it open he found what he was looking for. On the shelf was a steel box about eighteen inches long and six inches high and wide. He lifted it out, took it on deck, wrapped it in an old cork life jacket, then leaned over the rail and floated it away from the boat.

Billy watched him, eyes asking the question.

Mako said, "That, buddy, is a bomb." He watched as the device bobbed on the placid surface of the sea.

"There was no place down there to really hide it, so somebody stuck it right under the instrument panel."

Once again Billy scrutinized him, waiting for the rest of the explanation. In back of the *Clamdip* the thing was a small dot.

"I don't know what that was made of, but either the amount of metal drew that compass off or there were magnets in it."

Billy wagged his head. "But . . . a bomb, sar. Are you sure . . ."

The blast sound was dulled by distance, but the intensity of it was reflected in the brightness of the flash. A few moments later they felt the force of the concussion on their bodies.

"I'm sure, Billy."

"Mr. Hooker, sar, you are one smart city feller, that's for sure."

"Not so smart, Billy. I should have seen it sooner."

"Ha. But we are alive. You are smart."

"Okay, I'm smart."

"How do she get there, sar?"

"Billy, I am not that smart."

"Somebody, she want us dead, yes?"

"Yes."

"Since we are not dead like the fish . . ."

Hooker finished for him. "Yes, Billy, they will try again."

But Billy didn't answer him. He was staring over the side of the boat, then walked along the rail toward the stern, finally pointing toward the water. "He is there," he said. "Mr. Shark with your first name."

Hooker locked the wheel in place and went back to the transom. He saw what Billy did, the great, sinuous shape of the shark, death-gray in color but pulsating with vicious life. The great fish raised up, its eye coming out of the water. "It's a mako," Hooker said.

"Yes, sar," Billy told him. "He is your brother. He waits for you."

There was the white flash of teeth as the shark gaped, then his tail made a swirl in the water and it was gone. Hooker looked at Billy, grinned and went back to the wheel.

Chapter Six

The air had a sticky feel to it, and Mako switched on the old overhead fan. The draft cooled the sweat running down his spine and he leaned back against his chair to scratch the itch it caused, and cursed under his breath because a creepy feeling was all over him now, like a vast invisible cloud that seeped into the chinks of his armor, looking for soft places to spit poisonous darts.

He knew this was going to happen. He knew it when he took his walk out of the building that contained his whole life and he knew it when he bought his boat and when he settled into a routine that began to have some semblance of meaning other than killing or being killed.

Now he realized why some of the older guys had smiled knowingly, because it had happened to them too. They had tried to voluntarily exit a lifestyle they had voluntarily taken on and suddenly found out that nothing was voluntary anymore. You only thought it was voluntarily. You had a great aptitude for secrecy and stealth and violence, and some unseen force guided you to the right door, opened it and pushed you in, and there you were, right where you wanted to be. You were in with the killers, the secret brotherhood of legal, deadly killers, working against other secret brotherhoods almost as deadly as you were. Only you were better paid. Your government had heavier funding for this sort of thing. Their science and technology had made unbelievable things happen. All the spilled blood was blotted up and swept out of sight, and those who participated died as though they had never existed.

And although you were under contract, you could never really quit. Your contract never ran out as it was supposed to.

You only got out when you were dead.

So the other guys smiled. They knew.

And he wasn't dead yet.

They simply had to let him leave, knowing when the time came for him to be useful again, he would come back. The small communications box and the plastic bag of weaponry he had taken as mementos weren't trinkets to look at after all. They were there to be used.

Mako had concealed them well. He took the communications box out from its hiding place, making certain none of the telltale signs had been disturbed. The pretuned radio was an exquisite piece of miniaturization, powerful enough to reach any place on earth. He took four flashlight batteries out of their packs, shoved them into their clasps, and a tiny but mighty generator began turning noiselessly to power the unit. From a sealed plastic bag he took the receiver and stuck it in his ear.

Then he pushed the S button for send, heard slight little sounds as circuits were meshing together and a voice answered, "Base here." It had a mechanical sound so it couldn't leave an identifiable voiceprint.

"Catcher here," Mako identified himself, then looked at his watch.

When fourteen seconds had passed he said, "Catcher on-line."

Exactly five seconds had passed and the mechanical voice said, "Speak."

Mako didn't know how it worked, but now both ends were scrambled, and if anyone were tapped in they'd get beehive sounds because this technology was something they hadn't quite figured out yet.

He said, "BT 13 A."

They knew him now. The voice transmission broke down to CQ, and Morse code in an old cipher rapped out the message LIMITED USAGE BY RETIRED PERSONNEL ACCEPTED UNDER EMERGENCY CONDITIONS. PROCEED.

Base wasn't taking any chances with him, he thought. He went to a secondary code so that they'd know he was wise to their actions. His forefinger tapped on the small CQ key and sent back, REQUIRE CURRENT INFORMATION ANTHONY PALLATZO, MARCUS GREY. CQ TRANSMISSION ONLY. 1400 HOURS 8 15.

The time for the return transmission wasn't right, of course. There was always that possibility of the other side updating its technology, so the actual pre-arranged time would be an hour and a half later concealed inside a third code. He would have to review that one in his memory banks. Years had passed since he used it last.

Mako put the radio back in its box, touched the concealed self-destruct switch so that he wouldn't have to worry about its being stolen. Any motion without turning off the arming switch would automatically destroy the ultra-high-tech circuitry. He put the box back where he had gotten it, concealed the site and stood up.

That ought to start some mouths working, Hooker thought. They were a curious bunch at Base, and when his request numbers reached a certain level everybody was going to want to know what was going on. Most likely Chana would put in a request of her own and want to know what the hell he was doing on the site, and she'd really be put out when she didn't get an answer.

Nobody liked to believe in coincidences, especially when he was right on the spot where somebody was taking down ships. Hooker made a mental note to pick up some stateside newspapers and see what position was being taken by the pundits at the big desks.

Tomorrow at half past three he'd know. Base had great researchers and great connections. Right now he needed some sleep. He woke up twice. Each time, Judy had crept into his subconscious fantasies and jarred his eyes open. When he finally slept it was a welcome relief.

At sunup all the village fishermen were on the *Clamdip*. It was Billy's day to make the communal coffee and he threw in his own homemade biscuits to go with it. For a half hour Mako joined the morning festivities, then with a ceremonial crushing and tossing of the paper coffee cups in the metal trash can, everybody got off the *Clamdip*, went to their own boats and started up the engines.

Hooker let them all leave before he pulled away from the dock. They had serious fishing to do and every minute in their selected areas meant money. He was only going on an exploration trip to Scara Island.

This morning the wind and tide were in their favor and the tip of Scara showed on the horizon in forty minutes. No other boats were anchored off the shore and that was as he expected it to be. As the *Clamdip* closed in, Billy and Hooker could see the trunks of trees newly washed up on the sand and the wreckage of an old dinghy. Through his glasses Mako spotted the blast area where Chana had blown up the mine, but in front of the hole was another spherical shape covered with barnacle encrustation, but clearly identifiable by the studlike trigger mechanisms protruding from its body.

"You see she, sar?"

"When are you going to quit with that 'sar' business, Billy?"

"Right away, sar."

"Great," Hooker muttered. "And yes, I see she. That's a new baby up there."

"You think she could wreck a boat, sar?"

"Billy, that old ordnance can still be pretty hot. It may not do what it was supposed to do, but it sure could put a hole in anything around here."

"And now you want for me to put in the inflatable?"

"Would you rather swim?" Mako put to him. "That old shark he might still be around."

"He be your brother, sar, not mine." He didn't wait for any more talking. They dropped and set the anchor. Then Billy wrestled the inflatable over the side, lowered the small Johnson outboard down, got in and fitted it on the bracket and waved to Hooker. He came down the boarding ladder carrying a bag of tools, pulled the starter cord and headed for the beach.

At first glance there wasn't much to see on Scara. The windblown sand had laid a blanket over the rubble, but here and there protuberances jutted through the silicon cover, some identifiable, others not. There were old hatch covers and broken spars from ancient sailing ships, and, as if they were dropped haphazardly from the skies above, there were cut timbers from a wrecked cargo of home-building supplies. Now they were fuzzy and warped and of no use except for burning.

Mako and Billy dug around the base of three of the mines, and occasionally they chipped at the coral encasing the metal. Finally Mako found what he wanted. A metal plate was attached to the casing, giving identification numbers and place of origin. Hooker scrutinized it carefully and nodded. "It's American, all right.

The U.S.A. is heading right into a big international garbage pit."

"Sar . . . this I do not understand. There is no garbage pit . . ."

"It's political, Billy."

"Bad?"

"Very bad."

"We can't blow them like the sailor lady did?"

"There will only be more, Billy."

Billy thought about it a moment, then said, "You think, sar, she sink those boats?"

"It's a possibility."

"But sar . . . how does she make the teeth marks?"

"Beats me, Billy, but somehow I have the feeling that when we know that we'll know the answer to all of this."

"For sure, sar?"

"For sure, Billy."

"Peter-from-the-market, he say you don't have to see the shark who bite you to know who he is. The marks from his teeth, they tell you."

"He's got that right, pal."

"We both see the marks from the teeth on the *Soucan*. You remember she?"

"I remember."

"They were very big, sar."

"Huge."

"In mainland books is picture of shark mouth. Four men are standing there and they do not touch the jaws. That mouth could swallow one whole automobile."

"When do you read these books, Billy?" Mako looked at him incredulously.

The Carib made a noncommittal face. "Sometimes when I clean stateside people's big boats. They have books on shelves."

"That was a prehistoric great white shark that could grow to a hundred feet. The smart men refer to it as *Carcharodon megalodon*."

"What do you call him, sar?"

"I may call him by your front name if you don't quit giving me the 'sar' stuff."

Horrified, Billy drew back, stiffening. "Oh, no, sar, please don't do that! I do not want Mr. Shark to have my name."

"Billy . . . ," Mako said, "sharks don't speak our language."

Very solemnly Billy replied, "But Mr. Shark . . . he know. Just like big mako shark down there know you steal his front name too. He know, sar."

Mako grinned back. It was almost useless to argue with his friend on matters like these.

He watched Billy's eyes taking in his expression. "What're you thinking about, mate?"

Billy turned his head and stared at the old relics nestling in the sand. "These have to come up on the big tide, sar. Unless a great wind she blow, only when the moon is full does the tide come high enough to push them to here."

"What are you getting at, Billy?"

"Big month tide was three days ago."

Mako saw what he was getting at. The drop-off at

the edge of the beach was sharp and deep now, and those mines with so little buoyancy couldn't float up that slop at all. They would need the flood tide on the full moon to lift them up here.

"Then there has got to be a lot of them out there somewhere," Mako said.

"Yes." His word was clear, but there was a question in it.

"Nobody heard any explosions, did they?" Mako put to him.

"Nobody he say nothing," Billy confirmed. "They hear something, they tell. Make big story out of it."

"But if they were too far away . . ."

A spark of interest brought a crease to Billy's mouth. "You want to make one pop like *Tellig* lady did?" Hooker nodded. "We got no big gun," Billy added.

"Got matches?"

"Got that," Billy told him, with a frown.

"Then get a piece of lumber or something and scrape away those barnacles and that coral. I'll pick up some timbers and we'll blaze that baby apart."

Neither one had far to look. The beach was covered with old, dry lumber, some well tarred, some smelling of turpentine, but all ready enough to turn the cast-iron shell of a mine into a red-hot bubble of destruction.

While Billy was ripping into the white hulls of oversize barnacles, Mako gathered up the kindling, then went back for the heavier pieces that jutted out of the sand. They all came free easily enough, but the last one needed some hard prying to break loose. The end that had been exposed to the sun was weathered into gray fuzziness, but the other end had been well secured from the ravages of sunlight and salt spray, and what he had pulled loose was a hand-crafted beam from an ancient sailing ship. Carved into it by the knife blade of a seaman who had a lot of idle watch time was a beautiful image of an albatross in flight, wings fully outstretched, clutching in its feet a skull-and-crossbones emblem typical of those old pirate vessels. Beneath the carving was the date 1782.

The *Albatross*. Someplace in Mako's memory it rang a bell. But hell, it was a common name for a lot of ships. Even the carving could be the fantasy of a bored seaman with nothing to do. But he didn't put it in his woodpile. He dropped it back on the sand and turned it carving-side down so that he could find it again if he wanted to. Anyway, he had enough for what he wanted to do.

The two of them laid the fire up well, bedded down in the sand below the ball-shaped metal. When everything was ready and Billy had the Johnson outboard started up, Mako lit his match and touched it to the wood. He didn't need a second match at all. The kindling caught immediately and whatever chemicals had seeped into the wood still held their potency; the flames licked out like huge, snaky fingers and Mako got out of there. Billy backed the inflatable off while Mako was still climbing in and shoved the gear into forward, steering away from the beach.

A quarter mile offshore they watched while a roaring fire churned up a thick streamer of black smoke, pulling it skyward and to the east. They didn't have to wait long. The gigantic blast wasn't a bit like the one Chana had set off. This one threw sand and debris soaring into the sky and pieces of it spun uncontrollably in the sun, splashing down in water, one landing so close to them they heard it hissing as it sank.

Mako said, "Damn!"

"That one," Billy remarked, "she could sink a boat."

All Mako could do was nod. There was no way of telling how much force was left in those out-of-date explosives unless you blew them, and doing that in less than completely controlled situations would be dangerous.

One thing was for sure . . . they couldn't just stay there. Whether the government liked it or not, this was going to become a naval exercise in recovery or demolition.

Chana hit the off switch on the radio so hard that she hurt her finger. Charlie Berger and Lee Colbert sat across the room in quiet contemplation, seemingly placid, but with edges of a smile touching their mouths. Too often they had seen Chana lose her cool when something didn't live up to her expectations, and now she was going through a wild display of mental pyrotechnics at the Company because they had reaffirmed Hooker's statement about the ownership of Scara Island. It did, indeed, belong to a native government who had the power to keep anyone off it if they so chose.

"They wouldn't dare try to stop us," she stated harshly. "It's a damned collect-all and the next thing you know they'll be asking us to sweep it off for them. "

"I doubt it," Lee told her quietly.

"You doubt everything," she snapped back. "Whenever they ask anything from the U.S. they get it. Who knows what they'll want next?"

"Maybe they'll want us to get out of here," Charlie Berger pointed out. "Every time foreigners come in here they bring trouble. We dropped a war on them, our economy grabbed their output at rock-bottom prices and now we're salting their islands with mines from another age."

"Maybe they'll get to understand progress."

"Maybe they'll get to hate it too," Charlie said. "You heard about the explosion on Scara early today!"

Chana's jaw clamped tight. "Only what the kid said. Nobody else heard anything. The kid wasn't about to go looking to see what happened."

"What did they say at the naval operation?"

"Nothing. They had blown five underwater obstacles about the same time and weren't listening for anything out of their area."

Lee Colbert said, "Do you believe the kid, Chana?"

That muscle moved in her jawline again, but she didn't say anything.

"Those mines," Lee said, "can be as hot as when they were being delivered. They were made to be watertight and time may not have had as much erosion factor going for it as we might expect. Me . . . I'd just as soon keep away from them. But, if one did get washed up and turned when the tide went out from under it, the weight of the mine coming down on one of the spurs, it's conceivable that the crust of coral could have broken away and the plunger went in igniting the mechanism."

"Then we'd better see about it," Chana told him.

"Why?"

"It could happen again."

"So it would blow sand all over the place," Lee parried.

"If there are any U.S. markings on the wreckage, the Company will want to know about it." Chana looked at him for confirmation and he nodded. Before she could answer, the incoming message light on the radio flashed and she flicked the switch, easy this time.

The message came out of the printer in less than ten seconds. They all read it together. Very simply, it stated, COORDINATE ACTIONS WITH HOOKER. END.

This time Chana almost broke her forefinger hitting the off switch. It did break her fingernail and it hung like a tiny crescent moon from her fingertip, and the "Damn!" she spit out had the hatred of a dozen cobras in it.

Both the men hid their grins and got started readying the boat to leave the dock.

"That louse contacted the Company," she hissed.

"So he wasn't retired," Lee said. "He was on a leave of absence."

Chana's mood suddenly changed. Some degree of admiration shone in her eyes. "They're smarter than we think. They saw this situation coming on a long time ago and set it up."

Colbert and Berger looked at each other quickly. In a very small way it could make sense, but the logic wasn't there. "This wasn't planned, Chana," Colbert said.

"No, but it was anticipated," she said. "They had a contingency plan."

"Baloney. This was sheer coincidence. You don't plan for happenstances."

"The Company did, Lee. While everybody thought all those fiascoes in the nineties meant the end of us, the Company was working far ahead. Damn, they are smart!"

Hooker looked at his watch, and when he had two minutes to go he switched on the radio, flicked his ball point pen and let the point hover above his pad. Right on time the CQ message started to tick in his ears and he copied the letters down as he got them. When the end came he tapped in his own signing-off code and turned off the set. He decoded the message into English and read: PALLATZO LEGITIMATE WITH LOTUSLAND PRODUCTIONS. NO OUTSTANDING WARRANTS. NO CONNECTIONS WITH FORMER ASSOCIATES. STILL UNDER SURVEILLANCE BY FBI. ONE PARKING VIO-

LATION IN NEW YORK CITY. MARCUS GREY ARRANGED
FINANCING FOR MIDNIGHT CRUISE LINES THROUGH
THE BECKER BANK. BECKER SAID TO HAVE EUROPEAN
CONNECTIONS. FIRST BECKER PARTNER, MARSHALL PO-
DREY, MURDERED IN STREET MUGGING IN LONDON,
MAY 3, 1992. MIDNIGHT CRUISE LINES LEGITIMATE OP-
ERATION UNDER U.S. REGISTRATION. CHANA STERLING
IS TO COORDINATE WITH YOU. END.

For a full two minutes Mako read and reread the
message. The casual tone seemed strange, the word-
ing different from what he had experienced in the old
days. Maybe they had a new kid on the keyboard, he
thought, who hadn't looked at the full picture?

Marshall Podrey, a European banker, the kind who
would always have assistants, who would drive in
chauffeured limousines, who would never wander on
streets where he would be a target, gets hit by a mugger. And Arthur Durant got hit by a mugger too. But
in Arthur's case, he wasn't doing anything he never
did before. Miami was like a front porch to him.

A little feeling of uneasiness tightened the muscles
in his shoulder. Two coincidental muggings in the
same overall situation would make you think twice.
Like Tony Pell being a born-again businessman. He
just wasn't the type to take to legitimacy when there
was a dirty way out. Oh, it was possible, all right, but
the probability just wasn't there. Then again, Tony
Pell had seen plenty of his old buddies wind up doing
big time in federal or state pens, and he could have
had smart thoughts and gone straight, or at least
straight enough to survive in Hollywood.

One thing that did hit him was the name Becker Bank. It was a name that was familiar, one that he had run across in years past, but not with enough import to make him remember the details of what he had heard. But he had heard of the Becker Bank, and in his business even hearing of something gave reason to be suspicious of it.

Hooker grunted and very deliberately tore his pages into strips, laid them in the bottom of the galvanized pail he used for a trash basket and held a match to them. When they were all ash he stirred them up into a blackened powder and grinned at this handiwork. You'd think I was tied into some international criminal action, he said to himself.

Beside the hand-built house the metal windmill stirred in the constant breeze, pumping water when it was necessary or generating power for the electrical components. Hooker closed a knife switch and turned on his normal shortwave radio. The foreign station it was tuned to brought in the final act of Wagner's *Götterdämmerung* and Mako leaned back in his chair and closed his eyes, enjoying the driving tempo of the music.

When the piece ended he opened his eyes and turned the dial on the set. Nothing seemed to please him, so he went to American FM stations, wasn't satisfied there and switched to CQ. The code that came in was simple Morse, a position check from a craft named *Drifter* who was taking up station about twenty miles from Peolle for the night, off the course from normal sea traffic and reporting in on regular intervals.

There was no reply.

But to whom was *Drifter* sending? That area was well out of the shipping lanes. Unless they counted the comings and goings of the islanders' beat-up boats.

Hooker squinted and shook his head. This was another name that should have meant something to him, but it had been a long time since he had exercised those facilities he had been trained to use. He was annoyed enough to put his mind to it, then remembered *Drifter* and her robot photographing two sunken ships off the Atlantic coastline, bringing back evidence of a collision that had long been forgotten.

Drifter was another research vessel, and with the *Tellig* the Company had a pair of them fishing for the eater of ships. Somebody or something in Washington, D.C., had a lot of power going for him, and all they had to go on was the old Bermuda Triangle theory.

At twenty-five minutes past four Hooker's eyes snapped open and with the same motion he rolled to one side of the bed, his hand folding around the grip of the .45 he kept hung on the bed frame. The Colt was loaded with a full clip and there was a round in the chamber; his thumb pulled the hammer back in a motion so fluid that he surprised himself, and when Billy Bright burst into the room after a quick rap on the door he was surprised again that he recognized him in time to keep from shooting him.

In the dim light from the moon that angled in the

window Billy saw the empty bed, then the outline of Mako's head and the ugly snout of the .45 pointing at a spot right between his eyes.

Hooker eased the hammer down on the gun and stood up. "Damn, Billy . . ." He reached behind him and switched on the overhead light.

In one brief moment Billy realized just what had happened. He had thought he would have to awaken his friend, rouse him out of a deep sleep to give him the information that made his hands shake and gave his eyes a wide look. But his friend had heard him. He had the ears of a cat too, and the reactions of a wild one. He had awakened to full and complete activity so finely honed he was able to stop firing his gun with just a fraction of a second to identify his target. "Sar . . . !" was all he could get out.

With a grin, Hooker shook his head and stood up. "Sorry, pal. I sure didn't mean to scare you like that." Billy nodded and gulped. "Kind of a hangover from the old days, you know?" Billy didn't know and his expression asked for an answer.

Hooker said, "Military training. When I hear footsteps at night I react."

All Billy could do was stare at him for a second, then he began to understand.

"Now," Hooker went on, "what's happening?"

"It's Willie Pender."

"So?"

"His launch . . . he sets drift nets. He . . . he's caught the eater!"

"What?"

"Yes, he's out there!" Billy pointed wildly toward the beach outside the house.

"Come on, Billy, how do you know this?"

"Willie, he's got the CB radio. Not the VHF like we have. He call anybody. He wake up Poca and Lule Malli who leave radio on all the time. Something she hit Willie's boat then get caught in his net. He still out there, sar!"

Sourly, Hooker said, "And you want us to go out there too?"

The sudden horror of it stiffened Billy. It was dark and they would be walking right into the eater's mouth. They had no armament to tackle such a monster, no way of escaping its fury if they antagonized it, yet Billy's friend needed help.

He couldn't get the words out, so he simply nodded furiously so that his intent was clear.

"I don't suppose you asked anybody else, did you?"

"No, sar. Nobody."

"They'd go, you know?" Hooker reminded him.

"But first they would think. Then they would talk."

And by then it would be light, Hooker thought, and the venture wouldn't be quite so frightening.

"Let's go," he said.

When they boarded the *Clamdip* Hooker noticed the twinkle of lights on the other end of the island. There were others awake too, but the lights were moving between the houses, not on the dock. He flipped the blowers on, waited until any fumes were vented out of the bilge, then fired the engines, switched on the CB and VHF radios, and flicked on the running lights. Everyone on the island would know the sound of his motors and would damn well know where they were going. For a minute while Billy was throwing off the mooring lines he debated calling the *Tellig*, but they could be shut down for the night. He hit the throttle and slipped into the groove that took him past the coral heads and out to deeper water. Somehow Billy had gotten the coffee ready and brought him a cup. The dull light from the binnacle threw a glow over his face and Hooker saw the way it was set. Billy was scared silly, but he hadn't backed off a bit.

Hooker didn't plot a course. He simply followed Billy's finger, heading in a general southeast direction. They were running under full power, and although the old Matthews was a displacement-type boat, those classic old lines and newly renovated engines ensured a speed faster than most supposed.

The Malli brothers had a fifty-foot mast from an old racing sloop attached to their house, topping it with another ten feet of antennas. They could bring in a radio signal long before anybody else, but now Hooker was inside the range of Willie Pender's transmitter and he set the indicator on the channel the islanders used.

He called three times before Willie's excited voice came back to him and he said, "Easy, Willie, this is the *Clamdip*. I think I see your running lights. Are you all right?"

"Man, we got that thing! He a big one, he is. He tangled in my nets. He even bite at my boat!"

"You taking on water, Willie?" Mako kept his voice as calm as he could.

"Sure, we got water. Man, he didn't get time for a big bite."

"Your pumps handling it, Willie?" He flicked a glance at Billy, not knowing if Willie was all that concerned about pumps or not. Billy gave him back a harried look.

"No trouble, man. The pump, she do good, man. Real good. What do I do if that thing gets out of the nets?"

"Can you cut them loose from your boat?" Hooker asked him.

"Too messed up, man. Nobody here but me and young Jimbo and Jimbo so scared he can't even spit."

"Okay, then just hang tight. I have you spotted and ought to be right beside you in about twenty minutes. You got that?"

"I got that. Billy with you?"

Hooker grinned again. "Sure he is. He wants to see that eater thing. He wants to give it a name." He hung the microphone back on the set and looked at Billy, who watched him, horrified at what he had said. Then Billy's eyes went to the water frothing beside the boat, then back to Hooker.

"Mr. Mako is back again, sar." There was no quaver in his voice at all. Just a quiet knowing dignity tinged with fear of the unknown.

Hooker didn't even have to lean over the side of the boat at all. The great body of the mako shark arced up through the froth; he saw its eye and the eye was looking directly at him, then it slowly submerged out of sight. Hooker felt that chill again. "Mr. Mako Shark isn't afraid of the eater," he told Billy.

"Mr. Shark hasn't got that long name of the eater shark," he reminded him.

"Hey, I never said the eater was a *Carcharodon megalodon*."

"He one big mister, though."

"And he's extinct, Billy."

"What means that?"

"They don't make them anymore. They're all dead."

"How come you know them, then?"

"Fossil remains. What they find after they die."

"Dead sharks don't leave anything."

"Okay, smart guy." Hooker laughed. "Everything's cartilage except the teeth. They find these big choppers and can figure out how big the fish was."

"Why did they die?"

"I don't know," Mako said exasperatedly.

"Then how do you know they all dead, sar?"

"I read it in a book," Hooker told him. That Billy would believe. If it was written in a book it had to be true.

Up ahead the white mast light on Willie Pender's launch was rocking against the black of the sky. Hooker looked at his watch, then up to the east. In a little while they'd see the first gray of the false dawn, a hardly perceptible lightening of the horizon. The light wouldn't be enough to discern things by, but it would be a happy indication that soon it would be day again.

He reached for the night glasses on the instrument panel and adjusted them while he sighted on Willie's boat. The launch came in clear. It was backing off from the tangle of netting that stretched out over the bow. He could make out little Jimbo at the wheel under the cabin lights, not caring if it spoiled his night vision or not. Up ahead Willie Pender was trying to cut his boat loose from the long, glistening strands of nylon that ensnared it, but he wasn't having much luck with it at all.

The sea was flat, and with the little light that began to seep up from the horizon Hooker could follow the netting out from Willie's boat. It wasn't like he was fouled in a line at all. It looked more like he was fighting some great fish. The launch seemed to get pulled away from her course and dragged southward, and a couple hundred feet ahead the flat calm of the waters seemed to take on a new life of its own as something bubbled up out of it. Not high, simply a long, rounded form that twisted, and when it did the netting that had caught it snapped loose with an audible wet twang and Willie Pender fell back in his boat on the remains of the twisted nylon—and from inside the wheelhouse little Jimbo let out a wail of his own.

Beside him Hooker heard Billy let out his breath in a very long sigh.

The eater had disappeared. It was down below again and there was no telling where it could be.

Gently, Hooker nuzzled the *Clamdip* against the

side of the launch and Willie Pender and Billy rafted the boats together. There was no way little Jimbo was going to come out of the cabin, so Hooker had Billy go in with him and give him some calm talk. Under the lights of the oversize flashes they looked at the nets. They were of a fine gauge, but collectively they could hold a tremendous load. When they finally got the last of them pulled aboard they could see why they had broken loose. The net hadn't snapped at all. It was cut as cleanly and neatly as if someone had taken shears to it.

"The eater bit it off," Willie said simply. His voice had a new hoarseness to it.

Hooker wanted to tell him to forget that idea, but the signs were too clear. The netting had been cut through, not snapped. And he had seen that huge bulge that came up out of the sea, a huge mound of darkness. Now Willie was sniffing the air and Hooker caught it too. There was a smell, not an odor, a smell that said something terrible had been there and now that something terrible was back down there again.

There was no sense stowing the nets away neatly. They piled them on the deck, and when Hooker and Billy went back to the *Clamdip* they turned back toward Peolle Island, staying side by side for the feeling of mutual protection but knowing that there was no protection against that thing down there.

Twenty-two years ago the prime contact that the Company had set up in Paris had been compromised.

It was Mako who had uncovered the foreign infiltration, and after he reported the details, the Company had left the structure in place, using it to pass false information to the governments who thought they were using it for their own devices.

A pair of new business sites were secretly bought out and thereafter used as places to transfer money or information, secure new identity papers or arrange for any details necessary to the covert operations.

Mako had bypassed the official drop, a faceless company buried in the heart of Washington, D.C. Foreign operatives were as sharp as any the U.S. government had and they were working in their own backyard. It had taken a while, but Mako Hooker had installed his own drop. Only two people worked there, but they were a special duo. They had a mail-order business where they did the catalog advertising, and they sent the orders to the proper manufacturing outlets, who filled the requests; and everybody made a lot of money and there was a fine, legitimate reason for the Imogene company to have all those new high-tech computers.

The twice-weekly mail boat would be arriving at Peolle just before noon tomorrow and Mako would be another in the crowd sending out letters to friends and family in more civilized places. Mako's letter would be a semiyearly one requesting replacement parts for his Italian-made typewriter, an old manual model.

Included in his friendly letter was his order to get all details of the life and death of Marshall Podrey and of the Becker Bank and have the information inscribed on microdot that could be processed on Peolle.

When Mako gave the letter to the post office he knew it would be at least ten days before he had an answer. Any desire for a speedy transmission might alert somebody either nosy or smart.

Chapter Seven

The tide was a half hour away from being full and Willie Pender maneuvered his boat between the creosoted poles that marked the island's homemade "floating" dry dock. Boats that needed repairs or their bottoms repainted simply pulled in over the supports framed by the scavenged telephone poles, waited for the tide to go out and dropped the hull on positioned planks so that the workers could get on with the repair work.

Ordinarily, this was such a mundane sight that it was rare to have an audience, but this day everybody was there, crowding for the best space to see what had happened to the launch's bottom. Hooker tied up to the communal pier, grabbed a beer from the cooler and nodded toward Billy. "Want to see this?"

"Me?" Billy tried to sound surprised. "Why they want me to do the looking? Everybody else sees. They tell me later."

"Hey, pal, you were all gung ho to get out there." He waved his thumb toward the crowd. "Look at them, kiddo. They know what you did. Right now you're their hero."

Billy frowned. He didn't like to be pointed out as someone special. He looked pointedly at Mako. "Sar, you were there too. It was your boat. The eater could have bit us. I saw your face. You did not . . . have the scare."

"How do you know, Billy?"

"I see your face."

"Okay, I wasn't scared, but that's what makes you the hero. You were scared and did it anyway."

Billy started to grin at him and silent laughter shook his shoulders.

"What's so funny?" Hooker asked him.

Rather than answer, Billy's eyes moved toward the sea. When Hooker followed his glance he spotted the dot of a small outboard runabout heading straight for the *Clamdip*. Whoever was running it was crouched behind the windshield, running a good fifty or sixty miles an hour. As it got closer he saw a pair of the new black Johnson 130s powering it, but it was a craft he hadn't seen before.

"That's Miss Judy," Billy told him.

"Damn, and I haven't even had a bath," Hooker muttered.

Judy cut the power; the boat came off the plane and settled gradually, taking up a position at the dock behind the *Clamdip*. She tied the fore and aft lines off, then climbed the ladder, where Hooker gave her a hand to the dock.

"You were really flying there," Mako said.

"Was anybody hurt?"

"Willie's launch took a lick, but he won't know for a few hours yet. Nobody got a scratch. Little Jimbo was pretty shook up, but that was all."

"What did they see?"

"Something was there, all right. It got fouled in Willie's nets and right after we got there it snatched itself loose."

"Willie called in and said the nets were sliced through."

"I don't know," Hooker told her. "Could be."

Judy looked at Hooker very carefully. After a few seconds she stated, "You saw something, didn't you?"

"Yes, something."

"What was it?" she demanded softly.

"Keep it to yourself?"

She nodded seriously, her eyes wide.

"It was big," Hooker said.

"How big?"

"I only saw part of it. It was night, it was a hundred feet or more away and I only saw part of it . . . and it was big. In three seconds it was gone."

"How about Willie . . . did he see it?"

"I doubt it. He was too busy trying to haul in his nets to see anything. I think Billy got a glimpse of something out there, but he's not about to admit it now. Later he might tell about it around a campfire with his own friends, but he doesn't want to know if there is a boat eater or not. Right now he's not a very happy camper. At least you took his mind off the trip. How did you get the word?"

"My crew and I were washing down some pilings with the pressure hose. When one of them went back to get some coffee for us after sunup he heard the chatter on the radio. The way the story was blown up it sounded like the battle of Midway. Then when he said it was you out there helping . . ." Judy paused in mid-sentence and a look of confusion swept across her face.

Mako's mouth cracked in a smile. "Damn," he said, "you were worried about me."

"Don't be preposterous! I just thought . . ."

"Yeah?"

"Oh, hell." She grinned back. "Now I'm talking like a sailor."

Mako just kept looking and his grin got bigger.

"Okay, I was worried," she admitted.

He was close to her now. He could feel the warmth of her body and smell the sweetness she had brought with her. There was a strange brightness in her eyes and the breeze made her hair wave in its caress. Hooker said, "Lick your lips," and with a slow, sensuous move her tongue flicked out and did as he said; her lips were full and moist and a deep red, and when he kissed her gently and softly she shuddered under his hands. She reached out, her hands barely touching him, her eyes almost closed, then by mutual consent they drew back and this time when they looked at each other they both knew that something very strange had happened.

Billy tried to be quiet, but his audible gasp of pure delight broke into the stillness and Hooker said, "I am going to give you a shark name, Billy."

And Billy got quiet and moved down toward the end of the dock, where his admirers were waiting. Being named after a shark, any kind of shark, was something Billy certainly didn't want.

It was fat Charlie Berger who saw them coming and got up and held out his hand to invite them to his table. Lee Colbert pushed himself to his feet and Chana did the feminine thing and just sat there, politely smiling. Alley was on the spot with two extra chairs and they all managed to get seated again, but without any feeling of closeness whatever.

"I understand your reputation has grown to heroic proportions," Berger addressed Hooker.

"Anything can set that crowd off," Hooker told him. "Actually, nothing really happened."

"That's not what Willie Pender said," Chana cut in.

"Oh, something got snagged in his nets, all right. Those sports fishermen still come down here from Miami looking for that two-thousand-pound marlin and occasionally basking sharks show up. No boat eaters."

"What hit Willie's boat?"

"We'll know when the tide goes out," Hooker said.

Lee Colbert came right to the point. "What do you think it was, Hooker?"

After a few seconds' reflection, Mako said, "I don't know. All I got was a quick partial look. It was dark, something churned the water and then it was gone. Have you seen Willie's nets yet?"

"Billy Haines is down there now."

"Who brought in the robot?" Hooker asked suddenly.

The three of them were too well trained to give away information with a sudden, sly look. "Robot," Chana said. It was almost a question, but not quite.

Then Mako dropped the ax. "Your instructions were to . . . coordinate with me." His tone was cold and the message was clear.

Chana said, "I thought you were out of the business."

"So did I," he told her bluntly, "but the option is mine."

"The robot was the Company's idea," Chana said abruptly. "That group will act under our orders."

"Which are?"

This time Berger, Lee and Chana all looked at Judy Durant and said nothing. Hooker grinned and stood up. "Don't let Judy here shake you up, kids. She's in with some pretty heavy hitters too." He looked down at her and added, "Let's go, doll."

Alley gave Mako a strange look when he moved with Judy to a table near the bar and signaled for two coffees instead of the usual beer. Across the rooms he could see Chana and the two men in a serious discussion, but they gave no indication of what it was all about.

Judy noticed his casual glance and said, "What robot?"

Alley set the coffees down, gave Mako a knowing wink of approval and walked away.

"Underwater exploration," Mako told her.

"Why?"

"Because some agency of the United States wants to know what's happening around here. That team will lay out a grid pattern and let the robot send up TV pictures of everything on the bottom. They have other electronic equipment on board to scan for anything within range that moves."

Judy was watching him carefully now, sensing something she hadn't quite realized. She sipped at her coffee, then put the cup down. "Can I ask you something?"

"Shoot."

"You know these people pretty well, don't you?"

"Only Chana, but the others are types I am familiar with."

She looked puzzled now. "Billy said you were . . . a city man."

Hooker shrugged.

"You're a good fisherman." When he didn't answer she went on, "You have odd scars on you."

"I was in a war." He felt himself starting to go tight.

She paused, sipping at her coffee again. "Can you tell me what you . . . were?"

"Why?"

"Because everything seems to be coming apart. No matter where I look things are happening that I'm not used to seeing . . ."

"Judy . . . I was a government agent."

Her eyes went wide. "Oh." She stared at him hard. "The F.B.I.?"

His grin was almost imperceptible, but she saw it.

"My outfit was very unpublicized. Funding was circumspect, but we had plenty of it. Our jobs were . . . lethal." Hooker stopped smiling. He had told her nothing, but he had told her everything.

"Lethal," she whispered.

He knew she was thinking of the scars Billy had mentioned. "Not for me," he told her. "Not yet."

She was trying to assimilate this disturbing information and said, "What are you now, Mako?"

"A fisherman," he said. "I cut loose from the agency a long time ago. Being here is strictly accidental."

"You seemed to talk to . . . your friends . . . with great authority."

Mako nodded solemnly. "I said I cut loose from the agency, not that they just let me go. In this job they always keep a string on you, some lead, some damn wire that can reactivate you back into their fold whether you want to or not. It's nothing you do from eight to five, nothing you take a vacation from, it's something that's always with you. They let you out of the harness sometimes to retrofit, to let the wounds heal up, give you time to get your wheels back on the track again. Then when the time comes and they need you, it only takes the slightest little push to get you rolling again."

"Mako . . . are you rolling again?"

"No way."

"What are you doing, then?"

"I'm watching, doll. I'm looking. Nobody seems to realize it, but the players are all out there on the field trying to set the ball up for the big play and nobody even knows the game has been started in earnest. Sooner or later that ball is going to bounce off the field out-of-bounds and I'm going to grab it and run like hell with it."

Judy frowned. "I don't understand . . ."

"Without the ball there's no game," he told her.

"But what's the ball?" she asked him.

"I don't know," he said, grinning. "But I'll find out. First, though, let's go see what hit the bottom of Willie's launch." They left the bar and strolled down to the pier.

The crowd had thinned out with the tide. Willie and two carpenters were standing on the support beams studying the barnacle-encrusted planks of the boat's bottom, scraping away the crustaceans on the starboard side. There were no bite marks, no regular scraping indentations of teeth, just a three-foot gouge in the thick wood that did no discernible damage except to show where the boat encountered something fairly sharp underwater, the same kind of scar boats got from being beached, or hitting a partially submerged log in open water.

Hooker saw Billy work his way around the bow of the boat until he reached Willie, then put his own fingers tentatively into the grove mark, feeling it from one end to the other. He seemed satisfied at what he saw, but the expression on his face said he was leaving room for doubt. He spotted Mako, waved, then climbed the supports to where Mako and Judy were.

"What do you think, Billy?"

"Something hit ole Willie."

"Yeah, I know. You figure it out?"

His nod came reluctantly. "Wood very smooth. Like baby's skin. No marks like many teeth."

"Billy . . . forget teeth marks."

"Something very big . . . heavy like iron anchor maybe . . . it got dragged along bottom."

"Willie didn't have an anchor out. He was in two thousand feet of water," Mako reminded him.

"Yes," Billy said simply.

"Anchors don't float, Billy."

"Yes," he said again, as though Hooker were a simpleton.

"Just one tooth mark," Hooker suggested.

Billy's face brightened. He liked that scenario the best and he'd never seen the movie *Jaws*. He nodded vigorously. "Yes, just one tooth."

"I'll keep it in mind. You see the nets yet?"

"Sure. Now you can see. One big sharp tooth, that," Billy told him.

Judy nudged Hooker with her elbow. "Aren't you putting ideas into his head?"

"Not old Billy Bright. He knows what he knows and nobody is going to talk him out of it. There's an eater out there and until we lay the proof right in his hand, that's what's always going to be out there."

"Will it make a good movie?"

Hooker nudged her back. "You wouldn't mind that a bit, would you?"

The *Lotusland* had all the equipment at hand to film it. Why miss the opportunity? "Would you?"

"That all depends."

"On what?"

Hooker stopped walking and looked out at the area around him. Land development had not taken place yet. There were no signs of exploitation from the moneymen of the States, and the ocean wasn't dotted with expensive cabin cruisers or exotic marinas with mahogany bars and fake lighting to produce a South Seas setting. It was natural and almost primitive, a place where a hand pump sucking up groundwater was state-of the-art plumbing. There were soft sounds with no blaring horns or jam boxes blaring out rap music. People were polite and helpful, and if anybody was otherwise or did disgraceful things, they were cut off from the island society and had to move on if they wanted to survive.

"On what the islanders would get from it."

"With all the promotion and publicity . . ."

"They don't need that stuff."

"But . . . suppose Midnight Cruise ships put in here . . . would they profit? Wouldn't they . . ."

Mako cut her off. "They'd only be exposed to another culture and one that sure wouldn't be better than the one they have right now. The tourists would ruin this place. You'd be crammed with souvenir shops, T-shirt joints, sleazy motels . . ."

"What else could they have?"

"If it can't be better," Hooker said to her, "there shouldn't be anything at all."

Judy gave his hand a little squeeze, trying to understand him. "But what would be better for them?"

Hooker thought on that a moment, then said, "You know what a chandler shop is?"

"A store where they . . . fit out boats?"

"Pretty close. They'd need their own, supplying them with what they want, not what advertising agencies said they should have. Parts for older engines, for example. Top-quality fishing gear for their commercial needs. Navigation gear they can afford, that sort of thing."

"How would they get that?"

"Beats me," he said, "but that's what they deserve."

"Sar . . ."

"Yeah, Billy?"

"Do that *Carcharodon megalodon* come with only one tooth?"

Judy looked at the Carib in sheer amazement. "Billy . . . where did you come up with that?"

"Mr. Hooker, he one smart mister. He tell me what that big fish is."

She looked up at Mako. "That right?"

"Well, he asked me. He saw pictures in a book." He smiled at the look on her face. "If it come out of the sea, Billy wants to know about it."

"In that case, I have a library of nautical books he might like. What about that, Billy?"

The Carib's eyes had that impish look in them again. Hooker knew what he was thinking. Anything he could do that would keep Hooker and Judy together was as great as catching a black marlin on ten-pound test line. "That be very fine, missy," Billy said.

"What have you got for me?" Mako quizzed.

"A look at Willie's nets, that's what."

Willie had stretched out his nets to dry over a long double row of weathered two-by-fours. The torn ends were draped there and when Hooker ran his forearm under them and scrutinized them carefully, his mouth tightened and little creases appeared along his eyes. The tear wasn't haphazard, the way the netting would be if it had gotten hung up on an oyster bed or snagged in rotted pilings. It was cleanly cut, as if with a knife, and the slice was long and even, and no matter how Hooker looked at it, Billy's answer was closer than any. A one-toothed shark from the Miocene-Pliocene Age of many millions of years ago, the way the nutty evolutionists like to put it, seemed to be the culprit.

Hooker draped the nets back on the boards again. When he didn't say anything, Judy asked, "What do you think?"

"Well, if we haven't got an eater out there, we have a good taster. I wouldn't want to be the guy who has to photograph this baby."

"Oh," Judy answered pleasantly, "they'll find a way. Maybe with the robot."

"Sure," Hooker said.

Billy wanted to attend to the *Clamdip* and made a feeble excuse so that he could get back to the dock. Hooker grunted and muttered, "Who does he think he's fooling?"

"Why?" Judy squeezed his hand again.

"That sucker just wants us to be alone."

"Anything wrong with that?"

"On this island? Right now the gossip is going fast and hard."

"Then why don't we get in my boat and scoot back to my house. I can make you supper and we can pick out books for your friend."

"And how do I get home?"

"One of my crew can run you back." She stopped, smiled and looked up at him coyly. "That is, if you want to leave."

"Little lady," Hooker said, "something tells me I'm being suckered into a trap, but like any decent oversize fish, I'll take the bait and see if I can't throw the hook."

"And if you can't?"

"You don't know this fish, doll."

Unlike the last time, Judy's house was totally empty. Two of the boys on the dock had tied up the runabout, then gone back to packing the day's catch for shipment to Miami, shoveling ice down the chute into the hold of an old shrimper. A pair of local women who kept Judy's quarters in shape were disappearing over the dunes, and the only sound was the quiet music that seeped out of the screened windows and made Mako feel as if he were in a movie sequence where lovely sound suddenly came up out of nowhere.

Even supper had an unreal quality about it, making him feel as though he were someplace else. A smile made his mouth twitch and he said, "The last time I tasted this sauce was in a little restaurant outside Paris."

"My cook's mother was born near Paris. Her recipes are served on all the Midnight Cruise ships."

"And she taught everything to her daughter."

"Naturally."

"Judy . . . ," he said gently, "a meal like this takes about four hours to prepare."

She nodded and sipped at her wine. "At least."

"And it's not what you make for just one person."

Judy smiled at him, a sweet little smile that said everything without saying anything at all.

"I think I'm losing my touch," he said. "I knew I was being suckered, but not this much."

"You don't approve?"

"Gal, I love it. Someplace Billy Bright must be grinning all over the place. Just tell me something . . . who set this up, you or Billy?"

"Actually, neither."

"Oh?" He was wondering who else she had been expecting and it showed in his expression.

She let him simmer a few moments before she told him, "Nita suggested that since I was making such a mad dash across the island to see if you were all right, that I might as well bring you home for supper."

"And you agreed to your servant's suggestion."

"Naturally," she said again. "And I was hoping you'd come."

"I took the bait, all right."

"Now are you going to throw the hook?"

"Maybe I'll just play with it a while."

"That would be nice," Judy said in a strange tone.

Judy's father had had a very extensive library. There was a section for classics, an area that would have pleased any lawyer, another grouping on international financing and a dozen shelves of nautical volumes dealing with wooden sailing ships in the last three centuries. Mako pulled a couple out, glanced at the illustrations and put them back in their slots.

"My father loved the sea," Judy told him. "He said he would have been a pirate back then just for the fun of it."

"Most of that bunch died violent deaths. If they didn't get shot up in battle they were hung on the docks."

"Didn't any of them get away?" Judy asked him.

"A few," he said. "Some even became good citizens again." His eyes met hers and he added, "Not many, though."

"Wasn't Sir Francis Drake a pirate?"

"The Spanish called him one."

"He was a hero in England. The queen loved him."

"Could you blame her? After he dropped all that Spanish gold in her treasury he was one of her pet boys."

"Boy," she mouthed. "Daddy always thought he was a real man."

"He was."

"Then why . . ."

"It just depends on where you sit."

Judy knelt down and rummaged in the books on the bottom row. She tried two before she found what she was looking for, pulled it out and handed it to Mako. It was a volume on prehistoric sharks filled with illustrations and photos, including one of the men standing inside the jaws of *Carcharodon megalodon* to show the comparative size of the great fish. She said, "It was something like this that took Jonah. No whale did it. Their throats are generally very small and their food is krill and plankton, but a great white . . . now that's a fish, and he could swallow a man whole without any trouble."

"And keep him alive for three days?"

"Possibly."

"With no digestion process working on him?"

"Very probably."

"How?"

While she was searching through the index she said, "Some time ago a fisherman netted a great white and got it to shore alive. That's one species that's in great demand by aquarium owners and that fish was sold to one. They kept it in a tank for two weeks, but it wouldn't eat and gradually started to die, but before it did it regurgitated a human forearm that was as fresh as the day the owner lost it."

"Really," Mako said sourly.

"Yes, really. But there's more to it. They turned the arm over to the police, who took prints from the fingers, found the ID in their files and checked it out. They had belonged to a boxer on the mainland who hadn't been seen for two weeks and was reported missing by his roommate." She located what she had been looking for and turned the book over to Mako. "Here it is. When the police called on the guy's roommate the man almost fainted. He couldn't figure out how they had caught him. The two had had a fight out on the docks, he had knifed his friend to death, cut his body up into many parts and sailed out to sea and fed the pieces to the sharks. He had watched every bit go down a shark's gullet. Nobody was ever going to know what had happened."

"So what did happen?"

"Nothing extraordinary. It's just that a shark has an odd capacity to be able to retain food without digesting it for some time."

"And that took care of Jonah, right?"

"Well, let's say other forces came into play here too."

Judy waited while he read the entire account, then asked, "Satisfied?"

"They have things like this to read on the Midnight Cruise ships?"

"I wouldn't think so, although they do serve shark as a meal selection."

Mako handed the book back to her. "Let's keep Billy in ignorance of this little story. With his imagination who knows where he'd go next. The eater would turn out to be a real gourmet."

"For boats?"

"No, for people who were surrounded by a boat hull."

Judy made a wry face and nudged him with her elbow.

Mako pulled another volume from the shelf. It was dated from 1904 to 1920 and seemed to be a history of the local islands, well studded with black-and-white photos. Peolle and Ara were pretty much the same and the lone picture of Scara Island showed an accumulation of wreckage of small boats and one two-masted sloop that was pretty well smashed up. The naval base where the *Sentilla* was doing its exploration work was functioning where the German government previously had had a submarine refueling facility.

Mako showed the page to Judy. "You know about this sub base?"

"Oh, yes. Most do, but they weren't Nazis then," she stated.

"Those World War One submarines couldn't have made a trip this far at that time," Mako said, puzzled.

"Read on. You'll find they used a refueling sequence in those days too. Earlier, they had attempted to tow subs, but that proved too slow and dangerous. So they had supply ships meet them at designated spots at sea and resupplied their provisions."

"And they were going to hit U.S. shipping?"

"They never got that far. One of the islanders sailed a canoe up to the States and put them wise. He had landed on a Florida beach where the sailors guarding the area held him prisoner for three days before he got somebody to listen to him."

Mako frowned and shook his head. "I never heard of any subs being captured here then."

"They weren't. Their intelligence system got wind of it, radioed the boat commanders, and they blew the bottoms out of their subs before they were captured. Two more almost were caught, though."

Mako waited.

"They didn't get the message until they were fifty miles offshore. That's when they saw our destroyers in the area and made a run for the base. They were submerging when one took a direct hit from one of the destroyers' guns and went down with all hands before the destroyer could reach it."

"What happened to the other one?"

"Oh, he submerged and they laid depth charges all around the area. The bottom is about four hundred feet in that area, so either the depth charges got him or the pressure crumpled the hull. They didn't have the asdic devices then to pinpoint the wreckage, but they did a search thorough enough to make sure the U903 was gone. As a matter of fact, some graduate college students collecting data on World War One checked it out through the archives in Germany."

"It's a good story, doll. They ought to make a movie about it."

"Should I?" Her tone was serious, but there were laugh lines around her mouth.

"Well, you could afford it, I suppose. You think your dad would have approved?"

"Sure," Judy nodded. "He was a big risk-taker. Even when he was broke, if it looked good, he'd go for it."

"Your dad didn't inherit money?"

Judy busied herself putting the books back and straightening up the shelves. "Nope," she told him, "not daddy. Every cent he got he earned."

Mako made a small arc of motion with his head, taking in the room. "He did all right."

"He was a good businessman, Mako. He took advantage of every opportunity and built up his little empire the hard way."

"And now you have it all."

Judy gave a small shrug. "I have good advisors. The big money interests they take care of. I'm sort of the lucky charm for the movie company."

"How did Anthony Pell get into that?"

"Dad hired him. In fact, he brought him up from another company he owned."

"Movies?"

"As a matter of fact, yes," she answered.

"What studio?"

"He was an independent. He and dad made four low-budget films that were released in Europe before they came to the U.S. and they made a bundle. Dad brought him into his company as a partner after that and the profits have gone up fifty percent. Luckily, he had a good block of voting stock in the Midnight Cruise line and that venture floated them in the early days, so they made out just fine."

"Well . . . as long as it doesn't disturb the tranquillity of the islands . . ."

Judy tossed her head and her hair did a little dance in the air. "Oh, Mako, they're not the usual vacation tours. Those ships cater to casino towns where the rich can play the money games. I know it sounds awfully materialistic . . . and it is . . . but this is a wild generation that makes it hand over fist and spends it the same way. One-half the population has hunger pangs and the other half eats their way into a first-class casket. It's crazy."

"You can say that again."

"I suppose you want to know where I stand in all this."

Mako nodded. "I'm kind of wondering."

Judy's eyes met his with startling directness. "I don't," she said simply.

"You don't what?"

"Mess with all that. I live here. I own this place free and clear and run a damn good fishing business with top restaurants on the mainland. I have no partners, so nobody can own me. I still have major hunks of dad's old businesses, but I don't control them. I probably could, but I choose not to. Long ago he assigned others to handle his affairs and I have let it stay that way."

"What do you do with the money you make?"

"I pay taxes, bills, and bank the rest."

"You a millionaire?"

"I was that when I was twelve. Next question."

"What would you like to own?"

"A boat like yours," she said.

"Why don't you?"

"Because they don't make those antiques anymore."

Mako grinned at her. "I had a hard time finding mine, and it's not for sale."

"Got a classy name, though."

He grinned again. "Ah, yes, the *Clamdip*. Would you like to take a cruise on her?"

"I'd love it."

"We don't stop at any exotic ports of call, y'know."

"So I won't dress up. When can I go?"

"Tomorrow. We leave the dock at six in the morning. What would you like for breakfast?"

"Billy Bright will know."

"Good. I'll tell him to leave the eyes in."

"Certainly," she said, and he knew she meant it.

Chapter Eight

Mako watched the runabout disappear into the night, then turned and went to his house. While the coffee was perking on the stove he brought the transmitter out and made his contact; when the agency answered, he flipped the switch to scramble, identified himself and said, "Find out if Anthony Pallatzo operated inside the porn movie business. That would go back to at least twenty years ago."

The operator on the other end replied, "Right, hold on."

Only the faint hum of the generator was audible for a full ten minutes while a computer was busy scouring files, then the voice from the States said, "Got it. Tony Pell was active for six years, but nobody ever held him for anything. He was clean with Internal Revenue, none of the gals or guys they used ever laid a complaint on him and he just walked away from the business when it got too legal for him. There's a reference here to his association with a legitimate California-based studio called Alberta Productions. Nothing further has been recorded. There is no death notice on him."

"He's not dead."

"But he's not active, either."

Mako said, "That's because he's legitimate. He pays his taxes. His associates are reputable."

"That doesn't sound like Tony Pell."

"Sure makes a great cover."

"If it's real."

"Oh," Mako told him, "it's real, all right."

"You think he's staying clean?"

"I have my doubts," Mako said, then added, "Now, one more thing. The naval vessel *Sentilla* is engaged in an operation south of here. Please notify the captain that I want to meet with him shortly and be given what information I need."

"We can't interfere with naval missions, you know . . ."

"Quit the crap," Mako said abruptly. He wasn't about to try a bluff with the operator, but he knew how the Company worked in these matters. "They're operating hand in hand with our people and you damn well know it. You have my files there?"

"Yes, I have."

"Do I have the authority to make this request?"

"According to this you have unless . . ."

"Forget the unless. Just do it."

"I'm going to clear this with my supervisor, you know."

"Forget your supervisor. You clear it with Fennely and do it now."

"Director Fennely is . . ."

"I know who he is," Mako told him. "Just do it. Now."

Mako signed off and put the equipment back in its stall. This contact was going to rattle a few cages. Before long he'd have to give a full report on his actions, but they couldn't take any chances on trying to nudge him off to fit their plans. They had years of his activity in strange places and events that shook the world scene more than once, bringing down some pretty violent people and causing dangerous governments to change hands. At this point they didn't know how much or how little he knew, and throwing in Anthony Pallatzo would really make somebody scramble.

No formal charge would be made, but the bug would go in somebody's ear, new orders would go out to field agents and Tony Pell would be under scrutiny again. He'd know they were there, he'd smile and keep everything businesslike, and there would be nothing to report. Somehow he'd manage to do what he had to do, having a contingency plan for just this sort of thing. He'd keep it low-key and clean, but sooner or later some dirt would begin to show and the real Tony Pell would come out of his envelope.

Before he went to bed Mako retrieved his old .45 caliber Colt automatic, cleaned it thoroughly, even though it didn't need it, then oiled it, checked the mechanism until he was satisfied with its operation, and slammed in a fully loaded clip, slipping the rig into a niche between his bed and the wall.

He was getting that old feeling again. He didn't like it at all.

* * *

Billy Bright had scooped the eyes out of the fish heads in the stew. Judy expressed mild displeasure when Billy told her it was Mako's orders, but it was faked. Anyone who wanted fish stew for breakfast wouldn't make much of a fuss about eyes anyway. The rest of the meal would have cost a fortune in one of Miami's better restaurants, but here it was a simple island breakfast.

Judy made happy little sounds when she smelled the coffee aroma coming up from the galley. "Why is it your coffee smells so good, Mako?"

It wasn't a new question for him. "Because I get it fresh-ground in bags from Miami and keep it re-frigerated. On the island they buy the canned kind because the cans are as valuable to them as the cof-fee."

"Mako!"

"They have nice tight plastic tops and the painted metal takes a long time to rust out. You'd be sur-prised what they keep in them."

"Like what?"

"Like things you might keep in a medicine cabinet. Very personal items."

She stared at him for a moment, then smiled gently. "Are you almost talking dirty?"

"I'm talking about coffee cans."

Neither of them heard Billy come up behind them until he said, "Mr. Hooker, sar . . ."

Something was bothering his mate and Mako

knew it at once. His eyes tightened and he said, "Yeah, Billy?"

"The barometer . . ."

"So?"

"She is going to start to fall soon."

"You get a weather report on VHF?"

"No, sar. But she will fall, you betcha." There was a very worried expression on Billy's face.

"How would he know that?" Judy asked Mako.

Both of them scanned the sky for any indication of a weather change. It was cloudless and clear, a beautiful, hot day with waves running less than two feet, the wind gentle and from the southeast. There had been no notification of any change when they left the dock and from all indications it was no less than a perfect day to be going somewhere by boat. But still, Mako didn't argue the point. To Judy he said, "It's just something these islanders know."

"But the Miami weather station . . ."

"We're not in Miami."

Judy could read the seriousness in his tone and a frown wrinkled her forehead. "Are you going to turn back?"

"No . . . we're only two hours away from the *Sentilla*, and it's three hours back to Peolle."

Billy was watching him, quietly pleased that Mako had taken his warning seriously.

Mako said, "We won't do any night sailing, Billy, so quit sweating."

"Oh, I do not sweat, sar. We can make Reboka Island base before the glass she falls."

"Then why all the worry talk, Billy?"

The mate's eyes crinkled and Mako knew he was going to hear another of Billy's odd opinions or unfathomable judgments.

When he had his thoughts together, Billy said, "Sar, it is like this when the eater, he gets hungry."

"It's daytime, Billy."

"Yes, sar. If he is hungry, he will eat in the daytime."

"Tell me something, did the barometer always fall the other times when the boats . . . got 'et'?"

Very solemnly, Billy Bright nodded. "Every time. Yes, sar, every time."

"Your friends, they all notice it?"

"We talk about it. Yes, sar."

"They still went out in the daytimes, didn't they?"

His eyes roved the horizon. "So they can eat, they have to go out. Some think they can see the eater in time and maybe get away." He was remembering the *Soucan* with its bottom holed and Mako had seen the tooth marks himself. He was thinking about the eater being caught in Willie Pender's net and the way that tough nylon was neatly cut as if by a single great tooth.

"You scared, Billy?" Mako asked him.

A strained grin twitched at Billy's mouth and he shook his head. "If you and the missy are not scared, I'm not scared." Then he grinned very broadly and went back to the wheelhouse.

Judy turned her head and looked up at Mako. "You know, I really don't know just what's going on here between you two, but somehow I feel scared. I don't know what's happening but I'm beginning to feel that this little outing is more like a heavy business trip."

"You letting that 'eater' story bug you?"

"It's too ridiculous to be true. Those giant great white sharks are all extinct and you know it . . ."

"I've never dived that deep," he interrupted.

She knew he was making a joke of it, but she kept on anyway just to prove it to herself. "Never mind. If they were down there, and I said *were,* the enormous pressure change of coming to the surface would turn their bodies inside out." She ended with an emphatic nod.

But he still gave her something to chew on. "Whales dive deeper than sonar can track them. They lose touch below six thousand feet, yet they come up well fed and covered with sucker scars from giant squid."

Judy's eyes widened at the thought of his description and she let her breath out, not conscious of the way she had been holding it in. "You're just kidding about that . . . aren't you?"

"Nope. Besides, you're not scared."

"The hell I'm not."

"Can I put my arms around you and comfort you?"

She licked her lips and bobbed her head. "Sure."

Mako slid an arm around her shoulders. "How's that?"

"Big man," she said, "I'm real scared."

Before Mako could do anything about it, Billy's head poked out the wheelhouse window. "Mr. Hooker, sar, the glass, she has fallen two points."

"Call Miami and get a current report."

"I did that, sar. They said our barometer may be . . ."

"Defective?"

"Yes. That is the word they used."

"What do you think, Billy?"

"I can feel it, sar. The glass, she is good. Miami does not understand."

Under his hand he felt Judy shudder gently. On the horizon, both of them could see the thin darkening line of clouds starting to form. There was something ominous about them.

Mako said, "Quit calling me 'sar,' Billy."

"Yes, sar," Billy called right back. He had seen the clouds too. His hand nudged the throttle a little and the *Clamdip* picked up a few extra knots of speed toward Reboka Island.

Mako poured the both of them a Miller Lite beer and they leaned on the starboard rail, enjoying the moment, the only sound that of the waves lashing tiny tongues along the hull of the boat.

But moments like that were never made to last. Billy Bright had heard the click of a sending key, flipped the switch to the speaker and picked up the tight, disciplined voice of Chana Sterling saying, "*Drifter*, this is the *Tellig* calling. Please give us your position."

Almost immediately a heavy male voice responded with, "*Tellig*, this is *Drifter*. We are at B dash seven on your blue chart."

Mako grunted in disgust. They weren't using the regular nautical charts but had instituted one of their own so as not to give away their position.

"Roger, *Drifter*. We have located a disturbance. It

may be what we are looking for. We will need your diver. How soon can you join us?"

A hurried calculation was made and the voice came back, "Forty-five minutes will do it."

"Roger and out," Chana said.

Hesitantly, Judy asked, "Diver?"

"That would be the robot," Mako explained. "I'd sure like to know what kind of disturbance she was talking about."

"Could that be some kind of . . . ruse?"

"Not with Chana. She's all business."

"Why would she put it on the air like that?"

"Two reasons," Mako told her. "One is that she needs the robot. The other is that she wants everyone to know she nailed this sucker. In the area she works in, overt deeds of heroism make for rapid promotions."

"How high does she want to go?"

"Far enough to control the world."

"Or maybe just you," she added mischievously.

This time Mako gave her a sour glance. "She'd just like to shoot me again. In a way I hope she gets the chance."

"Why?"

"Then I can really kick her butt."

"What do you think that disturbance was she mentioned?"

"Could be a pod of whales."

Once again Billy's voice came out of the wheelhouse. "We can go see, sar. That is, if you want."

"I told you," Mako said, "that guy's got ears like a cat."

"Sar . . . ?"

"How would you know where they were, Billy?"

"The other day at the dock I see the big blue square on *Tellig*'s map. Others were in different colors. Blue part was over where Poca and Lule Malli catch the big marlin we all feast on."

"That was in open water, Billy. Poca didn't even have a map on board."

"I know the place," Billy said simply.

"But you don't really want to go there, do you?"

Instead of answering, Billy just shook his head.

"Okay, we continue on course. If they find the eater, good. They can take it back with them. If they get in trouble we'll go look for them."

"Suppose the eater gets them?" Judy suggested.

"Then we'll pour a cold beer over their watery grave. Or maybe half a beer."

At the wheel, Billy started whistling. They were staying on course and he was happy for everybody on board the *Clamdip*. But he was concerned about the *Tellig* and the *Drifter*. The clouds on the horizon were a little heavier now and the barometer had gone down another full point. The lady boss on the *Tellig* had said they had sighted a disturbance and whatever it was, he was sure it was the eater. And right now he was heading away from it. He touched the throttles again and the needles on the tachometer showed another ten RPM increase.

Fear was an emotion Chana Sterling would never admit to. Fear was something that belonged to cowards who fled from a confrontation with danger rather than face it. Right now the hair on the back of her neck felt a little stiff, but fear hadn't put a crimp in her actions.

Beside her Lee Colbert stood, one leg propped on the rail, the sporting rifle loaded with armor piercing explosive bullets held casually in his hand. It was that "masculine attitude" that annoyed Chana, that demeanor that didn't reek of fear at all but held the calmly interested expression she had seen on lab technicians peering into a microscope.

On their port side, ten miles out, the low cloud bank had a slow rolling motion. Every minute or so a yellow burst of light was visible along the line. "Lee," Chana asked, "did you ever see a weather front like that one?"

"Yeah, several times."

She knew he was deliberately making her wait, not finishing the explanation. Finally, exasperated, she said as quietly as she could, "Where?"

"Off the coast of Alaska during World War Two. They'd build up, then burst just as suddenly. Scared the hell out of the rookies." He gave her a meaningful glance and suppressed a smile.

Chana passed off this remark and kept staring at the ocean. The light chop that gave life to the water's surface suddenly flattened in a wild circle; the gulls that had been following the *Tellig* abruptly let out a series of raucous screams and wheeled off into disturbed flight. "There it is again," she said.

Lee Colbert's eyes were on her, but she wouldn't

acknowledge his unspoken question. She reached for the binoculars, focused them in and scanned the area. It hadn't changed in shape and seemed to be travelling in the same direction they were.

The big oval area seemed calm until it reached the rolling edges of its perimeter, where the waves chewed at it. The coloration was deeper, and blue in contrast to the green of the ocean itself. She stared even harder, analyzing what she was looking at. "There's a pressure under the surface," she said.

"Could it be a vent hole in the bottom spewing up magma?" He was grinning at her again.

"Lee, quit being an ass. This is the Atlantic," she spit at him, very annoyed now.

With the suddenness that it had appeared with, the flat calm gave way to the ocean's wave action again. She didn't put the glasses down. Here and there the surface would flatten again in a small area, then just as suddenly disappear.

When she took the binoculars away from her face, she said, "Lee . . ."

"What?"

"Something's down there."

He didn't answer her. Instead he pointed to the boat a few miles away coming up behind them. "There's the *Drifter.* Maybe now you'll know."

The bearded young man at the helm of the *Drifter* never would have been taken as an Annapolis graduate. His blue jeans were unwashed and cut off halfway between his knees and his bare feet, scraggly threads hanging down from the mock hems. His T-shirt advertised a suntan lotion and no hat covered his obviously home-cut hair.

But Commander Sullivan was among other things an underwater archaeologist, a trained diver, an expert in many things naval, and a Ph.D. in physics. His crew of six were equally disheveled and almost as well qualified in academic training. It was all a great cover. Being assigned to this present duty was like a paid vacation for all of them, because no way would there ever be a "ship eater" other than those in the stories you hear when happy hour is nearly over.

Sullivan recognized Chana's voice when she radioed, "*Drifter* from *Tellig*."

"Go ahead, *Tellig*."

"Can you see that flat spot on our port side?"

Through his glasses Sullivan surveyed the area. "There's a difference in the wave action, I think. You see anything?"

There seemed to be an anxious hesitancy in her voice when she said, "There seemed to be something there."

"Anybody else verify?"

"No. There was nothing to see. It was really a . . . condition."

"Hard to drop a depth charge on one of those things."

Chana's annoyance was clear. "There was something there, dammit!"

Sullivan tried not to chuckle in the microphone.

He pushed the throttles to full forward and told her, "We're coming up fast. Tell it to stick around."

She muttered something nasty and slipped her mike back in the holder hard. Lee tapped her arm and pointed off to the port. "It's back again, but this time it's leaving us."

Chana ran to the rail with the glasses to her eyes. A hump seemed to form on the surface, letting the small waves roll away to make a great oval again. She was holding her breath because it seemed almost likely that the "eater" would show itself, then the calmness quit and the oval grew smaller, and as Lee had said, it was beginning to flow past them.

Lee entered the time and sighting in the logbook, then tucked his pen in his pocket. He reached for the mike. To Chana he said, "Do we follow it or notify *Drifter*?"

"We'll stay clear, Lee. Tell him to get the robot out and pick it up underwater."

Lee pressed the mike button and said, "*Drifter*, you should be able to pick that disturbance up right about now. It's smaller, but it's heading back toward you. If you can release the robot you should be able to get some decent pictures."

"We have the area in sight, *Tellig*. The robot's going over the side now. Keep the area clear."

"Roger, *Drifter*. Out."

The engines on the *Tellig* lowered to one-quarter speed and the ship began a slow turn to the right. They could watch the activity on board the *Drifter*, saw the fat body of the eight-foot-long submersible being lowered into the water, then watched the team in the bow direct its movements from a handheld box.

The robot was one of the developments Sullivan had pioneered in the last five years. With miniaturization had come simplification, and handling the robot was much like flying a model airplane. The RV in the nose immediately sent back pictures that were taped and made you wonder why this wasn't done when they were diving on the *Titanic* or looking for the *Bismarck*. Everybody just wanted to make things bigger and more complicated, Sullivan thought. Maybe now he could prove something to them.

But his thoughts had interfered with his actions. What should have been immediate was delayed two seconds, and he didn't hit the lever fast enough to steer the robot where it should have gone. The ocean top suddenly changed as though huge hands just below its surface had waved upward, forming a huge wet hump, and out of the corner of his eye he caught something on the TV screen, but it wasn't something he was bothered about, because he would see it later on tape. But then the screen suddenly flashed and went white; the indicator on the box in his hand went dead and he knew he had lost the robot. The eater had gotten his equipment.

Then the flat spot on the water quietly disappeared. Whitey, his mate, said, "Something's coming this way, sir."

Barely discernible, the oval formed again, coming closer to the *Drifter* before seeming to go right under the ship itself.

The bite came with a shattering crunch and *Drifter* lurched in the water as though a dog had hold of their bottom, then she was tossed loose like a discarded bone and a hoarse voice from the cabin yelled, "We're taking on water!"

Drifter stopped rolling but listed five degrees off center.

Sullivan yelled, "Damage control . . . see what happened." He reached for the mike and called *Tellig*. What he said made the film of sweat on Chana's back suddenly go icy. "Something hit the robot, now it's hit us."

"What's your damage, *Drifter*?"

"We're holed, that's for sure. We're listing, but we have a double bottom under us and I think our pumps will hold. You'd better come alongside and we'll head for the *Sentilla*."

"You going to radio ahead?" Chana asked him.

In case anyone was monitoring the VHF, he said noncommittally, "You know our orders."

Which meant that anything like this was for secret communication only at this point.

But someone *was* listening. Hooker flipped the switch off and turned on his hi-fi. Judy saw him grinning and squinted at him. "What was that all about?"

Billy Bright stuck his head out to see what he had to say. "Looks like Billy's called the shots again. He knew something was going to happen."

A finger pointed toward the west. "Sar, those clouds that were rising . . . they are near gone now."

"What's the barometer reading now, Billy?"

After a quick glance, Billy told him, "She much better now, sar. I think the eater will not be back."

Judy said, "You believe that?"

The grin on Mako's mouth twisted into a puzzled scowl. "I like it better than what those guys on *Drifter* are thinking of right now."

She thought about what she was going to say for a moment, then looked at Hooker. "They're going to have more to think about next."

"Oh?"

"Yeah, *oh. Lotusland* is filming *Sentilla* and the naval exercise and the main ship of the Midnight Cruise lines are putting in to give the customers a show."

"Why didn't you tell me?" Hooker said, annoyed.

"Because it shouldn't have made any difference. Nobody expected this to happen."

Hooker grinned again. "Well," he said jokingly, "we'll blame it all on the Bermuda Triangle."

At the wheel Billy Bright let out a loud grunt of disdain.

Chapter Nine

The island was banana-shaped, a two-mile-long rising of green, fertile land, edged with a beach of blazingly white sand and populated with hordes of wheeling, screaming birds. The concave side faced the east, the bottom falling away quickly so larger boats could come in almost to the shore. The concrete blocks and support pilings still stood where they had once protected long-ranging German submarines during the First World War, and the rusting ruin of the single large machine shop still contained the aging remnants of forges and tooling to repair their charges.

To the left of all this was the orderly supply center for the *Sentilla*, crates and barrels of supplies, with two loading barges, their ramps down, ready to transport equipment out to the ship.

In the rear, under the trees, out of the glaring sunlight, were the nearly camouflaged outlines of the hutches the local workers occupied. Well away from the high tide line a dozen small craft sat ready, sails tied down, another two with those almost-antique

Johnson outboards that still ran smoothly, and another upside down where several boys were busy repairing the bottom.

The *Sentilla* was anchored a mile and a half offshore, three smaller boats in its lee. Tenders moved back and forth to the mother ship periodically, then there would be a cessation of activity, a dull boom could be heard, and a geyser of water erupted at the surface of the ocean. Immediately, the activity would resume and sailors with earphones and mouthpieces relayed information and instructions to others out of sight.

On board the *Clamdip* the three scanned the action while they cruised past the island. When the *Sentilla* didn't block their view they saw the sleek hull of *Lotusland,* her decks lined with avid studio hands waving to the small boats pulling away from the mother ship. The boats were all motorized and shot away rapidly, going around the naval vessel, heading northward. The first two had camera crews aboard, communicating with each other.

Hooker said, "They're using plain old CB radio there, Billy. See if you can pick them up."

"Yes, sar," Billy agreed.

"Damn it, Billy, quit with that 'sar' business, will you?"

"Your shark name is trouble, sar."

"Billy . . . do you eat mako sharks?"

"Only when I can catch him, sar."

"Then why are you afraid of them?"

"So I don't get 'et' first, sar."

Judy grinned at Hooker. "Good thinking. Maybe I should call you something else too."

"Like what?"

"Oh . . . good-looking, big boy . . . ," she teased.

Billy held his hand up and they stopped talking. Billy had nailed the CB frequency and the chatter told them that they were ready to cover anything that could be photographed around the *Drifter*. Divers were on board with underwater cameras while another crew would film any surface action that happened.

Mako realized that neither ship could try to order anybody away without revealing their identity, and that the only information that would be let out was that *Drifter* had sustained an accident, probably hitting a submerged object, and *Tellig* was assisting her to a safe place.

Judy took her glasses from her eyes and pointed toward the southeast. "Mako . . . check the horizon about one-thirty degrees."

He raised his binoculars and focused on the area she was pointing to. She was coming up fast, the big, proud hull of the main ship of the Midnight Cruise line. "There'll be a hot time in the old town tonight," he said.

"You can bet on it." Judy grimaced. "They're going to give the tourists just what they're paying for."

"And what's that?"

"Real action. Something to tell their friends about. Stuff from the Devil's Triangle, an eater tearing boats apart."

"You think that's going to impress them?"

For the first time she gave him a deep, serious look, her expression tinged with some hidden sadness. "There are a lot of jaded people on board, Mako. They're so damn rich they can buy anything they want. Now they're being given something they can't buy. Nothing better for them than the blood smell. It's impending danger. It sends their pulses sky-high and their feet back to the bar again to get back to normal."

"Judy . . . you are a part owner of Midnight Cruises."

"I didn't start it. Daddy did."

"You think this is what he planned?" Mako asked her.

She shook her head and stared out at the water. "No, it was to be something different. Daddy got . . . well, overwhelmed in business." She paused momentarily, then added, "It's tough when heavy money gets to be the big prize in life."

Hooker reached out and put his arm around her shoulder. With a childlike gesture she came against him, feeling the hardness of his arms and the taut musculature that pressed against her side. His fingers were wrapped very softly around her upper arm and she wondered briefly what power they could exert if he had wanted them to.

It only lasted a few moments when the radio came alive again with the *Drifter* and *Sentilla* both warning the small boats to stand off and saying that they were taking no responsibility for accidents. Divers were being told that they would be in a danger zone under the ships, but apparently nobody paid any attention. This was a once-in-a-lifetime situation and committed photographers would never pass up an opportunity like it at any cost. If they got nipped by a prop their names would go down in the record books of great underwater stuntmen. The occasion would never warn off other divers at all. They'd just want to make sure they stayed well away from ships' propellers.

Nobody seemed to care about the eater at all.

Commander Sullivan's face was set in a tight mask of anger. Whatever had slashed through the bottom hull had taken a small gouge out of the inner one and cut right through the main cable that powered the TV receiver on the deck above. Whatever the robot had picked up was lost forever. Disgustedly, he and his mate went back up the ladder, hooked the receiver into a secondary power circuit and flipped it on for a rerun.

And there was the robot's eye, peering into the green of the Atlantic, watching the flow of sea life slip around its contoured form. For thirty seconds the field of vision was good to seventy-five feet and in its lateral movements it picked up broken streamers of sargassum and a pair of unidentifiable fish darting out of range. Sullivan glanced at his watch. At any second the robot should be in the oval area he had pointed it at.

And suddenly there was something there. The visibility just as suddenly was shadowed into deep gloom, and before the automatic floodlight could cut in, the robot was hit with a wall of bubbles and for a single fraction of a second Sullivan thought he saw a set of the wildest, most formidable teeth he could ever imagine; then the set went blank.

The commander held a breath a moment before letting it hiss out. "You see that?"

"I saw something," the mate told him.

"Describe it."

"Beats me. It went by so fast . . ."

"Damn it, let's show it again until we know what it is."

"That's no guess."

"Well," the mate thought, "it was kind of angular."

"How big?"

"Who knows, Sully? We have nothing to reference it with. It was just there and gone. Hell, it could have been a piece of flotsam or a hunk of that sargassum that floats around out here." He stopped and squinted at the commander. "Why? What did you think it was?"

Very quietly and deliberately, Sullivan asked, "You think it could have been . . . teeth?"

"Come on, Sully, quit dreaming, will you?"

"Something hit us, pal."

"Sure, and there's a lot of somethings along the bottom here. Yesterday we fouled the prop twice on some old netting if you remember."

"And I remember whacking that rotted-out old

boat that was floating just beneath the surface, but it sure didn't hole our bottom."

"Some old wreck . . ."

Sullivan shook his head. "We would have picked it up on the gauges, pal. Nothing was there. Nothing."

"Something was there, Sully."

Outside, the shouting had started and he knew those idiots with the cameras were going to be all over the place. Well, they had been warned. They had acknowledged the warning. They came on anyway. He and the mate went outside the cabin and watched them. Their equipment was new and state-of-the-art, communication between divers and their boat was evident, and they worked in pairs with true professional detachment yet were extremely aware of the danger of their job.

Sullivan and the mate nodded approvingly. They weren't going to sweat out this team at all. They went back to the TV screen to review the flash shot of what the robot had transmitted before it went out of action.

Captain Don Watts personally welcomed Hooker and Judy aboard the *Sentilla*. None of them had met, but the captain had made a quick search of military records and media accounts of his guests to realize that these were no mere tourists. Mako's security clearance rate was ultra-high and a good portion of his service details were still secret. His agency had directed Watts to assist him in whatever area he needed help, stating that he and the crew of *Tellig* had a joint cooperation in place. However, it was intimated that Hooker's judgment took precedence in this matter.

On the stern, the three of them had tall glasses of iced tea while they went through the initial stages of investigative introductions. Judy let herself be dismissed as the heiress to Arthur Durant, with only a monetary interest in the Midnight Cruise line and Lotusland Productions.

She played the game well, having been in it a long time. She could seem aloof or distant during a conversation involving a great deal of technicalities, yet remain totally aware of its substance and intent.

The captain was one of those naval officers who thought the whole world should be wet. He was only happy when he was on the deck of a military vessel, engaged in a military action surrounded by military personnel. Anything else was a major nuisance, and although this had an interesting aspect to it, he preferred to deal with it quickly and get it over with without too much bother.

There was something imposing about the captain. A subdued military demeanor hinted that this man had been through the deadly fire of the war and come through intact and more wise than before because he was born to command and win; yet as imposing as he was, his attitude was direct and friendly.

He said, "Washington has sent me all your credentials, Colonel."

Judy's eyes made a small movement when she heard Mako called by rank.

"Forget the title, Captain. It'll make my work easier."

Captain Watts nodded. Being a player in any covert action wasn't part of his makeup, but if he had to be, he felt better being among friendlies. At least the army had a reservist here who was an old pro who knew what the angles were all about. "Tell me, how can I help you?" he asked, waving toward the deck chairs a sailor had brought out.

When they sat down Hooker said, "This operation you're on . . . what clearance do you have?"

"You don't know?"

Hooker shook his head. "This came up suddenly. I just happened to be on the spot so they called me in."

"There is no security risk on this operation at all, Colonel."

"Hooker . . . or Mako, okay? Forget the title."

"Certainly. Anyway, this is a very public and very standard type of action for us. This time we have been ordered to participate in an underwater exploration of certain geological movements of the earth's crust that seemed to emanate from this area. We have aboard twenty-three government specialists who are in charge of monitoring this activity, and their results and opinions have all been made public too. They go directly to Washington, uncoded, and are later published in scientific journals."

"Something's raising hell," Mako commented.

Watts shrugged and sipped at his iced tea. "That all started after the detonations were substituted for the electronic impulses. The equipment hasn't been repaired yet."

"That sure drew everybody's attention."

"Col . . . Hooker, when stories about boats being eaten by some strange sea creature leak to the press, on comes the sordid publicity that interrupts a scientific fact-finding operation."

"Something's doing it," Hooker told him.

"Something's always doing it. You know how many boats on the islands were lost last year? Just lost, not to hurricanes or collisions. Not to sea creatures, just plain lost?"

"How many?"

"There were fourteen by official records. There were twenty-seven rescued. Their reasons for losing the boats were sound enough. A loose plank, fire from cooking areas, gasoline leaks on outboard-powered crafts, a couple of collisions with subsurface debris. Nothing that ate them, though."

"How do you treat their stories, Captain?"

"I give them a great deal of thought, Hooker, a great deal. I've been out to sea too damn long not to pay attention to detail even if I don't understand it. This 'eater' concept is ridiculous. You agree?"

For a few seconds Hooker just stared at the sea. "I haven't given it a great deal of thought yet. You think those mines on the sunken hulk had anything to do with it?"

"Anything's possible, but after the few breakaways, we managed to secure the rest on the bottom for the time being. We know about those that reached Scara Island, but that's as far as they will go anyway. Later we'll dispatch a detonation team to blow them and that should end that. Two have already been destroyed. The *Tellig* took care of one."

"You planning anything for the rest of the mines on the wreckage?"

"They'll be wired before we leave the post and blown when everything's clear. It ought to make a real show for the Midnight Cruise lines."

Judy looked up and nodded toward the camera ship. "And *Lotusland.* You're giving them a million dollars' worth of publicity."

"Uncle Sam is happy to help," Watts offered. He looked over their heads toward the south and told them, "That crew of divers should add another million to the budget. *Drifter* and *Tellig* are getting major roles in this movie."

The three of them stood and went to the rail. Chana's crew had nudged *Drifter* to the large platform attached to *Sentilla's* hull, and two dozen sailors secured her properly and got lines from the *Sentilla's* cranes around her hull. In thirty minutes the area was cleared and the winch operator on the crane began the lift. The *Drifter* moved in its sling, then began to come out of the water like a toy.

Handheld cameras operated by the divers and others on their small boats recorded the entire event. Lenses zoomed in as *Drifter* rose and little by little closed in, and they all got a firsthand look at the single, six-foot-long gash in the bottom, the edges peeled upward into the hull as though a giant ax had slashed through the metal with one enormous stroke. Water poured out like a miniature Niagara and the crane held the ship in that one position until the flow ceased. Only then did one sailor walk up under the *Drifter* and snap close-up pictures of the bottom. When he walked away he waved off the divers with silent authority, then he stood back and gave a wave to the crane operator, and the *Drifter* started to rise to the *Sentilla's* deck.

Hooker nudged the captain and asked, "Would you have done that with a civilian vessel?"

"It would be an option under extreme circumstances. In this case it's a necessity."

"Then I take it *Drifter* is military equipment."

"So to speak, Hooker."

"The government's pretty raunchy, isn't it?"

"When it has to be," Watts told him. He looked at Hooker again, his smile grim. "That's why you're here, isn't it?"

"Not really," Hooker said. He took a deep breath and let it out slowly. "I'm more like an accident."

"Just waiting to happen," Watts put in.

"Something like that," Hooker told him.

Judy joined the men at the rail, watched while *Drifter* was lowered down onto chocks on the deck, then said, "The captain of the Midnight Cruise line has requested that the three of us join him and his passengers for supper on the beach tonight."

Watts gave her a sharp glance. "Requested how?"

She pointed toward the cruise ship off their side and waved. A light flashed on the bridge, so they knew they were being watched through a telescope.

"Answer?" Judy queried.

"That's code," the captain said sharply.

"I can read Morse, Captain. Well?"

"How's he going to get all those passengers on the beach?"

Judy let out a gentle laugh. "Not that many will want to go, Captain. Some will be adventurous, but the rest will prefer the bar or the gaming tables. One thing you can be sure of: the food will be exceptional. In fact, the whole evening might be exciting. I'm inviting the crew of the *Tellig* there too."

Hooker gave her a questioning look, but she didn't explain any further.

Very gradually, the sun was completing its arc in the heavens, beginning its slow descent into the ocean. Seabirds winged their way back to the islands and the shadows that danced off the wave tips grew longer. A lone palm tree, somehow uprooted from its island, bobbed aimlessly. The branches slapped the surface and the small, fingerlike clump of root system made eerie wriggling motions, the tips white with salt froth. Its shadow had no mass to it, just a black streak that formed and broke continuously.

Small fish that liked to dive and play around floating objects and their shadows made a myriad of sparkles and splashes, and here and there a small, violent disturbance indicated something bigger had zeroed in on them for a quick kill and fast meal. The reaction would be immediate as the others fled to safety, but their memories were short and they returned within minutes as though nothing at all had happened.

Outside the perimeter of the great palm the predators waited, darting in at their own convenience, selecting their victim when they were ready, not conscious of any danger, because in this area they were safe. They would eat at their own pace, and when they were sated, they would move off as a group to other natural activities.

They knew no danger.

Here they were the only predators.

Realization took time, even for them. They felt a pressure from below, an upward push that shouldn't have been there at all, and the predators knew that something else was there, something bigger and more deadly than anything they had ever experienced before—and instinct told them to flee. They left fluorescent streaks in the water that was beginning to darken with the dusk, and a great oval calmness started to form as though the ocean suddenly had a gelatin shell, and the ghastly blue form of it just below the surface seemed to turn in an agony of birth; then, as sheet lightning lit up the sky in the east, the thing glided away and the sea returned to normal.

The great palm was totally unconcerned by it all. The few frightened forms of sea life that had stayed hidden in its branches swam out, but not too far. They too were guided by instinct.

Chapter Ten

The Midnight Cruise ship was well prepared for any contingency. A spur-of-the-moment beach party dinner was a simple matter to arrange, even with an elaborate menu of gourmet items. A sturdy motor transporter ferried the stoves, tables and place settings while another carried all the foodstuffs. The operation was so efficient that hardly anybody noticed. The guests were formed into teams and prepared to do some exploring before dinner.

Chana and Lee Colbert had let the initial teams go ahead to pick their way around the rubble of the old submarine base. Chana shook her head and said, "Listen to them. You'd think they were in Disney World. All they're doing is traipsing through wreckage."

"In their world, lady, they don't see junk. They only see money and what it can buy. This is a new adventure for them."

"Come on, Lee, they're tourists."

He gave her a tight smile. "Sure they are. Millionaire tourists. Hell, you can't even get a boarding pass on that ship unless you have a seven-digit income. Not capital. Income from the capital. Get the picture?"

The frown Chana turned on him showed pure displeasure. "That's disgusting!"

"That's what the last report from the Company indicated. I take it you didn't read it."

"No. I was busy with other matters. It was filed under general correspondence. I'll read it later."

Lee waved his hand at the backs of the retreating passengers. All of them were uniformed in white or khaki hiking clothes, some with Frank Buck jungle helmets and others with cute kepi-style coverings from expensive tailoring shops.

For a minute, Chana studied them again, then asked, "Why are they all waving like that?"

"They're off the beach," he told her.

"So?"

"They're on the grass and they haven't been issued any bug spray. Somebody is going to catch hell."

Lee had barely spoken when they saw a young sailor in the ship's colors running hard to catch the plodding assembly. Two canvas bags were over his shoulders and when he reached them he began passing out the canisters with instructions on their use and made sure everyone was well equipped before he started back.

When he reached Hooker and Judy he stopped and grinned at them. "Sure appreciate you telling me about that."

"No trouble."

"It would be for me if the boss man knew about it."

Judy thought Mako was going to say something and gave him a nudge, but all he said was, "Just give us a wink when we eat. I want a seat close to the kitchen."

The boy gave him a wink and said, "You got it, man."

Judy took Mako's arm, stuffed her bug spray in her pocket and started walking toward the remains of the repair shed on the beach. "He wouldn't have believed you anyway," she said.

Mako didn't answer.

"Do I look like a part owner of the fleet?"

This time Mako nodded. "Sure you do."

He was so matter-of-fact about it that she stopped and faced him, her brow furrowed. "Why?" she demanded. "Why would I?"

"Because you're with me," he told her. Then he grinned and said, "I'm the dominant male, wouldn't you say?"

"Damn!" She laughed and kicked sand at his feet.

The perfumed chemical smell of the insect repellent hung over the island. Laboratory technology had improved the performance of the insecticide a thousand percent since the jungle warfare of World War II. There was no wild waving at clouds of minute flying things because they were either dead or held at bay by man's chemical expertise.

Flashbulbs from small cameras were capturing the maze of bent steel girders, and inquisitive tourists were prying in and around ancient tooling devices and rotted cranes. Here and there a shriek would erupt as some furry thing dashed out of a hiding place, or a scorpion would suddenly become alert and make a threatening gesture at a portly millionaire who wasn't used to violence of this sort at all. One tried bug spray on the terrestrial arachnid and all it did was spur the little beast into a charge. The man's eyes bugged and sheer fright immobilized him, but the scorpion abruptly stopped and the man swallowed hard without being seen, then stepped back.

His pudgy little wife beamed at his bravery and said, "Dear, that was marvelous!"

"Yes" was all he could answer. His voice was quite humble. Inside all he could think was that that little bugger had scared the crap out of him.

Hooker and Judy were outside the scene, but they had found something of their own. Protruding from the sand was a huge piece of curved, shaped metal. Unlike most of the iron and steel around the base, this one showed no trace of rust at all. Hooker pried up a piece of board and began shoveling away the sand until four feet of it showed plainly. Judy said, "Is that what I think it is?"

Hooker nodded. "Part of it, anyway." He poked away just below it and hit something solid. "A blade of a propeller. And here's another one."

"That second one's awfully close to the other one, isn't it?"

"Well, it's more than a four-bladed baby, that's for sure. At the angle I see here, this prop must have carried eight or ten blades."

"How big across, would you say?"

"The circumference of rotation would have to have been at least twelve feet." He started pushing the sand back into its original position. "That was a big bastard for World War One." His face had a puzzled expression and Judy noticed it when he joined her.

"What's the matter, Mako?"

"There's no rust on that prop."

"What about it?"

"The thing isn't stainless steel, but it's in better shape than what we're producing today."

"But it's just laying there."

"I know," he told her. "Apparently the German metallurgists were way ahead of their time. They didn't even bother to try to hide what they had. They just used it, figuring they were going to win the war anyway."

"Hooker . . . is it that important?"

"No, not now. We can produce hardened, nonrusting metals ourselves, but back then it would have been quite a coup, as the Indians say."

"Then why did you cover it up?"

"Because there might be something there that needs looking into. We'll let Captain Watts send a team in to recover it." He scanned Judy's half-closed eyes. "What's bothering you now?"

"That propeller had been here since 1918. How come nobody else ever spotted it?"

"Maybe they did, but who cared? The war was over. Nobody wanted this island, it was all history and destined to rust."

"Except that it didn't rust."

"No, and neither do your zippers on your jacket. We caught up, okay?"

She thought a moment, then agreeably nodded. "Okay."

Mako took her hand and led her back into the maze of aging girders. In the rubble was the culture of another generation; a single shoe of heavy leather, a piece of striped cloth—part of an apron—both too rotted to touch. The mouth of a whiskey bottle protruded from the sand and in one corner was a heap of old beer bottles, some with corks still in them.

At the far end was the office or what was left of the office. The furniture was not what any native would use, so it was sand-covered, but recognizable. The wooden filing cabinets had come apart and only shards of papers were to be seen, but an ancient typewriter, still covered by a cracked rubber hood, sat on a sturdy table, looking totally untouched.

Judy asked why.

"Natives could have been superstitious. This was the home area of the place to them. They didn't like the unexplainable, so this place could have been taboo. Anyway, who knows?"

"The others from the ship could have taken souvenirs from here."

"Not likely, kid. This was adventure, not an auction. It'll all look better in photographs. You hungry?"

"Starved."

Mako glanced at his watch. "We can beat them to the tables if we shake it a little."

From a good distance away, Lee Colbert put down

his binoculars. For an hour he and Chana had stayed out of sight but kept a close watch on Judy and Mako. "They're just kicking up sand," he said.

"Balls. Hooker's up to something."

"Chana, knock it off," Lee told her testily. "They haven't been looking for anything and they haven't found anything."

"Then why is he here?"

"Damn it, Chana, he's here because he's got a woman with him!"

"What difference does that make?" she spit back.

Very quietly, but very nastily, Lee said, "At least he knows she won't shoot him."

Captain Don Watts wasn't about to miss a meal on the beach. For too long he had been exposed to the superb elegance of French and Italian trainee chefs on board the ship, and now he wanted the smell of charcoal fires and to hear the sizzling of plain old hamburgers on the grill. A pair of the islanders who worked on the *Sentilla* had already buried yams and a fresh-caught fish in leaf wrappings, and the aroma hung over the beach like a pleasant cloud.

A portable plank bar had been set up above the high tide mark, bottles of distilled spirits glistening like jewels, but the glassware was heavy and old-fashioned. A half keg of beer was chocked in place at the end of the bar, an old wooden spigot rammed into the bung. Thick mugs with heavy handles were grouped around it.

"A miniature Sloppy Joe's," Judy said.

"Anything for a change," Hooker told her. "They'll be lining up at a keg and spilling the suds all over the place. I wonder when was the last time these old boys bellied up to a beer bar?"

She looked up at him and grinned. "Oh, these old boys have been there and back, believe me. Two in that crowd started out in pushcarts."

"Selling what?"

"War surplus," she said. "The government threw it away and they sold it back to use in Korea."

Before he could answer, he spotted Captain Watts coming up the beach and waved. Watts was sipping the foam off a mug of cold suds, washing down a mouthful of hamburger with apparent relish.

When he got closer he yelled, "You'd better get into the chow before the crowd gets here."

"We intend to," he said, pulling Judy to an angle to intercept the bar. When they all had a beer and burger they curled down into the sand far enough away from the squealing of the happy crowd so that they could talk without shouting.

Judy asked, "How long are you staying, Don?"

"When they dry up the bar they'll be ready to go back. This bunch is always ready for a little extracurricular activity. They never miss an outing. Some of them wanted to go skin diving, but none were qualified."

"You need a certificate out here?" Judy put in.

Watts shook his head. "Didn't have to explain. We just pointed out the sharks the boys had piled up on

the dock and that slowed them down pretty quickly."
The captain stopped and stared over Mako's and
Judy's heads a moment, then said, "Company com-
ing," and stood up.

Hooker got up with him and let out a tight smile at
Chana and Lee Colbert. Judy waved from her position in the sand. There was another girl with them,
and this one was no tourist. The sun had burned her
almost as dark as Mako, but she had gremlin eyes
where diving goggles had given her a strange mask of
white, and in the dimming light it was almost impossible to tell if she was plain or pretty.

Captain Watts made the introductions. The girl
was Kim Sebring, an oceanographer from Woods
Hole who was researching ocean currents around the
area where the *Sentilla* was operating.

When everybody was back in the sand again, Judy
asked her why Woods Hole would be interested in
this area.

"You know the history of Reboka Island?" Kim
asked.

"Only that it was a German sub base in World War
One," Hooker told her. "Was there more to it?"

The girl shrugged. "Historically, it's a question mark.
Submarine warfare was in its infancy at that time, but
the German government realized its potential. Unfortunately for them, their technology was limited and
their production capabilities didn't measure up to their
plans."

"How did they pick this place?" Watts queried.

"Probably through information gathered from

their shipping trade. Most likely the subs were towed as far as they could be. In some instances the records show they were towed all the way. Incidentally, did you see those low spots in back of the buildings?"

Mako said, "I saw them through the office windows. They sure weren't foundation excavations."

"They were blowout holes," Kim told them. "Originally, huge steel tanks were buried there. Fuel cells, loaded with oil for the subs."

"What happened to them, Kim?" Judy asked.

"The operation ceased," the diver told her. "The war ended. They had used up all the oil anyway and when a hurricane hit here and flooded the island, those big, empty drums just burst through the sand and floated away. Apparently the vents were left open, because they were never seen again."

Hooker finished off his beer and wiped his mouth. "You trying to locate them?"

"No way." Kim laughed. "They were made of thin metal that has long since been eroded away. No, I've been checking out the odd currents in the area. The way everything gets dumped on Scara Island, for one thing."

"Those mines that drifted there were a surprise."

"Not really. All sorts of odd things wind up on that beach. There are parts of old ships from the eighteen hundreds, wreckage from torpedoed boats during World War Two. There were even two houses that drifted down from Florida during a hurricane. They didn't last long, though. Whatever hits the sun and the sand doesn't last long."

Hooker said, "You'd think the kids with metal detectors would be scouring the area."

"Why, metal doesn't float. Buoyancy and a strange tidal current keep the junk on Scara Island."

"Too bad."

"Except for a float sent up from a sunken submarine."

"A float?"

"Yeah. Apparently one of the subs assigned to the base here submerged and couldn't blow its tanks to come up. When they had tried everything the captain shot the float up through one of the torpedo tubes."

"You're a real seagoing encyclopedia, lady."

Kim gave him a small laugh. "You know what the Kingston valve is?"

"Tell me."

"It's the valve that controls the flow of compressed air. When the sub was submerged the air was compacted into high-pressure containers while seawater flooded chambers that gave the sub negative buoyancy to take it down. To go up, the compressed air was released, blew out the seawater and the sub rose to the top. Only in this case, the valve stuck."

"Who's got the float now?"

"It's in the Naval Academy at Annapolis."

"How'd you wind up here?"

"Magazine assignment. Our bunch at Woods Hole get some beauties since we work closely with government projects."

"They sent you out by yourself?"

Kim shook her head at Hooker. "I'm not alone.

There are four of us on the dive and we're well equipped."

For the first time Chana spoke up, the tone of her voice tinged with a note of superiority. "You're not afraid of the eater, I take it."

Kim laughed again. "Lady, I'm afraid of everything I'm not prepared for."

"Then how do you prepare for an eater?"

A casual shrug touched the girl's shoulders. "Hell," she said, "I'm not a boat." She turned her head abruptly and grinned at Judy and Hooker. "Either of you two divers?"

"I've got a ticket," Mako told her.

When Judy said she was certified too, Mako gave her a curious glance. "You get around, kiddo."

"Daddy let me dive for three seasons with the sponge fleet. We were using hard hats then."

Hooker said to Kim, "You need some extra hands on your project?"

"Two of our divers have head colds you wouldn't believe. They take a shallow dive off the boat and it's like eating a cold ice cream cone and having that hammer hit you in the forehead."

"I remember the feeling," Hooker said. He nudged Judy and asked, "You want to lend a helping hand?"

"Sure, but I'm not an oceanographer."

"No sweat," Kim told her. "All you have to do is stick plastic pennants on wire rods into the sand. We'll be at fifty feet to seventy feet with hundred-foot clear visibility. Nothing dangerous down there we can't handle, and when we're done we can drop on down to the wreck of an old submarine. It's been there since 1918."

"Interesting," Judy said. "What about the diving gear?"

Hooker said, "I have equipment for four on board the *Clamdip*."

"Tanks?" Kim asked.

"Eight fully filled," Mako told her. "There's a four-stage compressor on board if we need to recharge."

Chana's eyes narrowed slightly. "Why would you carry all that equipment for, Hooker?"

"I'm a sports fan," he told her. Then, "Why don't you come along, Chana. Diving is one of your specialties, isn't it?"

There was more in his tone than an invitation. This time it was a direct order given so that no one would suspect he had the commanding position. Chana's hands tightened involuntarily, then she gave a small smile of pleasure and nodded her acceptance.

Hooker grinned back and squeezed Judy's hand. "What time do we leave, Kim? We'd better take the *Clamdip* instead of your little boat. We're up to our ears in supplies and the *Tellig* will be staying on station with the *Sentilla*, right?"

Lee Colbert was pleased with the idea. He could get the official business done with Captain Watts without Chana looking over his shoulder, and Chana would have a good opportunity to find out just what role Hooker had in this game.

Kim said, "We'll leave at six A.M. It's about a forty-minute ride to the dive site, so we should be in the water at seven-thirty. That sound okay?"

"Suits me," Hooker said for Judy and himself. "Where are you tied up?"

"On the other side of the *Sentilla* at the floating dock."

"Good, I'll pick you up there." To Chana he said, "You staying on board your boat tonight?"

"Where else?"

"Then I'll pick you up after I get Kim and her partner."

"I'll be ready," Chana said, then looked at Judy. "Thanks for inviting us to the beach party."

"My pleasure," Judy told her. "It was fun."

When Lee and Chana walked away Captain Watts eased up from his cross-legged position in the sand and brushed his pants off. Down by the water's edge the last of the cruise ship's passengers were boarding the boats to get back to the main ship. A handful of sailors were packing away the picnic equipment and when they were ready the captain said, "I suppose you two are going to get in on the cruise ship's festivities, right?" He gave them a wry grin. "I understand they have two major shows, two lounge shows and a fully equipped gaming section."

"They have everything on that ship," Judy reminded him.

"Except spare quarters," Captain Watts laughed. "I hear they are completely sold out."

"For three years in advance." Judy smiled back. "Even being a part owner doesn't mean a thing."

Watts gave her back a broad smile. "Just think of the money you're making."

"The name of the game." She smirked. "Anyway, I have my own cabin on the *Clamdip*." When Hooker didn't say anything she prodded. "Well, don't I?"

"Hell, a hammock on deck isn't so bad," Hooker mumbled.

"No wonder Chana shot you."

Watts glanced up sharply. "What?"

With phony fierceness Judy nodded and said, "That's right, she put a bullet right in him."

"That true?" the captain asked.

"Yeah, but she missed."

"Missed what?"

"Killing me," Hooker said, his voice cold.

"Damn! How'd that happen?"

"Women and guns make an unhappy combination."

Watts didn't ask anything further, but the half-concealed smile begged an answer.

Hooker said, "I'll keep her guessing on that dive. I'll stay in back of her and she'll never know if I'm going to jab a knife into her or not."

Quietly, Judy asked, "Would you?"

"No," he answered softly, "but I'd like to. Trouble is, it would draw blood, then the sharks would come, then maybe the eater would come and we'd all be in one heck of a mess. Anyway, Captain, we'll cancel on your invitation for tonight."

"Maybe tomorrow night, then?"

"Good. You're on."

On the way back to the *Clamdip* in the dinghy they enjoyed the whine of the small Johnson outboard and the salt taste of the spray on their faces. The night was warm, the air a little heavy, but the moonlight sparkled off the waves. Ahead of them was their boat, lights blazing on deck and below. When they got close they could see Billy Bright pacing in the wheelhouse and Judy asked, "What's wrong with him?"

"He's alone, it's nighttime and he's scared witless that the eater is going to make a snack of him."

But it wasn't that at all.

Billy had caught a radio message directed to the ship *Tellig*. A cameraman in a light plane sent up by the *Lotusland* had gotten clear shots of the eater. It was plainly seen by the pilot, the copilot and the cameraman, although they could not determine the depth below the surface. The day was clear, the sunlight bright and the plane was headed back to process the negatives.

The answer from the *Tellig* was direct. They identified themselves as a government agency and the film was to be delivered to the *Tellig* immediately upon development. Five minutes went by before the *Lotusland* chiefs acknowledged in the positive. Nothing was said about it being the sole copy. This time the government was dealing with Hollywood, and movieland wasn't going to let any U.S. agency get away with a prize like this.

Billy brought them a cold Miller Lite after he lashed the dinghy down, joining Mako and Judy in the deck chairs. Simply knowing that the eater had been photographed brought him a sense of satisfaction. The unknown had suddenly become known and now it was something they could go to war over.

Judy said, "How are they going to get this before the public, Mako?"

"Probably TV. That *Lotusland* group will go over every detail of that film for their own use before they get it to the *Tellig*. Chana might have come down hard with her demands, but there's no way they can force the issue. Not at this point, anyway."

"Would it be to anybody's advantage to hold it back?"

"Uh-uh. This 'eater' story is big news, a damn sight bigger than the Bermuda Triangle jive. The public will eat it up."

"Mako . . . what do you think it is?"

Billy squeezed his empty beer can into an aluminum ball, wondering if he should listen to his boss or not.

Hooker said, "Beats me." He turned to Billy then. "Our TV working out here?"

"Not for long time, sar. Only in port," Billy replied.

"We can pick up the transmission on the cruise ship," Judy said. "If we radio Don Watts he can monitor the stations and tape the broadcast."

"Sar . . . will we really see the eater?" Billy asked.

"Why, don't you want to?"

"If the eater . . . he was dead . . . then I wouldn't mind." He swallowed hard and added, "He still down there, sar."

"Mako . . ." Judy's voice was very quiet. "*Lotusland* is only a couple hours from here."

"So?"

"We're still in its . . . operational area."

Hooker headed for the wheelhouse. "Then let's see if we can find out what it looks like," he said over his shoulder.

Judy and Billy watched him silently as he contacted the Midnight Cruise ship. They avoided looking directly at each other but scanned the darkened sea every so often. It was a vast blackness out there, then something would make a wild dash below the surface, leaving a bright streak of fluorescence in its path. At times a body would lift out of the water and come down again in a muted splash. Twice a living thing felt its way along the keel and twice the hull was rammed softly by some sort of creature as long as the boat. They weren't new experiences to Mako or Billy, but for the first time, Judy realized just how alive the ocean was and how small their boat seemed and how helpless they would be in a foreign element like the Black Sea.

When Mako came back on deck she had to stifle a sigh of relief.

But he knew what she was thinking. "Relax," he told her. "It's always noisy out there. As a matter of fact, this is a quiet night."

"Why haven't I noticed it before?"

"Because you've always been in a cabin or the band was playing too loud or somebody was whispering in your ear."

"The next time I'll be listening." She paused a moment. "What did the ship say?"

"They'll monitor all the stations. Whatever is made public, we'll see."

"Could you go to Chana . . ."

"Forget it, Judy. She'd make every move difficult. Unless we know . . . are absolutely sure of what we're dealing with. All we have is speculation."

Billy sensed his annoyance and brought him another cold Lite. Mako opened it with an automatic gesture and sipped at it.

Judy left her chair and stood next to Mako at the rail. "Why is a government ship here at all?"

"Because the *Sentilla* is a government operation. Supposedly, *Tellig* is resupplying them."

"That's a cover story, Hooker."

"Sure it is."

"Then why are they here?"

"Judy, there are some incidents that can go around the world in one hour. You think this 'eater' business isn't being gobbled up in every city on earth? Hell, even if it was only around our islands it would be big news, but when the *Arico Queen* got hit, we're on the front page."

"Mako . . . accidents happen all the time!"

"Damn it, this was no accident."

She felt a sudden coldness in the air, chilled by the tone of his voice. "What do you think it is?"

His shoulders shrugged his answer. Finally he said, "Something is prowling around, that's for sure. As long as it's something it's big news. It's the monster out there in the dark. It's got teeth and it's got power and everybody is scared to death of it."

"Suppose it's identified?"

"Then we'll know how to deal with it."

"You're thinking something else, Mister Hooker."

Mako nodded slowly and took another pull of his beer. "I'm thinking of all the cute political moves that are going to come down on us. Those playboys in Washington will make more out of this than the Panama bit."

"Like how?"

"Like how and where to apply funding to something that will improve the politicians' positions. This has all the earmarks of one hell of a publicity angle that can't be overlooked. Every paper and TV show in the world will be locked in on it, and before long every publicity-hungry pol will be drooling over the potential for reelection that it offers."

Mako's facial expression had darkened and she didn't pursue the conversation.

Billy Bright had been bent over the starboard railing. Now he pulled up the line in his hand and took the readings off the thermometers that had recorded temperatures at different depths. He squinted at the readings and took them under a brighter light to verify what he saw. He jotted numbers down on a pad and handed them to Mako. "She be high, sar. Four degrees over last night."

Mako checked the readings and compared them to the other nightly numbers. "Odd," he stated.

"No flying fish," Billy told him. "Plenty last night."

Puzzled, Judy said, "What's flying fish got to do with anything?"

Mako shrugged again. "Just odd, is all. The islanders have something about rising water temperatures and no flying fish."

"Billy?"

He gave her a noncommittal look and shrugged too.

Once again, the night air seemed cooler than it actually was and she wished she had another sweater.

Almost as if it knew that its picture had been taken, the formless mass reacted to the nature of its environment and gently let its own world smother it. There was no hurrying in its movements, just easy responding to its elements, knowing that it would go to the right place. The elongated form drove other things out of its path simply by being there, as if the smell of it were as offensive as its size and character.

Only the smaller fish seemed protected by its presence, the way pilot fish are by a shark, or like suckerfish adhered to a predator's belly. When the mass rose, the small fish rose with it. When it turned in those very wide curves they would be alongside. Their safety was ignorance. Overhead daylight had put a pale glow on the surface and the movement of the great body caused it to ascend, bare inches at a time. Now it seemed to be looking. On the surface was the dark bottom of a boat and not far away was another, but the great thing was not looking for them. When it was ready, it would find what it was looking for.

Chapter Eleven

The diving party reached the assigned area thirty minutes after leaving the *Sentilla*'s floating dock. The bottom was thirty-two feet below the surface, but every detail, every contour was clearly visible. The ocean itself was placid, barely undulating at all. Only fish jumping here and there made an impression in that great greenish-blue expanse. For a change there were no strands of sargassum floating about, buoyed up by the bubbles along their fronds.

When Kim gave the signal the divers began dropping off the inflatables at regular intervals, going to the bottom, where they fanned out to follow the grid pattern Kim had given them. As he had said he would, Mako stayed behind Chana, thirty feet to the right of Judy but in plain sight of her.

The task was simple enough, pushing the marker flags eighteen inches into the sand, making sure their plastic triangles were fully unfurled. At preselected points they angled westward about twenty degrees, sloping downward very gradually. Twice the team went up to the inflatables to take another bundle of markers, then dove back to their positions for the final placements.

Nature was a living thing, the ocean currents part of her fluid mobility. Their changes in course and pattern were slight, but each variation caused some other force to alter its way and conform to a new avenue that could possibly alter conditions and situations above. Even here, in the warm, placid waters where they placed the flags, the recordings would indicate movements and speed that Woods Hole personnel would be able to sense and interpret.

Mako looked at his watch. They had been down for almost two hours but in shallow waters. There was no need for decompression, but the work was monotonous and he was beginning to think of how nice an ice-cold Lite beer would be. He waved over toward Judy and got her eye.

He got the eye of something else too. Suddenly it came up out of the sand, huge and black, its initial movement clouding the waters so all he could see was something gaping, something wide and monstrous, a horribly big and long thing that had no name, dangerously alive and vital. Its movements had a thrashing motion, powerful enough to churn the water into momentary, sandy translucency, and when it swept past Chana the force of its movements flipped her upside down, her arms and legs waving wildly. Judy had spotted it as soon as Mako did and she dove into the sand, fingers clawed to anchor herself. Up ahead some of the others had felt the pressure of movement in the sea, looked back and kicked furiously to get out of the area.

Mako's back brushed the bottom and he was looking upward, a dive knife a futile weapon in his hand. He watched the extremities of the thing whip past him, estimated the length at least two hundred feet, made a slash with the knife at the very trailing edge and flipped over as the thing passed and disappeared out of sight.

When he reached Judy he saw that she was all right, her eyes behind the glass of the mask devoid of fear, but looking at him with a questioning expression. Mako nodded and pointed to the surface. Ten feet from the top the water cleared and they could see legs being pulled in over the sides of the inflatables.

With a single lunge Mako pulled himself into the boat, then reached down to give Judy a lift in. "You okay?" he asked her.

"Ask me that when my heart stops pounding." She took a deep breath and gave him a small grin. "Damn, I don't like that kind of excitement."

Chana had stripped off her gear. It was evident that her diving was finished for the day. "Did you see that? Did you see that!"

There was no answer. Everybody had seen it, all right.

"That was as big as a football field!" She glanced at Mako, who just sat there quietly. "You saw it, didn't you?"

He looked at her hands. They were shaking. Chana could stare down a gun barrel or charge a tank, but out of her element she was one scared operative. "I saw it, Chana," he told her blandly.

"Was it . . . the eater?"

Deliberately he looked around at all the faces. "Well, nobody seems to be missing here and they got all their body parts."

A flush started in Chana's neck and Mako saw her torso stiffen. A touch of her inward fury at Mako's nonchalance crept into her face and she almost hissed, "That was no joking matter, Mako."

"Nobody's laughing, lady."

"Hell, we could all be dead."

"But we're not."

Chana's composure was coming back slowly. Finally she announced very coolly, "I'd like a written, personal observation from everyone here. If you can accurately sketch what you saw, please add that." She caught Mako's eyes, suddenly heavy-lidded. "Do you agree, Mr. Hooker?"

"Oh, sure," he said, but his tone told her that he wasn't going to stand for anyone running in front of him. He smiled. Chana smiled back. There was no friendliness in either smile at all.

A news flash had already announced the possibility of the eater having been photographed by a camera plane from the *Lotusland*, promising viewers that the results would be seen on the evening news. Chana realized immediately what had happened and told Mako, "That original print is going to be on the movie ship. What we get will be a copy."

"And there's nothing you can do about it. Legally, that is."

"This is still a U.S. operation."

"Not out here, lady. We're in foreign territory right now. This event you play with diplomacy, not guns."

"So?"

"So we see the original print. They can show it for us on the *Lotusland*."

"How do we get aboard?" she demanded.

Mako shrugged and grinned. "Just ask Judy. It's her boat."

"Damn you, Mako . . ."

"Hey . . . I'm only a bystander," he said.

The projection room on *Lotusland* had been set up for a limited number of viewers. There were two rows of three seats and standing room for about six more behind them. Chana and Lee Colbert took the front seats and Lee said to Mako, "You want to sit up here with us?"

"I feel better back here," Mako told him. He looked back toward the photographer and motioned with his hand. "Why don't you get up here and give us your summary."

The young guy nodded and edged forward. "Not much to tell. This was one quick shot, that's all. We didn't have a monitor in the plane and I don't know what the hell we're going to see. I know what I saw through the viewfinder . . . I think."

Somebody switched the overhead lights off and the camera motor began to hum. There were half a dozen separate shots taken of the ocean's surface from various altitudes. One showed a family of porpoises playing in the waves and another a million tiny bait fish turning the placid ocean top into a rolling scene of activity. Three fish leaped and dove into the mass, filling their bellies, then a cloud of seagulls dove into the feast, ate, took off, then dove again.

The cameraman said, "Here it comes."

Everybody leaned forward. Only the camera motor made a sound. Nobody even breathed hard.

The plane was in a mild bank, the camera pointed down at a forty-five-degree angle, panning slowly as if it were looking for something. Then at the top of the frame the water suddenly stilled, became darker, not because it itself changed color, but because something below was making itself known.

Had the plane continued in its turn the camera would have caught it, but now it was sweeping away from the deadly thing below. Before anybody could say anything the cameraman put in, "I was the only one who saw it. I kept yelling for Al to go back and he finally heard me."

The camera was still focused on the blackness below. The plane banked to the right now, hard in the turn, skidding enough to throw the camera a little off, then there it was, the dark thing again, its shape indeterminate, but for one second you got the impression that you weren't looking at its length, but down onto it, and it was looking up at the camera, knowing what was happening. And it just dissolved. The darkness wasn't there any longer.

Lee said, "Could it have been a shadow of the plane?"

"The sun was in front of us," the pilot said.

"Bait fish?"

"Nothing. There was nothing there, that's why I was turning away. We were looking for some action on the surface."

They ran the scene four more times, but all they could see was what their imaginations told them to see. "You're going to put this on national TV?" Chana asked flatly.

"You bet," the cameraman told her.

"There's nothing there."

"Oh, there's something there, all right. With the right music and our guy with the beautiful throat doing the voice-over, the entire viewing audience will see their own picture. The eater is suddenly going to be famous."

"We might have even had a better view," Chana said quietly.

She knew all the eyes were watching her and the moment belonged to her. A factual eyewitness account from a team of divers who experienced something they could recount and draw pictures of and tell about would carry more weight than a dubious strip of film. But backing up the film would add to the importance of the actual photography, enough to make the operation extremely newsworthy. Played right, political funding could be enhanced and upgrades in rank considered.

Chana smiled silently. She might even get to outrank

Mako Hooker no matter where he stood in the Company. It would be her turn to lean on him next time.

The suddenly inquisitive murmur of voices stopped abruptly when a voice from the door said, "What did you people see?"

Mako recognized the voice. It was Anthony Pell, and though his tone was seemingly one of polite curiosity, there was an edge to it.

Chana wasn't going to leave herself open to any interrogation from a civilian, so she simply said over her shoulder, "Tell him, Mako. You seemed to have had the best look at it."

He decided to really spruce up the episode enough to rattle Chana for putting him on the spot. He said, "Well, I'm no paleontologist but it was nothing like I ever saw before. It was big, damn big. It came up out of the sand like a pure burst of energy and went right over our heads. Visibility went from a hundred feet to a few yards from the violent disturbance of the sand and it moved fast. The whole thing took a good ten seconds to pass us and get out of sight."

"And nobody even got nipped," a voice said sarcastically.

Mako couldn't see who it was, but the voice wasn't new to him. He had heard it before, and he was running the sound and the inflection through his mind trying to identify the speaker. He couldn't get an immediate make on it, but he kept the impression fresh and knew that the next time he heard it, the name would be there.

When the light came on he saw that more personnel from the ship had crowded into the screening
room. It was their ship and their project too, so they
had a right. He reached out and took Judy's hand.
"You got a bar on this boat?"

"Of course. This is Hollywood afloat."

"Then let's get Mr. Pell up for a drink. Think you
can do that?"

"For me Mr. Pell would do anything."

"Who made that smart remark about not getting
nipped?"

Judy frowned, then said, "I think that was Gary
Foster. At least I think I recognized his voice."

"What's he do?"

"He's the assistant prop boy," Judy told him.
"Why?"

Without answering her question, Mako said, "Who
does the hiring for the company?"

For a moment she was silent, thinking, then: "If
I'm not mistaken, the heads of the departments notify Mr. Pell. He contacts agents or unions for proper
help." Her eyes drifted up to his. "What are you looking for?"

Mako shook his head. "Nothing special at the moment."

"Yes you are," Judy stated.

"Like what?"

"This inquiry about Gary Foster."

He let another few moments pass, then asked her,
"Can you find out just what he does?"

"I can tell you now. When the prop boy goes over

the scripts to pick out things they'll need on the set, principally for the actors, his assistant will get the items out of our own inventory, or if they're not in our stock, he will locate and purchase them. All items will be okayed by the head prop boy and paid for by Mr. Pell."

"How big is your inventory?"

"Beats me," she told him, "but I think it will handle most details. *Lotusland* doesn't make *Gone with the Wind* pictures. The main projects have been TV documentaries that seem to have gotten ahead of the motion picture end."

"But all economically successful?"

"Very." She gave him one of her impish grins. "Want to buy some stock?"

"Nope."

"You just want to be a fisherman all your life?"

"If I'm lucky," he said. "At least I'll always be able to eat."

"And live in a funny house on a sandy beach?"

"You forgot my army surplus dinnerware."

Judy gave him a light punch on the arm. "I'm only kidding," she said softly. "If Daddy thought I was pulling any rich-kid stuff on you, he'd turn over in his grave."

"He knew his way around, didn't he?"

"With the money he made, he'd have to." Her eyes got a momentary misty film on them and she said, "I wish I had known him better."

"You ever find out what he was doing in Miami the night he got killed?"

Judy pursed her lips. Her eyes squinted a little and she shook her head. "It was business, that's all."

"In that part of Miami? That wasn't any part of a business district."

"Then why would he be there?"

"How about a woman?"

She wasn't offended by the suggestion at all. It had been put to her before. "My father was no kid," she said. "He didn't have women on his mind at all. If he really wanted somebody she'd be only one phone call away, if you know what I mean. Besides, the section where he was mugged was not a place where prostitutes hung out. It was a seedy, small industrial area. Garages, used auto parts places, junkyards, things like that."

"And he was mugged."

Judy nodded. "He was well dressed. He was a perfect target."

"And he should have known better."

"Yes," she answered sadly.

"I was just thinking."

"Thinking what?"

"Somebody else might have known better."

Very gradually a frown began to crease Judy's forehead. She folded her lower lip between her teeth a moment before she asked, "What are you telling me, Mako?"

"Could your father have been lured there, Judy?"

"No." Her statement was emphatic. "He'd be too smart for that. Under unusual circumstances he'd always be well protected."

"He carry a gun?"

"He didn't have to. He had professional guards who did." She let her breath out with a small hiss. "I've wondered about that too . . . his being alone, that is. It was as if . . . he were going to meet somebody . . . but he certainly wouldn't have picked that sort of a place to conduct business." She paused, her mind wandering back to that night. "I contacted his security offices and he had not asked for any protection at all. His business in Miami was with reputable people and conducted in an office. When it had been completed, Daddy shook hands with everyone and went down to his car."

"He drive himself?"

"No, he always rented a small town car and driver."

"And where did the driver take him?"

"He didn't. He said Daddy told him he was going to walk and dismissed him right there. In fact he even signed the trip ticket so the driver wouldn't get into trouble. He was one of the Mariel Cubans trying to make a go of it in Miami, but he couldn't speak good English yet."

"The cops checked all of this out, then?"

"Every detail."

"They missed one," Mako told her.

"What's that?"

"Why it happened."

"Mako . . . he was mugged. He just decided to walk and went in the wrong direction."

"But he didn't do things like that, did he?"

"I don't know. Everybody else says it was unusual

and not very smart, but Daddy did things that were unusual too."

"But smart," Mako added.

"Yes."

"Was his business meeting successful?"

"Yes. The police checked that out too." She stopped then, turned and looked up at Mako thoughtfully. "What are you getting to?" she demanded.

Again he shook his head. "It's like not getting the punch line on a joke. It's not supposed to happen that way."

"The Miami police suggested that too. Then they found out that Daddy was a walker. He frequently took long strolls wherever he was."

"With somebody?"

"Yes. He always . . . or nearly always, had a companion or two. But there were enough times that he walked alone to satisfy the investigators."

"In places like where he was mugged?"

Judy didn't answer. The logic was all scrambled. It was evident that the same thoughts had run through her mind too. Now her father was dead, nothing could bring him back, his death hadn't caused her any loss except an emotional one and nothing had erupted in business to make his demise seem suspicious at all.

"Can I ask you something?" Judy suddenly said.

"Sure. Shoot."

"When we were underwater . . . that thing that came at us . . . was that the eater?"

Mako let a few long moments go by before he said solemnly, "Not the one we're looking for."

Anthony Pell was in an exuberant mood this night. Having twice photographed evidence of the surreal thing that was wreaking such havoc among the boats, then having an agent of the federal government report an encounter by something huge and unidentifiable, backed up by other witnesses, was making this side trip of Lotusland Productions an economically satisfying one. Bids from the networks had been coming in steadily and the home office was preparing for a gigantic motion picture effort. What they needed was an ending. It had to be so sensational that nothing would ever touch it. The photography had to be exceptional and no expense was to be spared to get the desired result.

The home office had already assigned writers to prepare the script and plot out an ending. It was evident that they thought the whole affair was all wind and no substance, but that's what made people buy tickets and no matter what, the studio would give it all the substance it needed. How many books had been written about the Bermuda Triangle and how many movies made and how many incidents distorted to make it all look real?

And look what *Jaws* did for the great white shark.

Smelling big money was what Anthony Pell did best, and he smelled it now. His was only a small percentage of the whole, but it was worth millions and

Anthony Pell knew his cut was sufficient for him. He could buy anything he wanted, go where he desired and do what he pleased. As long as he did not get greedy and did his job to his bosses' satisfaction. For a moment he thought of Tony Pallatzo and grimaced. He didn't like himself very well then.

A jigsaw puzzle is a box full of unrelated pieces, but if you can separate out the parts that make four ninety-degree angles, you have the corners and everything else fits inside them. They were the easiest parts. The real work is sorting out the bits and pieces that make up the body of the picture. Mako could mentally visualize the corners, now he had to start arranging all the loose parts into reasonable order.

And he didn't like that word, "reasonable."

Anthony Pell was beyond reason. He was a piece from another puzzle, another time. He was out of place in this one, but why and how, Mako couldn't quite fathom. But it would come. It would need some prodding and some urging, but it would come.

Mako gave a single sharp rap on the door to the stateroom and heard footsteps, and there was the new face of an old streetwise punk he had known a long time; he decided to play along in the game, and he gave Judy's hand a soft squeeze under his arm.

Hooker shook Anthony Pell's hand and felt the hardness in his grip. The clasp was stronger than it had to be for an ordinary greeting. It was like a warning, Hooker thought, that Anthony Pell was a very determined man, a hard man, one who let nothing get in his way. You knew it in the strength of his hand, even though his smile was affable and his eyes laughing.

Hooker played the same game too. Nothing gave in his fingers and he was smiling too. For the briefest of a second, Pell looked surprised, then reconsidered any ideas he might have had that they were simply two physically fit men meeting again.

"You certainly have brought good fortune to this trip, Mr. Hooker. The film we have . . . with reenactments and additional coverage, is going to make a great movie."

"You missed the big show on the island," Hooker told him.

"Oh, not at all. We had somebody covering the boat that caught the eater in its nets . . . all that activity looking at the tooth mark. Hell, you are even in some of the film, Mr. Hooker."

"I'll have to get a SAG card," Mako said.

Pell went on as if he hadn't heard him at all. "Even the natives were great. The stories they had to tell! They probably exaggerated them, but there's no doubt that they were completely unrehearsed. And what actors they were, the way they agreed to everything we said."

"How'd you get them to hold still for a camera? I didn't see any equipment on the beach."

"Technology, Mr. Hooker. We have the latest miniaturized equipment made. Film sensitive beyond belief. It can be carried in a woman's purse, a lunch box, practically anything that makes it unseen. You'd never even suspect that a movie with sound, in full color, was shot."

Caustically, Mako asked him, "How is it powered?"

"That, my friend," Pell told him, "is our secret."

As though he had never heard of the new use of handheld digital cameras, Mako simply said a quiet, "Oh?"

The way Mako said that made Pell's eyebrows come together. Then he smiled and said, "It's not solar power, Mr. Hooker."

Very offhandedly, Hooker said, "No, of course not." Then he smiled too.

"It's a bit of a secret," Pell explained, for a moment unsettled by Hooker's tone.

"You think you'll have enough material for a movie?"

Pell laughed softly. "Hollywood, Mr. Hooker. If we don't have enough, we'll invent it. No trouble at all."

Hooker asked, "What do you think this eater thing is?"

"Does it really matter? Even if it's only a figment of some islander's imagination, it will make a great story. Besides, whatever it is, we can come up with something better."

Judy stepped forward and held up her hand. "Just supposing, though, that this . . . this eater is real . . . "

"Look, you know . . . "

"We don't know, Mr. Pell. We just know that something is there and something is doing all these things. We're not in an international conspiracy or a political squabble . . . we're in the middle of something that has never happened before, something . . ."

"Extraterrestrial?" Pell interrupted.

"Who can tell," Judy blurted, her face turning red.

Changing the subject, Mako said, "Could be better than *The Lost King* or *Mineshaft*."

"Oh, you saw them?"

"Enjoyed them too. Pretty damn exciting. I know how the demolition company took down those old hotels, but how'd you get those close-ups?"

"The new technology, Mr. Hooker. We had already planted cameras that gave almost on-scene photography. No special lens work . . . just our new equipment. Great stuff, hey?"

"Sensational. What really got me was blowing up those bridges. Somebody is great at making miniature sets and . . ."

"Ah, no. No miniaturization at all. Those were real bridges."

"How did you arrange for that?" Judy asked in a tone that was unbelieving.

Anthony Pell took on a subtle air of superiority. "Very simple. There still are several old unused bridges built by the railroads early in this century. There were two more in South America we used for covering shots too. We did a public service by taking them down; they were in such bad disrepair. Made a fine movie sequence, didn't it?"

"Who handled the charges? You get some of the old army pros from World War Two?"

Pell gave his smug laugh again. "No, we simply hired a genius right out of the ranks of the experts that took down those condemned buildings."

"Great," Hooker said.

"Cost a pretty penny," Pell added.

Hooker thought, And what is he making being an assistant prop boy and making snide remarks without getting his behind kicked? And what kind of a cussing-out did he get for not blowing up Hooker's boat like he was supposed to? The slob might have known explosives, but he was a loser when it came to the intricacies of magnetic compasses. That son of a bitch had tried to take him out, but the order had come from somewhere else and for some good reason. Why?

The bartender came over and took their empty glasses. "Another?" he asked. All three held up their hands in a "had enough" sign.

Judy explained that they were going to the Midnight Cruise ship for a visit and invited Anthony Pell, but he declined, saying he had work to do on board *Lotusland.*

When they got to the boarding ladder Chana and Lee Colbert were there and Lee wanted to go back to the *Tellig,* but Kim accepted Judy's invitation to join them on the cruise ship for a while. When Chana and Lee stepped into one inflatable, they slid into the other. The sailor handling the big Johnson outboard touched the ignition button and the engine came alive; and when he put it in gear, it started skimming its way toward the porthole lights and the bunting-and-flag-decorated decks of the great vessel.

It was a quiet night, the ocean flat again, a warm breeze churning up a delicious salty smell in the night air. This time there were no luminous streaks trailing behind fast-moving night predators in the water. Nothing flapped on the surface. Behind the inflatable the trail of the propeller made a bubbly path barely visible in the light of the rising moon.

Had anyone been looking, they would have seen a sudden break in the propeller track. It was wide and momentary. It was moving. It wiped out the track, then it was gone. But something had been there.

They were approaching the cruise ship from the starboard side; the sailor listened to a voice from his handheld radio, received an order and acknowledged it, then turned toward the stern, cleared it nicely and came up on the port side of the ship. As they skirted alongside, Mako's eyes roamed the steel sides, scanning the portholes, taking in the large cargo doors that opened at dockside to take on supplies. Another smaller one was closer to the waterline and just before they reached the loading platform there was another, its sliding door slowly coming down, several sailors inside the ship guiding it, apparently repairing a malfunction.

When the outboard was cut off, muted music flowed down from the deck above, and over it were the squeals of delighted women and the louder voices of the men. Uniformed sailors helped them out of the inflatable, most of them recognizing Judy and saying hello to her. She treated them like they were friends, not hired hands in her business.

Mako said, "You have a lot of admirers here, kiddo."

"Oh, they all worked for my father in the old days."

"The young ones too?"

Judy laughed pleasantly. "They've just heard about me."

"You leave quite an impression, lady."

When they reached the deck Marcus Grey was waiting for them. He took Judy's hand as if she were the queen, helped Kim onto the deck, then jokingly said to Mako, "I assume you're much too vigorous to need any help from me, young man."

"Oh, I could use a little push now and then," Mako told him.

"Not from what I hear, sir. You seem to have quite a reputation of your own."

"And what would that be, Marcus?" Judy inquired.

"For one thing, that business on the dive today. You seem to have come up something of a hero."

"I don't remember doing anything special except getting out of there."

Marcus Grey smiled a little bit, creases forming around his mouth. "One of the divers saw you with a knife in your hand taking a big swipe at whatever it was attacking you."

"Pure reflex, Mr. Grey. I was in the rear and had more time to size the situation up."

"And what did you see?" Plain curiosity edged his voice.

"Frankly, nothing identifiable," Mako told him. "It was simply big. The sand cloud obscured everything."

"The diver said you stabbed at it . . ."

"Come on, Mr. Grey. What good would a six-inch blade be against something that huge? Everybody saw that much anyway. The damn thing came right toward us so fast, the current made us tumble around like driftwood. Hell, that was about all any of us felt."

Strangely enough, just that much seemed to please the old man. There was a real future to be made in the unknown. It could be given teeth and direction and with the right promotion a mystic quality, a "something" that lurked. A "something" that was always there, ready to have a new story built around it, a new moneymaking prospect.

"Well," Grey said, "the whole episode has really given the passengers something to talk about. This has been the most exciting part of the entire trip for them." He paused and tilted his head to a listening position. "And what have you for them tomorrow?"

Before he could answer, Kim said, "We're going on another dive. Why don't you have the old folks ride on top of us in the inflatables? The weather is supposed to be clear and the seas calm."

"Miss Sebring . . ."

"Oh, come on. Because they're still dancing waltzes doesn't mean they're out of action. I bet plenty of them are experienced small boaters. They may not see anything, but just thinking about it ought to give them a kick."

"Yes, quite. I see what you mean. Well, I certainly will suggest it and see what happens. I just hope they don't want to take up deep-sea diving as a sport. It would be a rather strange bit to advertise, don't you think?"

"Whatever they can afford, give them," Kim told him.

"My dear Miss Sebring," Grey said, with his accent showing, "these people can afford anything they want. Anything at all. Money is merely a toy to them."

"Toys can break," Kim said.

"And they can be repaired or new ones bought. Theirs is another world, young lady."

"Fine, Kim, fine. Let him see what he's missing. Unfortunately, all the ships are completely sold out for the next three months, but after we get the new ports opened and built, we'll be adding two more vessels to the line."

Just going to the main ballroom, Mako was amazed at the brazen effrontery of luxury. There were the rich and the rich rich, but this group was in a class by itself. The jewels on the ladies were so big that they seemed artificial, but the men's finery was nearly the opposite. The clothes they wore were made by the most expensive tailors in the world, yet worn with casual indifference. Here and there would be a man in knee breeches and another in Bermuda shorts, but the mark of the money was there in every detail. A simple nod would bring them a drink and one word was enough to send the wife or mistress away while they had a business conference in a corner somewhere.

Silently Mako took it all in. At the casino he looked at bored faces winning or losing millions, not caring one way or another. Well-built waitresses made them smile and the liveried stewards took care of the women's needs.

There were six gambling casinos on board, all well filled, and Mako said, "Vegas should do this good."

"Now you know why the Midnight Cruise lines were set up."

"How long do the passengers ship out for?"

"Oh, they can leave anytime," Judy said. "Generally they take the full cruise for three months, but they always come back. I'd say that nearly everybody on this trip has been on two others. They like the excitement, you know."

"Baloney. They should be home in bed."

"Try telling them that." Judy glanced at her watch. "Let's go down a deck and you can see what makes this ship tick."

It wasn't the first time Hooker had been in the bowels of a ship. This was one of the new breed, well constructed, designed for comfort and speed, the first to benefit the clients, the second to outrace storm systems. No expense had been spared in its construction, including a completely equipped hospital operating room and a helicopter kept below deck on a lift ready to be hoisted to the deck for emergency action. They walked past the still-opened cargo hatch doors, where the off duty crew gathered to have a beer and talk about girls. Judy knew some of them too. A little farther down a door was built into the bulkhead unlike any other doors. This one was of solid steel, hung on extra large but practically concealed hinges.

"Captain's lounge?" Mako joked.

"No, the money room," Judy said. "It's right beneath the bank upstairs. Cash from the games comes down the chutes to be counted and wrapped."

"And . . . ?"

"Beats me. It's only money." She waved her thumb toward the overhead. "To them, play money."

"The government ever check on this operation?"

"Not on the high seas," Judy told him.

Mako nodded, thinking about that little door almost at the waterline. It would have been an entry to the money room. Or an exit. But what the hell for? He hoped it was mighty watertight.

"It is." Judy laughed.

"What?"

"Watertight. That's what you were thinking, weren't you?"

"Yeah. You a mind reader?"

"No, but I'll tell you what it's for. When we go into different ports where we have our own landings, the passengers who want to gamble onshore have to use local currency. The funds are delivered through that lock. And believe me, it isn't just a cargo door . . . it's more like an airlock on a space orbiter."

"Foolproof?"

"As much as possible. It can't be assaulted by a team, it's easily defended and has twenty-four-hour security. Money may be spent easily around here, but our passengers want good care taken of it."

"Any attempts at robbery?"

"Don't be silly. One government tried a bribery scam, but their head man had a fifteen-minute chat with one of the passengers and came away white as a sheet and shaking like a kid sent to the principal's office."

"Who was the passenger?"

"You wouldn't want to know," Judy told him. "He runs huge corporations, dictates to senators and congressmen and gets called for advice by the president."

"Cute," Mako said.

"Very," she answered.

The storm came in just before midnight. It was one of those freakish upheavals of nature that in one hour can turn a flat sea into rolling waves with tops whipped into white froth by a screaming wind. The gale ripped and tore at anything movable, as if it had teeth and jaws, wrenching apart metal things and smashing whatever offered it resistance.

Mako had smelled it coming and got Judy into the cabin of the *Clamdip* while Billy Bright did a final check on the lines. There were three anchors out, the oversize ones Billy had suggested when Mako bought the boat. The chains were new and the bow of the boat headed into the wind, splitting the waves that charged down on it. The rain was a vicious, driving enemy that tried to smash the windows out, but they held in spite of the pressure.

Talking was almost impossible. The wild fury of the wind was a pounding symphony, pure almost deafening noise only a driver of a Sherman tank in a raging battle could understand.

Judy put her mouth to Mako's ear. He couldn't hear what she said, but he knew and nodded, made an okay sign with his fingers and gave her a big grin.

Billy Bright knew his boss was faking it, yet for some reason he felt secure. They all stood there bundled in their life jackets, each one equipped with an electronic beacon device that would alert air traffic to their positions if they got knocked overboard. He touched the throttles up a bit as the wind got stronger, letting the engines keep the strain off the anchor lines. He had a funny look on his dark face and when Mako looked at him he knew what it meant.

The Carib wasn't frightened by the storm. He had lived with them enough during his lifetime to know them. He knew the boat, and although it was an old wooden one, it was maintained beautifully. It could take the beating the storm was giving it.

What bothered Billy was the night. And the eater. A surface storm could be enough to rouse that thing below and there would be no way at all to avoid it. They were held tightly to the bottom in seventy feet of water and if the eater could roam in that depth, they could be dead meat.

Mako and Judy were holding hands. With their free ones, they grasped the built-in handholds of another sort. Nobody heard Billy when he said, "Crazy 'Mericans. Storm up here, eater down below. Pretty soon they be kissing!" He grinned at the thought and shut up.

A half mile away there was an awakening below. It was a subtle rolling motion, a mere disturbance. The storm had come in too quickly, spending its force with a single, paralyzing punch that might destroy an unprepared opponent but just stagger a real pro who was ready for it. The force of its might was on the surface only, never quite gravitating down to any appreciable depth. The disturbance was merely a nudge that didn't awaken the sleeping giant at all. The gentle drift of the current kept it in constant movement and when it was ready it would find what it wanted.

Chapter Twelve

The storm didn't ease up. It stopped with the startling suddenness of tropical disturbances in that area, the low clouds rolling away like a retreating army. The nasty chop of the waves rounded off into gentle swells, and overhead the flickering light of the stars made the sky come alive.

Judy looked at Hooker and he nodded. Billy Bright let a smile grow on his face, wiping out the concern that had etched it earlier. Mako said, "Where are we, Billy?"

"Over the deep coral heads, sar. You want anchors to get lifted?"

"Weighed, Billy."

"I know how much she weigh. You want I lift them?"

Hooker didn't argue the point. "You go ahead and lift 'em, then."

When Billy went up to the bow Judy asked, "Aren't you going to help him?"

"Lady," he said pleasantly, "when I outfitted this boat I didn't plan to mess around with big old navy-style anchors. They got motors to do those things."

"Sorry I asked."

"Only way you'll ever learn, doll," he told her, with a grin, then switched on his fish finder. In a few moments the face of the instrument blossomed into life, registering depths below, showing the flurry of action schools of fish made and picking up images of big singles that still lurked below, wary of the power of nature that could rile up the ocean to its very bottom.

Judy pointed to the odd shadowy things on the screen. "What are those?"

"Coral heads. They're stretched out for another three miles."

She put her finger on the numbers indicating the depth. "Aren't they down awfully deep? Most of the ones I've seen were in one atmosphere, about thirty feet."

"No telling what's happened to the bottom in this area. Undersea disturbances are pretty damn common. How do you think all these islands were formed? Right now the *Sentilla* is probing beneath the sea for an indication of activity."

They heard the growl of the chains coming in and the final *thunk* as the anchors were snaked onto the deck. And while Billy Bright was lashing them into place, Hooker nudged the throttles and the *Clamdip*, almost as if she were happy, dug her forefoot into the chop and picked up speed.

Above them the dots of the stars gave way to the grayish light of dawn, disappearing slowly, and were gone when the sun let a tip of itself show above the horizon to the east.

A soft, rain-cooled breeze came across the boat. Billy had made the coffee, gave one to Judy in the stern and brought another to Mako. He put it down beside the wheel along with two pink packets of sweetener. "Why that stuff work, sar?"

"Because," Hooker explained to him, and Billy nodded as though it made some sense.

But Hooker had forgotten about the coffee. He was watching the fish finder and very gently pulling the throttles back as Billy walked away and picked up the binoculars to search the area ahead, as though looking for the *Sentilla*. Billy and Judy, who had re-acted to the boat slowing down, knew what Mako was doing but didn't pay any more attention.

Mako wasn't looking ahead. He was staring at the images on the fish finder, wondering if what he was seeing was real. Something was there, all right. It had no definite form, but there it lay amongst the coral heads like some strange, deadly anomaly, a something that didn't belong.

The sun hadn't penetrated deep enough to define the thing; it was a great, dark blob, distorted along its outlines, the coral heads making the whole scene seem unreal. It could well have been a trench area, or an underwater garden of weed. Had he fished this area often he would have known what the mass was, but Billy had always put him over the top spots where the fish they wanted fed. For a minute he thought of calling to his mate, but there was no sense in upset-ting Billy again. He had survived the night into a new day and that dark thing whose shape wasn't really discernible at all made it an ambiguous deal not worth pursuing.

Suddenly it was not there anymore and the coral heads thinned out until they were gone altogether. Up ahead on the surface he could see the tiny shapes of the *Sentilla* and the cruise ship. Nearly blanked out by their sizes would be *Lotusland*. He looked back at Judy and pointed up ahead.

A minute later Billy joined Hooker at the wheel, waited a few seconds, then said, "Sar, what is it you see?"

Hooker scowled and glanced at the Carib. "What are you talking about, Billy?"

The mate nodded at the fish finder. It was off and the screen was blank. "This thing you see down there."

"What thing?"

"The one you don't want to tell me about." Before he could ask, Billy explained, "Easier to see through glasses when at speed in this boat, sar." He looked directly at his boss and grinned. "So . . . ?"

"I saw something big and dark."

"Many things big and dark down there, sar."

"How come you're not scared, Billy?"

Billy pointed to the barometer. "The glass, sar, she is steady." His finger pointed off the starboard side at the splashes in the water and the low cloud of what looked like low-flying birds and said, "The flying fish, sar." His nose went skyward and he breathed deeply, filling his lungs with air. He did it again. "It is not a day for the eater, sar. Today is a good day."

"And when it gets dark?"

A little frown clouded Billy's eyes momentarily,

and then the grin came back. "Like the man says, sar, what will be will sure as hell be."

"Tell me that when something comes up out of the water and breathes on you."

Billy twisted his head very slowly and stared at Mako for a long time. "Sar, you are fooling me?"

"Yeah," Hooker told him, "I'm fooling you." He let out a small snort and hoped Billy believed him.

Captain Watts ushered Mako into the wheelhouse of the *Sentilla*, checked the gauges, then pulled out a couple of high-backed stools to sit in. "You're a big believer in this eater business, aren't you?"

"Somebody has to be. You pick up anything on sonar yet?"

"Nothing that couldn't be explained. We put out three scout boats with some new technology aboard and they covered everything in this site for three miles. There's nothing under us except the usual species of fish. One of them located an old hulk from World War Two and the burned remains of a fishing schooner. If you're making another dive, believe me, nothing is going to eat you."

"I sure appreciate the effort."

"Couldn't do anything less, Colonel. Your credentials come from understood high places."

"High enough to get me a special favor?"

"Just ask."

Hooker wrote the name down on a piece of paper and slid it over to Don Watts. "I want his history. He may have used other names, but I'm pretty sure the last outfit he worked for would have checked him out pretty thoroughly."

"What are you looking for?"

"Anything, but let's start with a police record. In this computer age any contact with the cops gets you down on paper. A lot may be illegal, but if you're clean it won't matter. If you're dirty, you can buy the farm . . . six feet deep." Mako tore another sheet off the small pad and wrote on it. "I'm giving you a number that identifies me. Memorize it and use it if anyone puts a block in your path." He handed the paper to Watts. For a minute and a half he stared at it, unblinking, then handed it back. Hooker lit a match and held the paper to it.

"That big, huh?" Watts said.

"That big," Hooker confirmed.

Before Hooker could add anything else, the phone rang and Watts picked it up. He listened for a moment and switched on the overhead speaker. He said, "Say again."

A muffled radio voice said, "This is Paul Vernon on the twenty-two boat, captain. We just got a signal on CB radio from one of the native fishing boats a couple of miles from here. He's hooked into something huge about fifty feet below him. Whatever it is, the head of the thing is a few hundred feet away from his short line."

"How long will it take you to get to him?"

"Fifteen minutes, sir."

"Good. Stand by when you get there. Take that fisherman and his crew on your boat and attach a marker buoy to the line he has out. Keep that thing in sight."

When he ended the transmission, Watts said, "Seems like something's about to happen."

"Are you going to cover this?" Hooker queried.

Watts shook his head. "Unless there's a war, this ship is on permanent station until our jobs are finished. This situation isn't serious enough to call for other ships to converge and I've instituted an action already that could handle any contingency." He stared at Mako and let a grin cross his face. "Especially since I have a gung-ho army colonel ready to take a stab at this himself."

"I didn't ask for this," Hooker said.

"But you wouldn't turn it down," Watts proposed.

"No way."

"Who are you taking?"

"Kim Sebring and a few of her top diving team."

"Need any special armament?"

"What can I have?"

"Your security clearance will get you anything under a destroyer, but I'd suggest a mobile rocket launcher. You won't be in a naval engagement so it should take only one shot. Those rockets are armor-piercing explosive shells, and what they hit goes to never-never land. Have you ever fired them?"

"Trained with them and used them in the field."

Watts didn't ask him where. The expression on Hooker's face told almost the whole story.

✧ ✧ ✧

Kim Sebring picked her two best divers and left the others grumbling on the dock. No information was given out on the mission but everyone knew this was top priority. Sebring consoled those left behind by telling them to be ready for an emergency call. That seemed to satisfy them.

On the *Clamdip* Billy and Judy had engaged the compressor engine and were recharging the empty diving tanks while Kim Sebring was going over a notebook full of diagrams with her divers. Finally the three of them opened up a large oceanographic map of the seabed below them, sat on the corners and discussed one specific area. Hooker came over and watched them trying to make sense out of all the penciled markings and crayon-shaded sections.

Kim looked up and said, "I think we've figured out the secret of Scara Island."

"That sounds like the title of a spooky movie."

"Doesn't it, though. And it almost is."

"What's happening?" Mako asked her.

She tapped the map with her forefinger. "This area has undergone a recent change. Not last week or last year, but a couple of centuries ago. The old Confederate ship *Savannah*, whose captain detailed everything, made soundings all around here. Note these large rises."

Hooker studied them a moment and nodded. They were large hillocks that swelled up from the sandy bottom, some rising to within thirty feet of the surface. In those days a line of them had run nearly to Peolle, with another branching off like a scimitar, nearly touching what was now Scara Island.

Kim suddenly sketched in other shapes and when she was done she said, "This is the way it is now. Undersea movements have flattened out those rises, and now a channel runs on the left side of where they were. It isn't a very deep crevice but it causes a flowing action that ends up on Scara Island."

"That affects objects down deep?"

"No," Kim explained. "It's generally surface material that's directed to the island. There are many currents in the ocean itself that nobody can fully explain. Some are proven and used, like the westerly and the easterlies. Sailing ships used these conditions to travel around the world."

Billy suddenly called over his shoulder, "Mr. Hooker, sar, that boat she be straight ahead."

Hooker leaned over the side, spotting the naval boat and one of the islander's single outboard dories. "Whose boat is that, Billy?"

"She belong to Peter-from-the-market, sar. He buy that boat in Miami."

"Get him on the CB and tell him we're coming alongside. Ask him if it's clear."

While Billy contacted his friend, Hooker picked up the VHF microphone and said, "*Sentilla* scout, this is *Clamdip*. What's the situation?"

"Sir, that fisherman has got something down there, all right. You look off about thirty degrees to his right and you'll see the commotion in the water. Something barely surfaces there every once in a while."

"Right. I think I see what you mean." He pointed with his finger and everybody on board looked out, fascinated. "I'm coming alongside you for a closer inspection."

"Whatever it is down there is pretty damn big, sir."

"Well, the divers will go down and take a look at it."

"Sir!"

"You're off the hook, sailor. Confirm with your captain if you want to."

The way he said "Yes, sir," left no doubt about his doing just that.

But there was a different look on the faces of Kim Sebring and her divers. There was no apprehension at all, just anticipation, the excitement of the dive, the anticipation of possibly seeing firsthand some incredible thing that no one had ever seen before. All three of them had strapped on underwater cameras with small-sized but powerful floodlights and each carried a long aluminum tube that fired a twelve-gauge shotgun shell that could take out practically any predator.

Above the noise of voices Billy suddenly said, "They won't need those bang guns, sar."

"What?" Mako looked sharply at his mate. He wore his usual placid expression that showed no concern at all. Quickly he scanned the water around them and saw no flying fish at all. Then he looked at the barometer. It hadn't changed at all. It was still a nice day.

"It is not the eater, sar."

"You sure, Billy?"

"Like you say, I am one smart Carib. I am very sure."

"Then go get some equipment and you can dive with us," Mako suggested.

Billy's expression didn't change, but his mind did. And he told Mako, "Maybe I am not so sure, sar."

Mako knew his buddy would add another excuse he *could* be a little more certain of. He said, "Oh?"

"The shark with your front name, sar, he . . ."

"You see him, Billy?"

"He is a quiet mister, that one, sar."

"But he's not here, Billy."

Very solemnly, Billy Bright said, "Everything's got to be *someplace*, sar."

This time Hooker let out a short laugh. No way was he ever going to get the better of the Carib. "Okay, pal, you take care of topsides while we check this thing out." He paused a moment and added, "You *sure* this isn't the eater, Billy?"

Billy, still very solemn, nodded his head. "Sar, I am very sure."

And Hooker stopped grinning because Judy had come up from the cabin carrying her dive mask and fins and for a second he thought she was totally naked, until he saw the tiny pink bikini she was wearing, and all he could say was, "You diving like that?"

Judy's eyes flashed over to Kim Sebring, who was hoisting her single tank onto her back. She had on the same outfit in black.

When she smiled coyly Hooker said, "Yeah, but she sure isn't built like you, doll."

"We're going after something that won't notice the difference, aren't we?"

Hooker just shook his head and she leaned over and kissed him on the cheek. Then she walked over to get her tank out of the rack and check its pressure. When she was satisfied it was okay she started to lift it into position and a young diver started to give her a hand. But he was too slow. Hooker jumped in himself, adjusting her bindings, then she gave him another kiss on the cheek.

How Billy saw the action he didn't know, but Hooker heard him say very softly, "Yes, sar, *everybody's* got to be *someplace.*"

Mako slipped on his tank, got squared away and jumped in right after Kim Sebring. Judy followed with the two young divers behind them. The group dropped down twenty feet below the *Clamdip,* where they all checked the compasses on their wrists, then fanned out and swam toward the dory of Peter-from-the-market, whose line was still snagged into an unknown thing another fifty feet below them—where visibility was cloudy, and the unknown, no matter what it was, posed a threat like walking through a minefield.

They all felt it. Unconsciously, they tightened up their small formation, well within sight of each other. Mako saw the men firm their grip on the bang sticks and then the movement of their flippers stopped.

The eighty-pound nylon test line that started at Peter-from-the-market's dory angled right down in front of them. There was no slack in the line at all, and as they watched, it began to veer to the left as something on the other end pulled it that way.

It was Hooker's move now. He reached out and felt

the line between his fingers, sensed the vibration coursing up it. Undoubtedly, old Peter had tied on a number 14/0 hook used for marlin and sharks. He had snagged something and wasn't about to lose his rig no matter what it was. Peter had already had a brush with the eater, and from his initial radio contact to his staying on the scene without cutting his line, he had the same feeling about what he had caught that Billy had.

The divers were watching him closely now, then Judy and Kim came up beside him and he was thinking how stupid it was to have the girls down there on a trial run like this. Judy's eyes were clear behind the mask and he knew that whatever he did, she would follow, so he pointed down and they followed the heavy strand of nylon.

About three hundred feet of line was run out, taking them down to eighty feet. Churned-up sand made the water murkier than ever. Twice, fish about three feet long passed languidly in front of them, then swam away leisurely with no sign of fear.

Fish have no sense, Hooker thought.

And at that moment he saw the waving black thing in front of them, a hideous mass that seemed to have no dimensions at all, and the nylon line was tied in securely to its body and it was pulling forward, ever so slowly, but pulling. Peter-from-the-market had put no anchor out, and Hooker knew the dory would be following whatever was on the line and that the scout boat from the *Sentilla* and the *Clamdip* would be following right along. Right about now, no matter what he believed, Billy Bright would be having a fit. He would be able to see the bubbles coming up from their diving gear, but if they stopped there was no telling what Billy would do.

Hooker went hand over hand down the line. The thing hit him in the face before he got to the first hook and with one hand he tried to wave it away, but his fingers sank into it and before he could shake loose he knew what it was and hung on.

They all saw him turn, wave them up, shaking the other arm that was seemingly into the very flesh of the indescribably wild *thing*, then up close they could see what it was. Peter-from-the-market had inadvertently hooked into an old drift net that had been floating loose in the sea.

But something else was caught in the other end.

Hooker gave a thumbs-up sign to return to the top and the team swam toward the surface.

On board the *Clamdip* Mako gave the two men the end of the three-quarter-inch braided nylon anchor rope to take down and tie around the net. The other end ran around the pulleys on the ship's winch. When the divers came back up, Hooker started up the auxiliary engine, put the lever in gear and began to pull in the line.

"What do you think it is?" Judy asked him.

"We'll know in a few minutes."

The end of the net came over the side and Hooker stopped the winch. All hands began taking in the net, and when the weight got too great they tied it off, reset it into the winch and powered it in some more. At least a football-field length was piled on the deck and right below them was the monstrous, nearly dead body of a manta ray, its wings spreading well over twenty-five feet across.

Billy said, "That is one big mister for sure."

"And he only eats krill. Little tiny krill."

"How he get so big, sar?"

"He ate a lot of krill," Mako told him. He looked up and smiled. "You feel like eating this baby?"

"Maybe I like him better if we cut him loose."

Kim Sebring came away from studying the giant ray still entangled in the net below the boat and said, "You know what this is, don't you?"

"Sure," Hooker said cheerfully, "this is what scared the hell out of us when it came up out of the sand and took off dragging that net behind it. Here we were thinking the damn *eater* had us and we got all shook up."

"I think Billy had the best idea, Mako."

Judy stood there, wet and glistening, that tiny bikini seemingly highlighting her chilling beauty. Hooker wondered if he was the only one who could feel whatever it was that radiated from her.

What Judy had said was almost like an order. Minutes later the net was cut free and the manta ray was loose. It sensed its freedom and its giant wings waved slowly, gratefully, and it swam away from the boat. Almost as one, they started to clap.

On board the *Sentilla*, Captain Don Watts saw the underwater action, and the capture and release of the manta ray, and he grunted his approval. "That's first-class photography, Colonel Hooker. No wonder the guests on the cruise ships passed up your invitation of a dive. Just watching what the cameras caught raised their heart rate up considerably. That manta was gigantic."

"And totally harmless," Hooker said, then added, "unless they get tangled in an anchor line and tow some poor sucker miles from home."

"The *Lotusland* people like it?"

"Did they! Right now a story conference is going on and they're going to rebuild some of the boats that have been hit, principally the *Soucan*. Their money men got right to the ones who photographed the damage on the *Arico Queen*. The story is almost writing itself, and with the real-live action stuff that will go in, they'll have one hell of a hit."

Captain Watts leaned back in his chair and took a sip of his coffee. "But what about the main star?"

Hooker saw what he was getting at and a grin toyed with his mouth. "The *eater* has to go. Whatever it is has got to be caught and destroyed. Or at least photographed. There's been too much publicity about that . . . that *thing* to have it just disappear."

"You have any idea about it?"

"What it looks like? No. What it does I can tell you. How it does it is beyond me. If we knew, a full report would have gone in to Washington from Chana and they'd be champing at the bit to find out if those mines on Scara Island tie in with this boat eater." Hooker paused and frowned at Watts. "What have you heard?"

"The satellites are covering every inch of our area. The navy has made a dozen photographic missions as well and so far . . . zilch. All they could report was that this was a peaceful section. The planes photographed three more mines on Scara and a team of Navy Seals are coming in to destroy all the old explosives left on the wreck below."

"And the *Lotusland* will get all this on film?"

Watts shrugged. "No way of keeping them out of it without raising a ruckus. Hell, as long as the publicity is favorable to the navy, why fight it? You say they're doing a story on it now? They probably already have copyrights on it in hand and a script registered in Hollywood."

"They haven't got the *big* thing, Don."

"What's that?"

"The ending," Hooker said. "The multimillion-dollar ending."

"Did you ever think all this could have been accidental?" Watts asked.

"No," Hooker told him softly, *"something's down there, all right."*

Across the desk the two stared at each other, lost in their thoughts. It was a strange moment for them because they knew that in many places in worldly governments consternation was touching certain individuals, because in this day of high technology and scientific investigation something was happening that they couldn't understand at all and couldn't focus on with any of their expertise. Again Watts sipped at his coffee. "No idea at all?"

"Just that there are things here that shouldn't be. They don't mesh. Events in the past suddenly pop up, like this eater baby is a catalyst and that keeps the pot boiling."

"Which came first, Hooker?"

"I think the eater has the edge," Mako said, and refilled his cup. "Did you make that call for me?"

"Oh, yes, I sure did. In one hour I had the answer. It's three pages long and for your eyes only." He opened the drawer of the desk and took out the stapled sheets, handing them across the desk. "This answer came back on a very secure channel."

"That's because they don't have an idea of what's going on, but you can bet the Company will be doing a follow-up investigation of their own."

"It's really that hot?"

"Considering the status of world affairs it's hot as hell. There isn't a truly stable government on the globe right now. They're all in trouble. If they're not at war, they have an insurrection, or an internal collapse, or an economic crisis. In 1956 you could buy a new Cadillac for around five grand. Now you don't get a decent used car for that. Money was worth something, now a dinner out can ruin a hundred-dollar bill. The politicians deal millions, hell, billions out like shovels full of sand to change the way other nations feel about us . . . and that's our hard-earned cash."

"What did Shakespeare say, Hooker? 'First, let's kill all the lawyers.'"

Mako let out a laugh. "And nick the politicians a little bit."

"Come on, Mako, those guys duck blows like a slicker does rain."

Mako unfolded the sheets in his hand and scanned the history of Gary Foster. He skipped over the details of his early life, noting that he had two years of college and was studying chemistry before leaving school to join the army, where he was put into an outfit specializing in explosives. After an altercation with an officer, he was court-martialed and eased out of service with a Discharge Without Honor, which didn't bother him at all. He had three arrest records, two for using dynamite in an illegal manner. A clever lawyer got him off with severe warnings. For several years he apparently was without a job, but most likely he had some illicit scam going where no tax monies were paid. A year later he was hired by Donnell and Johnson, a demolition company that took down buildings in tight city quarters with an impeccable work record. He was let go on suspicion of having stolen a considerable amount of explosive material and associated items. His next employer was Lotusland Productions. They were aware of his previous history. His work record to date was excellent.

"Did you read this?" Mako asked.

"It was for your eyes only . . . after mine. Anything you can tell me?"

"Nope. It just confirms a suspicion that I had."

Watts waited.

"He could have been in an action designed to kill me and my mate on the *Clamdip*."

"What good would that have done?"

"Keep me from probing into somebody else's background who thinks he's under deep cover."

"Didn't work, did it?"

"Damn near did," Hooker said.

"You need any other favors, Mako?"

"Just one for the moment. I need access to a radio, voice only."

Watts stood up and waved for Hooker to follow him. "I'll take you up to the radio shack myself. Our chief radioman up there is ten years past normal retirement and doesn't appreciate intruders on his domain. Can you handle the equipment?"

"No trouble."

The chief radioman must have lied about his age. The navy was his home and he wasn't about to live any other place. Even Mako's being in company of the captain wasn't enough for him. He interrogated Hooker until he was sure he knew what he was doing, then stepped outside with Don Watts very reluctantly and didn't stray far from the door.

It took Hooker two minutes to contact his source in the Company; then he gave his ID with the number and coded words that attested to his status, security rating and current operative position. When the computer gave back a confirmation, the line was open to the director, who spoke with a soft voice that hid all the nails in his makeup. "I'm glad you're working with us again, Mako."

"It wasn't my idea."

"Yes, I understand. But it's always been that way, hasn't it?"

"That's why I retired," Hooker said.

A laugh came through Mako's headset. "There are a lot of people here who wish *you* had stayed that way." He heard the metal clang of a steel door being opened, then shut, followed by the rustling of papers. The voice finally said, "You requested information about the Becker Bank. After the founder was killed during a robbery, the French government moved in, initiated an audit, and although nothing was found out of order, some of the bank's depositors had a questionable ring to them."

"Like how?" Mako queried.

"They wouldn't release all the information to us at first, but it seems that several had mob connections in the United States."

"Definite?"

"The investigators seemed satisfied. There was no proof of any wrongdoing, but the suspicion was enough. They are still following the lead."

"What the hell are they after? You can't prosecute a suspicion."

"Our man who is handling this thinks a very large loan was made to somebody in the mob."

"Come on, the mob doesn't go to banks for money. What would they use for security?"

"Good question."

"I have a better one," Hooker offered. "What would they do with it?"

"Tomorrow," the voice of the director said, "we are flying in a specialist in this operation. He'll arrive at nine A.M. and check in on the *Sentilla*. You talk to him."

"Good deal," Hooker said.

The connection was broken and Hooker called in Don Watts to tell him what was going on. The captain nodded sagely, wondering just how high Hooker stood in the chain of command. Then he realized that there was no chain of command in Hooker's line of work. The last man alive was the top dog.

At dawn Alley Ander's boat sidled in next to the anchored *Clamdip*. Billy Bright yelled hello and invited him aboard for coffee, and when Hooker came on deck he said, "You're pretty far from your bar, Alley."

"Come on, man, I heard there was lots going on down here. Can't let you old spooks have all the fun. Besides, I need a vacation." His eyes went to the *Tellig*, which was riding at anchor an eighth of a mile away. "She been shooting at you any more?"

"She knows better," Hooker said. "Come on over and get some java."

Alley rafted up to the *Clamdip* rather than drop an anchor and Mako shook his head. "Once a city boy . . ."

"Hey, buddy, I wasn't a navy man in my war. I was an old jungle rat who walked and climbed and jumped and clawed my way through everything that had stickers, and my best buddy was bug repellent."

"Then you'll love it here, pal. All we have are giant manta rays, an invisible eater, and a shark that's been tailing us for days."

Suddenly Alley looked concerned. "Don't kid around, Hooker."

Mako said, "Tell him, Billy."

"Yes. It is right. The shark who had his name stolen by my boss man here, he has followed us. I tell my boss, 'Give him his name back,' but my boss, he keeps it. Mr. Shark, he stays close so that he can kill my boss *and* get his name back."

"Mako . . ."

"Billy believes it, Alley."

"*You* believe it, Hooker?"

With a light shrug, Mako glanced out at the ocean. "I've seen him, pal. He's been with us all the way since we left Peolle."

"I didn't ask you that."

"Hey, if Billy believes it, so do I."

"Then why the hell don't you give it back?"

"How, Alley?"

The bartender gave him a sheepish grin and made a face. "Damn, you're making me think like the islanders."

"We think pretty good," Billy put in as he handed Alley his coffee. "And Mr. Shark, he sure be out there, all right. You look hard, maybe you see he."

Alley turned his head and took in the ships on the port side. "Doesn't look like much action going on today."

"Give it another hour, Alley."

"What's happening?"

"There's another showing of the film we took snagging that giant manta. Want to see it?"

"Yeah, man. I heard about that on the radio! But that wasn't the thing that ate the boats, was it?"

"No way. The eater is still out there looking. It's a wonder you didn't run into him, coming down here at night."

Alley's eyes squinted again. Facing a raging fire was nothing for him. Climbing up sixty feet on a ladder into an inferno was commonplace. Being alone at night on a great expanse of water that housed some incredible wild creature was a shattering experience.

Hooker hid his grin and said, "If you're going to see the showing on the cruise ship, how about taking my passenger with you? I have another appointment."

"Out there?"

"Guy's flying in. Business."

"Oh," Alley said. "Sure. Who's the passenger?"

Behind him Judy said, "Me, Alley, or do you object to having women on your boat?"

There was no bikini this time, but the sarong did just as well. It revealed everything, yet showed nothing. Even though you knew this vision was real, she was almost too good to be true. Her dark hair had taken on natural sun-streaked glints, her tanned skin alive with the vitality inside her.

Alley said, "Good grief!"

With another grin, Hooker told him, "Watch it, pal, she's tough. She went down on that dive that got us the manta. Now she wants to nail the eater."

Alley slid his coffee cup back to Billy, gave everybody a silly smile, and after one more look at Judy said, "I don't think I can stand this."

Chapter Thirteen

The seaplane with the navy markings landed three hundred yards off the *Sentilla,* taxied halfway back to meet the launch the ship sent out, discharged its sole passenger, then, when the launch was clear, turned into the wind and took off again.

Five minutes later the tall, middle-aged man was shaking hands with the captain, handing him his ID papers, then letting his eyes roam the deck until he spotted Mako leaning on the starboard rail. "That's him, isn't it?"

"That's him," Watts repeated.

"Damn, he hasn't changed. Haven't seen him for twelve years and he still looks the same."

"Nice fellow."

Helmut Wilkins said, "Yeah?" The tone of his voice made Don Watts look at him sharply. "That nice fellow was the Company's top shooter. He took out more unfriendlies than you can count, and some friendlies too. The director was glad he retired. So were our enemies."

"He hasn't taken out anybody around here," Watts said.

"Don't worry," Wilkins said, "he will, he will."

Hooker let go of the rail and walked up to the pair, his hand out. He said, "Hello, bean counter. How goes it?"

Wilkins's smile was noncommittal. He was glad to see Hooker again but didn't seem to enjoy the reunion at all. "Can't quite quit, can you?"

"Things seem to follow me around."

"Sure, like major crises."

"I wouldn't go that far," Hooker told him.

"You don't watch television or read newspapers anymore, either."

"There's enough excitement right here."

Wilkins addressed the captain with "Someplace we can talk privately?"

"Plenty of that during working hours. Come on with me." He took them to a small library with books stacked along each wall and a half dozen comfortable chairs scattered around. There was a desk in one corner with an electric typewriter and a fax machine, a jar filled with ballpoint pens and pencils. "Lock the door and make yourselves comfortable," he told them. "Nobody will bother you."

Hooker locked the door, then sat down facing Wilkins, who already had his attaché case open and was extracting several sheets of paper. The red printed CONFIDENTIAL stamped at the top indicated only moderate security, not worthy of being transported by a top-level agent like Wilkins. So he waited. Wilkins was playing that damn fool amateur routine of trying to get him talking first, but Hooker didn't buy it.

Wilkins knew what Hooker was doing. He smiled

indulgently and stated, "You made a request from the Company." His eyes flashed up to Mako's for confirmation.

"The Becker Bank," Hooker said.

This time Wilkins waited.

"And any Durant connection."

"Yes." He paused, reread the information on the sheet in his hand and made another one of those meaningful nods. "Becker and Durant had been friends for some time. According to Becker's business records, they met several times, in Europe and the Americas. It is assumed that these were business meetings."

"Why an assumption?"

"Because Becker's pleasure was gambling and Durant's was fishing. You couldn't get Becker on a boat or Durant in a casino but they both were business tycoons." Suddenly he stopped and asked, "As a matter of curiosity, would you mind telling me why you want this information?"

"They're both dead."

"True."

"Murdered, both the same way. An ocean apart."

"Street muggings," Wilkins muttered. "They happen here, they happen in Europe."

"Neither one was guarded."

"That's not unusual. Millionaires walk all over the cities these days."

"Not in unlikely places where these two were killed. Neither one had much cash in their pockets."

"They weren't wearing cheap clothes, Hooker."

"Nobody stole the clothes either. They got a watch off Durant. What was Becker missing?"

"A watch, two rings and a diamond stickpin."

"Glad you noticed," Hooker said. "Now you know as well as I do that something was fishy."

"It wasn't big news to us, pal. The French have a pretty good spook system going for them too, and sometime back a money courier from the States opened a sizable account with the Becker Bank. Sheerly by accident, that courier was identified as having close association with mob figures in New York. Unfortunately, the person who made the ID died in a car wreck."

"What are the big numbers, Wilkins?"

"The Company and the French police did one hell of a thorough investigation. Our side ran the lead down and a bundle of francs from our contingency fund dug something out. Becker had a male secretary, a little on the cute side, but nobody accused him of any sexual deviation. It didn't take much pressure to make him mention that just before Durant's death, Becker had sent him a fax message to meet Durant on a certain date in a certain place in Miami."

"How did Becker send the fax?"

"The memo was on the secretary's desk where Becker dropped his usual requests when he was going out."

"Okay, got it."

"The guy did what Becker had ordered. He sent the fax. A copy was in the files. The date and place of the meeting were when and where Durant was killed."

"Wasn't the secretary a little suspicious of the deal?"

"Not a bit. He said that Becker often did that. He thought they were assignations Becker had arranged."

"Pure sex, huh?"

"I told you, the guy was cute."

"But you didn't tell me all of it."

Wilkins grinned again and said, "Just before Becker was killed, the secretary died in a car accident. The police said it could have been arranged."

"The usual mob touch," Hooker said.

"That's still speculation, Mako."

"Then try this. That supposed courier opened an account. What's wrong with that? Was it big enough to warrant Becker's attention?"

"It must have been, because not long afterward Becker met with his advisors about a sizable loan to a U.S. client. There were no specific details given, but it seemed acceptable to all. Not that it mattered, since Becker called all the shots, but he wanted to have other thoughts on it before he moved."

"Did it happen?"

"A two-hundred-million-dollar loan was negotiated, the money transferred to a bank in Grand Cayman, the account owned by a corporation that got lost in the maze of paperwork those slick deals entail."

"The U.S. client who requested the loan, then, would have been the one who owned the account opened by the courier?" Hooker suggested.

"Right."

"And the identity of the courier was guaranteed by the passport he carried."

"Yes."

"Easy to counterfeit, of course. No need to go into a security check when he was putting money in, not taking it out."

Wilkins agreed with a motion of his head. "Money talks, Mako."

"Hell, it yells. What security was given for the loan?"

Wilkins said, "The twenty-million bank account and a carton of bonds as good as gold and not traceable to anyone. We assume they are stolen."

Hooker let it all sink in before he asked, "Is there anybody who could identify that courier?"

"There were three who saw him. The descriptions were all identical but, when you look at it, all very ambiguous. He was tall, well built, well dressed, had stylishly cut gray hair, rather heavy eyebrows and a dark mustache and beard. He wore heavy reading glasses, kept them in the breast pocket of his suit coat, and was very pleasant."

"What about his coloring?"

"They all noticed that he had a tan, not unusual for Americans at that time of the year."

Hooker said, "The guy was clever. Great descriptions, but nothing that couldn't be faked. Anything about his voice?"

"Yep. Well modulated, well spoken and very American." Wilkins leaned back in his chair, watching

Hooker closely. "You have somebody in mind for this caper, Mako?"

"Not really."

"You're lying, pal."

Hooker shook his head. "I'm just playing a close hand."

"Look, dammit, you got everybody all shook up with your contact . . ."

"Quit the crap, Wilkins. I'm an old retired hand. Right now the Company is down in the garbage heap and is ready to do anything to claw its way out of the mess it got itself into. It needs restructuring, refinancing and respect, and they're looking for that big touchdown pass to win the game for them, and this eater business popping up like a publicity hound's best dream and me being on the scene have given them one big last-ditch chance to get back in the lineup. Just don't try to crap me, old buddy."

For a full minute there was silence between them, Wilkins folding the papers back in his attaché case. Hooker swung around and asked, "What's new on the mob scene in the States?"

"Quiet. When the bosses start to go to prison things get stale for a while. Not that that means much. They've been going legitimate for a long time now and let the families that handle drugs, prostitution and all that stuff take the heat."

"What's the scam on the drug scene?"

"Nothing new. The poorer countries grow it with their government's protection and the affluent places buy the junk. Our narcotics agencies confiscate tonnages of the stuff, but that's only a drop in the bucket."

"Think it'll ever change?"

"Not in this system of things." Suddenly Wilkins stared at Hooker, his eyes half closed. "You think drugs are involved in this mess?"

"Nope."

"What, then?"

"Money, pal. It's always money. It's what makes this old world go round."

"Yeah."

"One other thing, Wilkins." The agent paused in snapping the lock on his attaché case. "Becker had his own investigative group working for him, didn't he?"

Wilkins said nothing, just nodding slightly.

"He would have had them look into that loan, wouldn't he?"

"It was standard procedure."

Now Hooker let the grin develop slowly. He wanted the uptown spook across from him to know that the old-time spooks could still mix up the batter and make a pie. "I bet you, old buddy, that Becker had some second thoughts about that loan and was going to recall it before it went through."

He waited. Wilkins licked his lips, grimaced slightly and pulled at his earlobe.

"Yes. Something happened that Becker didn't like. He could have put an order through canceling the check, but he was mugged and killed before that happened. The deal went through."

Hooker leaned forward, propping his chin on his hands. "One more quickie, Wilkins. How did the loan pan out? If anything big had hit the bank, the financial pages would have broadcast it."

"The debt was paid off. It was legitimate from front to back."

"Except for the killings."

Without bothering to answer him, Wilkins stood up and both of them went back on deck. Captain Watts came out to join them and see the agent into the launch that took him out to the seaplane, and they both watched it take off back to its Florida base.

They could hear the sound of the party long before they reached the side of the cruise ship. Decorative lights turned the decks into a rainbow of colors, the music of the band crisp and clear, the dancers a flowing swirl of vivacious animation. Two large bars had been set up, mainly for the men, the ones who gave orders to the captains of industry in faraway places. Their shipboard uniforms were gleaming-white and the fading sun still glinted off the medals some of them wore.

Billy Bright surveyed the excitement ahead and said, "Is this like a marriage thing the stateside people do in Miami?"

"Not this party, buddy. Something has happened we don't know about."

"They catch the eater, maybe?"

Hooker shook his head. "Nope. *Lotusland* is still dark. They'd be out photographing if they had the eater." He pulled the glasses out and scrutinized the faces on the deck. "Hell, Billy, the whole crew from *Lotusland* and *Tellig* are there too. Chana's at the bar with Colbert . . . and there's Judy with Pell and . . ."

He stopped there. Billy gave him that curious look again and said, "You hate that Pell man, sar?"

"Just don't like him, Billy."

"Think you'll knock him on the head, sar?"

Mako let out a snort and grinned at his mate. But Billy Bright's expression was serious.

"Sar, why don't you like him?"

"A long time ago he was bad. Very bad. Now he's far worse. Now it doesn't show and nobody knows just how bad he really is."

"You know this for sure, sar?"

"No," Hooker said, "I don't know . . . but I do know."

Billy Bright's eyes had the wisdom of the world in them. He nodded very slowly and very deliberately and answered, "Sar, I know just what you mean." While Hooker was still amazed at his understanding, Billy pointed off the side and told Mako, "There he be again, sar. He be waiting for his name back."

The huge shape of the mako shark rose to the surface again, rolled slightly, eyeing the boat, then slid back into the depth below.

"He follow us," Billy said.

"There's a lot of them around here."

"This big mister, he stay close."

"You just threw that bucket of bait fish over the transom."

"He has a fight scar on his head. His tail has two notches near the tip."

Hooker let out a soft "Damn" under his breath because Billy had spotted the same thing he had known. That mako was the same fish they had seen days ago. And it was looking. It was traveling at its own pace, knowing that sooner or later it would get what it wanted. The grin was hard and deadly. That mako shark was just like him.

As if he heard Hooker's thoughts, Billy said, "Yes, you are brothers, sar. Different from the way we are brothers."

Judy had spotted the *Clamdip* coming alongside the cruise ship and wormed her way through the happy crowd to get down the gangway to welcome Hooker aboard. Billy practically pushed him into her arms as he was climbing over the side and Judy thanked him with a wink. While they went up to the deck, Billy took the *Clamdip* out to anchorage, dropped the hook and came back to the cruise ship in an inflatable.

Judy led Mako to the nearest bar and, knowing what he liked, called for a Miller Lite. The bartender said, "And you, ma'am?"

"I'll have the same."

The toast was brief and Mako put half the beer down, wiped his lips and asked Judy, "Okay, doll, what's the party all about?"

She gave his arm a squeeze and waved to the well-dressed man further down who was laughing with the group around him. "Suppose I let Marcus Grey give you the details."

Marcus saw the wave and excused himself, coming to Judy's side. "Ah, my dear, you haven't been mingling. After all the great news I'd think you would be enjoying yourself more."

"I was waiting for my . . . friend to get here, Marcus. You remember Mako Hooker."

"The name I could never forget." He held out his hand and Mako took it. It was pudgy and soft and he wanted to squish it but didn't. "Haven't seen much of you since Judy's party."

"Well, I've been a little busy, Marcus. That eater out there has been giving us fits."

"So I've heard. Too bad, it only brings bad publicity. Rumors like that . . ."

"They're not rumors," Mako interrupted.

"Surely you don't think . . ."

"Something's out there. It's done a lot of damage."

Marcus Grey made a noncommittal gesture with his head. "Well, it's unlikely that it will interfere with our project any longer. Has Judy told you the good news?"

"She hasn't had time. I just got here."

"Well, then, we just got a radio confirmation that four other islands have opened up ports for our cruise ship landings. Certain corporations have agreed to fund the casino operations, other retail groups are bidding for exclusive commercial rights. The big thing is, we have the backing of the local governments, and with what we have, the value of our holdings will be over a billion dollars."

"I thought you were considering Peolle and Ara Islands."

"Unfortunately, that idea has been discontinued. This story about that . . . that eater had gone world-wide and been embellished in the tabloids and foreign television . . . it just wouldn't do, you understand."

"Those islanders were counting on that project, especially since it was already under way."

"Well, Mr. Hooker, all I can say is business is business." He looked at Judy and added, "Wouldn't you say, my dear?"

"No, Marcus, I wouldn't say that at all. Nor would Daddy if he were alive."

"Unfortunately, that is not the case, but fortunately for all these people here who have shares in the company, and me . . . and you too, my dear, I have control of the Midnight Cruise line and all that it entails and that's just the way it has to be."

At no time did Marcus Grey lose his smile. He took Judy's hand and kissed it and said to Hooker, "Good evening, sir. It was nice talking to you."

Watching him walk away, Mako wanted to put his foot up his tail. This time Judy got as bad as Billy Bright and read his thoughts. "Why didn't you do it, then?" she asked him.

"Do what?"

"Kick his fat behind."

"I didn't want to get anything on my shoe," he told her. "Has he really got that kind of control?"

"Yup, and there's nothing that I can do about it. I have shares and they'll pay off, but the control is his. Daddy didn't want me bothered by business details. To him women were for being taken care of, not laboring for money."

"He should see you now." Hooker laughed. "Supplying fish to Miami restaurants isn't a very ladylike occupation."

"But you should see the money it makes." She pulled free a moment and looked at the dancers on the floor and the bunch gathered at the bar and said, "I'm not like them, Mako. I'm damned independent. My inheritance is still in the bank. It grows and grows and never gets touched. If I want something I buy it with the money I earn myself."

Behind her, Mako grinned. "Nice speech."

She spun around, a frown on her face. "I meant every word of it!"

"I know you did."

"And you have the same feeling for the islanders and Peolle and Ara as I have."

"You'd better believe it, doll."

"Then why . . ."

"I said it was a nice speech."

The way she folded herself into his arms was so natural he could hardly believe it. Women were something he had never needed. They were always there, but he had never felt the desire to keep one around very long. On occasions they were very useful, but generally speaking, there was very little they could do that he couldn't do better and faster, without having to be perpetually obligated.

The smell of her hair was fresh, salt-air fresh, and there was the smell of flowers from some distant place, soft and pleasant, that made him think of being off the Florida Keys on a warm spring night, going someplace, yet no place special, just enjoying the long, soft moments.

"What are you thinking of, Mako?"

"The *Clamdip*," he replied.

She tilted her head up to look at him.

Mako said, "You were there, doll."

"What were you doing?"

"Just what I am now."

His hands could feel the warmth of her body and under his fingers a tiny pulse was racing much faster than he would've expected.

"Mako . . ."

"What?"

"This is all Billy's fault, you know. He's been telling me about you ever since you moved to the island."

Mako blew some strands of dark hair away from her ear and nodded. "I got the same treatment."

"Were you interested?" she asked him.

"No. Were you?"

"No. I had enough society types running after my money."

"What about now?"

Judy rubbed her head against his chin, then turned her head to look up at him. "I'm just crazy about your boat."

"And about its captain?"

"Ummmm."

The dance music on the deck suddenly changed tempo. Ravel's *Bolero* came in with its sensuous beat and nobody dared put movement to it. Instead they all headed toward the bar or their tables.

But Judy moved. In his arms her torso did things that were hardly noticeable, but Mako felt every one. Muscles in her stomach rippled against his hands, saying quiet things that he could hardly believe. She wouldn't stop, swaying exquisitely in tempo with the driving throb. Very subtly, Mako turned so his back was to the dance floor; she gave him a hungry smile as her spine arched and she pulled him to her as the wild song pounded to its wild climax.

When he kissed her it was a warm touch that began to blaze and when he pulled his mouth away he could say nothing at all for a full minute. He could still taste her and her eyes were watching him, waiting for him to speak.

"Think we could make it, Judy?"

"Uh-huh." It was spoken very softly.

"Would your dad have approved?"

"He would have been delighted."

"You can take your money and shove it, you know," he said.

"Why? It's only money."

"I got enough for us, pretty girl."

"And we have everything we want right now." She smiled at him again, an inquisitive, questioning kind of smile that only women in love know how to do.

But Hooker was an old pro in the game too. He had seen life and death, been part of situations that blew up like a time bomb, and he was in one right now. He knew it, he could feel it, the way the cold wind blows in ahead of a violent storm.

"Soon, doll. When this is over and we're still here, I'll say what you want me to say."

"Mako . . ."

He shook his head, his eyes emphasizing his decision. "There are some pretty big things going on, Judy. There are only a few of us against one hell of a lot of power and money. The chances are that they'll win, but when you play that game the nasties always make mistakes and they can never quite cover them up. Some might get away with it, but sooner or later the ax comes down."

"And you're the ax?"

"I'd like one more shot at it," he said simply.

"Think you can do it?"

"Until now, I always have, kiddo. I'm not a new boy in the game."

This time she kissed him, a light, wet kiss that told him to go to it, but hurry.

From the opposite side of the deck, in his white shorts and Hooker's Hawaiian shirt, Billy Bright was grinning more broadly than he ever had before. He heard some voices shouting from the deck below and peered over the side. Three big lights were playing over the surface of the water, and in the middle one the huge, sleek form of the mako shark emerged, his dorsal fin cutting the ocean, the tail slicing neatly eight feet in back. Billy saw the familiar nicks on the tail before the shark submerged.

It was Hooker's brother. He was still waiting.

Chapter Fourteen

The cruise ship was on no definite schedule. It stayed in safe waters and went where the passengers chose to go. They all wanted excitement, but quiet excitement that they could stand. They weren't interested in warring nations or poverty-stricken countries, but places where they could play and enjoy themselves out of harm's way. When the dive team from the navy arrived to blow the submerged mines, one of the ship's passengers, a former senator, made arrangements for the action to be shown on live television. There was no difficulty with the production. It would be a valuable promotional piece for the party in power, and his was arranging it.

Everyone had comfortable chairs, waiters passed among them handing out drinks, others balancing canapé trays, and a young sailor was delegated to give a running account of what was happening.

Marcus Grey watched them closely, saw his charges happily enjoying themselves, excited, but not *too* excited. They oohed and aahed at the shots of fish gliding past the lens of the camera, making distraught noises when a squid appeared or a heavily toothed mouth seemed to jump out of the blue-green darkness to swallow up another smaller predator, leaving parts of it and making the water murky with blood.

On the wreck the divers worked slowly, chipping away the coral, then cutting the chains that had held the old mines on the sunken deck. Only two began to rise of their own volition and divers guided them to the surface. The divers attached a small box to the top of each one, then swam to the dive boat and took off their gear. Down below, the other divers had done their work, come up as a team and climbed into the boat.

On the cruise ship, the sailor doing the commentary told the audience that they wouldn't actually see much, but these old World War II mines posed a threat to shipping and had to be destroyed. Only the two that they could see some way off had enough positive buoyancy to float and these were the dangerous ones. The others most likely had rusted through and seawater destroyed their potency. At any rate, they would see for themselves.

They had all pulled the chairs up and had their eyes glued to the TV. On the navy launch the diver in the bow held up his hand. The sailor at the TV saw it and began counting down, all the voices chiming in with him after three. When he reached ten the diver touched the button in his hand and the first mine blew, just a little eruption from the box on top of it, then the whole shell exploded into pieces and dust particles. The area had hardly cleared when the next and the next disintegrated from the explosive charge. Then one, a maverick, gave off a mighty blast that sent a column of water thirty feet above the surface, and blew another one next to it that gave off a smaller but unexpected blast that left the TV screen a dark, blurry square that gradually lightened as the current cleared away the debris.

The sailor spoke into his microphone and said, "You have just seen explosives that have been underwater eighty-two years go off with enough impact to sink a ship." He pointed out at the open water where the two floating mines had been dragged. This time when he lifted his arm, the sailor on the launch saw it and did the same. The countdown began again. At "ten" the diver on the launch triggered the blast and the pair of mines tore a hole in the water and sent pieces of coral-encrusted metal into the sky; when the nearest landed a few hundred yards from the cruise ship, the passengers had all the excitement they could stand. The crowd headed back to the bar.

Just before they began their trek the sailor said, "Now you can see what possibly 'ate' those boats." Their eyebrows raised and they all nodded in agreement.

Marcus Grey looked at the sailor and smiled gently. The kid would find a fat envelope delivered to him soon. Hooker and Judy had been standing in the back, watching the show from a distance. When the sailor had intimated that loose mines could be the eater, he said, "Smart move."

Judy squinted at him, a silent question.

"You have powerful people out there. They can control things. They just saw firsthand what old mines could do, corroborated by the navy, and as far as they are concerned, everything that has happened, the destroyed boats, the dead islanders . . . all that speculation about an 'eater' is rumor."

"Rumor," she said softly. "You think it should stay that way?" she asked.

This was a situation Marcus Grey had studied very carefully and his answer was quite direct. "Most of our guests are possibly . . . and likely persons we will include in financing the Midnight Cruise projects," he told her.

"And you don't think rumors would panic them?" There was no accusation in her tone at all, just a simple curious question.

With studied seriousness Marcus shook his head. "Not rumors. Only facts, and the navy has offered us just that . . . visual facts."

For several seconds she stared at Marcus Grey, her eyes locked on his. After a long pause she said, "*Something* has destroyed the boats. There certainly will be a big investigation into what hit the *Arico Queen*."

Very solemnly Marcus nodded. "And I'm sure they will agree with the navy's capable deduction. Pure logic tells us that there is nothing that 'eats' boats." Without waiting for Judy to speculate on his answer he added, "You know how far they've gotten with that movie script on the 'eater'?" He pronounced the last word quietly.

"Pell seems to think they were pretty well along.

There's very big money ready to go into this if they can get a decent story out of it."

A small, satisfied smile creased Marcus Grey's mouth. He said, "Well, if the story, the real thing, isn't all that big or threatening, they can still go into the studio labs and make a film about it. The publicity is as big as the Bermuda Triangle story, and they've made a half dozen films about that. But if the eater actually exists and their footage is real, that's where the big money is. Right now the public is on the edge of their seats waiting to see what happens next. Tomorrow everything shot on those mines will be national news."

"Featuring Midnight Cruise lines."

"Can't help that."

"With *Lotusland* standing by, ready to shoot. In the background lending dramatic authenticity is the *Tellig*, featuring super-secret electronics, representing our government's interest in this affair. All this with the *Sentilla* proudly doing a public works favor, very nonbelligerent."

"That really bothers you," she asked Hooker, "doesn't it?"

"Yeah, it does. Everybody is after the money. The setup and the cast came naturally. The threat is still there. Nobody cares what it's *really* all about."

"Mako, you're wrong."

He looked at her, his eyes tight.

"We care, don't we?"

The fury left his eyes and the grin touched his lips. She touched them with her forefinger and said, "Let's go find a phone."

It was the odd tone of her voice that made Hooker stare at her. "Something important?" he asked her.

"I want to speak to Pell," she said.

Mako narrowed his eyes slightly, wondering what she was thinking of. When Judy turned he followed her back to the communications room and watched while she dialed. "You want me to leave?" he asked her.

Judy just shook her head.

In about twenty seconds somebody brought Pell to the line, and even though Judy had the receiver to her ear Mako could hear the snarl of Pell's voice when he answered. But as soon as he recognized Judy the voice got syrupy again.

Judy was cold and direct when she said, "Anthony, I've been thinking that this picture we're considering producing could be a detriment to the Midnight Cruise lines. I've discussed it with some of the principals, and they seem to agree with me."

This time Anthony Pell's voice lost all its syrup. He quietly exploded with, "Dammit, Judy, we're not about to dump this feature! You realize how much we have invested already? Hell, I even have distributors banging away at each other to get the release before we even shoot a foot of film. With all this publicity there's no way we can dump this film!"

Judy was just as fiercely quiet when she said, "I'm part of this deal too, Anthony."

"Baby, you're on the money end. Or maybe you didn't read our contract yourself. Don't give me a hard time on this or we'll wind up in court, and I'll win hands down."

From the expression on her face Mako knew Judy *had* let something slip by her. Somebody else had scanned the contract and she had okayed it, probably while she was tied up with some other project.

Pell's voice came back on the phone and he asked, "Who you been talking to, kiddo?" And this time it was the old Brooklyn Tony Pallatzo voice Mako remembered so well. He grinned and waved at Judy, making a throat-slicing gesture that meant to cut off the call.

This time, quietly, Judy gave in with, "Well, you're probably right. We'll go ahead with it."

"Real good, baby. All we need is that big—and I mean *BIG* ending—and we have the world in our pocket." He paused, said, "Take care, kiddo," and hung up.

Judy cradled the phone and looked up at Hooker. "He's a snake, isn't he?"

"A real live one."

"So how do I protect myself?"

"I'll think of something," Hooker told her. He had a tight grin on his face that she couldn't quite read and she felt a shudder cross her shoulders.

Back on the deck the portable bars were busy again. The men were sipping gently at drinks that were more flowery than potent. Some had miniature Japanese parasols spouting out of the glass and others looked more like fruit punches than highballs. At least there were no sloppy drunks mouthing off and Hooker let a little grin crease his mouth.

"Self-control is why they're rich," Judy said.

"What?"

"You were wondering, weren't you?"

"Damn, can you read my mind?" Hooker blurted.

"Sometimes."

This time Hooker grinned. "Then watch it," he said. "I might just embarrass the hell out of you."

"Good," Judy answered, then gave his hand a squeeze. Without letting go she turned and started to walk toward the stern of the ship. There the area was empty, the hum of voices from the bow barely audible. No personnel monitored the passageways and the only sound was that of the waves slapping against the hull.

Judy sidled toward the rail, leaned on it and stared out over the water for a long minute before she turned and said to Mako, "I want to hear more about Anthony Pell."

"You don't believe me, do you?"

A few seconds flicked by and she said, "Yes, I do. But I want to know more."

"Why?"

"It's nice to have confirmation. Wouldn't you?"

"Will you believe me? I mean, totally believe me without reservations?"

Her answer was quick and direct. "Yes."

Hooker stared into her eyes and told her. "His name is Tony Pallatzo and he started as a street bum in Brooklyn."

For a full ten minutes he filled her in on what he knew and what he thought of Anthony Pell, speculating on what could have been when he was out of the jurisdiction of his own outfit. His information was sketchy about Pell's later life, but one thing he was sure of was that Anthony Pell hadn't changed a bit. Right now he was rich and important with an attitude of being well educated, but Hooker knew that he was still a street bum at heart underneath the facade.

Judy let it all sink in, then asked Mako, "Daddy was a pretty shrewd judge of character. I remember some pretty heavy operators trying to con him in business situations and he took them to the cleaners. In fact, several wound up in prison."

"Your dad could have been good, doll, but there are others who can be just as good and sometimes even better."

"But Anthony Pell never tried to cheat my father!"

"Not yet," Hooker said simply.

"Everything they did together was successful," she insisted. "Do you know they made millions? Even Anthony's lesser share has made him rich."

"No doubt."

With a touch of exasperation, Judy said, "Then what are you getting to?"

"How much was his employer getting?"

"Anthony Pell worked for himself. He had no employer."

Mako just looked at her. There were taut lines around his mouth. Finally he said, "Pell *had* a boss. He couldn't walk away from him, he couldn't be retired from him and no way could he quit. His boss is one hell of a big businessman with enough power and money to control governments and an army big enough to back up his demands. In plain words it's called the mob. Organized crime."

"But . . ."

He anticipated her question and shook his head. "I don't care what you read or hear. They made a big deal of stopping the Gambino family and they put on a show when Colombo got hit. When John Gotti did his thing it took all the heat off the background action, and when Gotti got sent up you'd think crime had gone down the drain."

"But . . . ," she started.

"Judy, don't fool yourself. The lawyers and the bright boys have control of things these days. The lesser rackets they give over to their street people, but where the heavy dough is, there *they* are. Industry is fleeced out of billions, tonnages of merchandise diverted into *their* channels of disposal, wars fought and religions invaded to suit their demands. Their needs never cease and keep on getting bigger. You think they can't get choice personnel to pull off their stunts for them?"

"*And you think Pell is one of them?*" she demanded.

Hooker didn't answer her. He simply nodded.

"You're sure?"

"Not yet," he told her.

"When will you know?"

"Pell is a smart one. He thinks. He knew that street mobs get knocked off by other mobs or the law itself. It didn't take him long to see that big money on the streets is pocket change to the real bosses. One thing they know is how to spend it. The heads of families still had homes in old ethnic neighborhoods, living by old European standards, and rarely got past the capitals of their crime industry. Oh, maybe a run to Vegas or a side trip to Atlantic City, and all very hush-hush with bodyguards beside them and damn near a midnight military approach to a hotel they probably own."

"How did Pell do it?"

Mako glanced down at her, reading the expression on her face. "You don't believe all this, do you?"

"You're describing a world I've never been part of."

Hooker took a deep breath of the fresh sea air. For a few seconds they watched the activity in the water below, listening to the delicate splashes as a predator snapped up a surface meal, flipping its tail in a dive.

"You've been part of it, Judy. At least you were on the fringes of it."

"Are you telling me Daddy was inside things like that?" Her loyalty to her father was showing in her face and she let her fingers fall away from his forearm.

"I don't think your dad knew anything of what was *really* going on."

"Mako, he was a brilliant businessman!"

"In his own field, yes."

"If Anthony Pell was doing anything illegal he would have known about it!"

"That's the point. Pell *wasn't* doing anything illegal. He was working the best kind of con game of all . . . one where everybody made a pile, business expanded and the future looked great from every angle."

"Then what's the catch?"

"Someplace along the line *somebody* was *really* going to hit the big time. Legally."

Hooker felt her fingers go around his arm again, then she asked, "That's the good part?"

"Uh-huh."

"What's the bad part?"

Hooker spit down into the ocean. Even thinking about all this had given him a bad taste in his mouth. "Somebody always has to die," he told her.

It took her the better part of a minute to see what he was driving at. Very quietly, she whispered, "Daddy?"

"He was one."

"Mr. Becker . . . ?"

"Yes. He was another."

Judy clenched her lower lip in her teeth and her face looked drawn.

"Is this . . . just the beginning?" she asked him.

"Things this big just don't happen suddenly. It's a planned operation that was laid out with a lot of thought. There was money to back up every move and it wasn't being done for a minimum return."

"Why, Mako? Why would they go to so much trouble?"

"Simple. It's legitimate. They could get all the money they could ever want without having cops breathing down their necks or knowing the Feds were planting listening devices in their houses or business offices."

"And Anthony Pell is part of it." It was a statement this time.

Hooker nodded again.

"Do you think . . . he'd try to kill you?"

"I *think* he already has." He watched the frown form on her forehead but didn't explain any further. Instead he said, "Don't worry about me, Judy. I've been down that road more than he has and he's not about to catch me off base."

The tone of his voice was too light to please her at all. "What would you do, Mako?"

"You don't want to know, Judy."

"Yes," she insisted, "I really do."

"I'd kill him," he told her.

Down below him Mako saw the sea bathed in the soft glow from the open portholes of empty staterooms. There was no movement of the surface, no fish feeding, just some gentle swells reacting to the pressure of the ocean around the area. For those few moments it seemed placid again, peaceful and quiet with no indication of death and destruction at all. A quiet, empty sea.

Unnaturally quiet.

Judy's eyes had been following his and slowly she pointed her finger to the minor disturbance astern that was angling toward them, the rigid dorsal fin of a large, deadly shark that rolled slightly when he was beneath them, and Mako knew that black eye in the sleek body was staring straight up at him.

"Mako . . . ," she started to say.

"Are you talking to me or to *him*?"

"Do you think . . . could that be the one Billy Bright . . ."

"It's just a fish, Judy."

"But it was a mako shark."

"Yes."

"We were diving in waters with *those* around us!"

"Sharks have a deadlier reputation than they deserve, honey. People are not on their menu. Most attacks are because they were mistaken for something lower on the food chain."

"But Billy thinks . . ."

"Sometimes Billy lets all that beach talk get involved with real life. Do you really think that shark is annoyed because I have his name?"

She looked at him very gravely, then shuddered slightly and grinned. "Maybe I've been in the islands too long," she said to him.

"Maybe."

"But don't take me away from them."

She turned under his arms and her hands came up behind his head. In the semidarkness he saw her mouth glisten, her lips part slowly, then he lowered his mouth to meet hers and they melted together, their bodies tense, each knowing what their emotions were demanding, each realizing that they had walked to the edge of the cliff and there was no way back and they had to jump, not knowing if they would land in the soft snow or on the jagged rocks.

Mako pushed Judy away gently and said, "Careful, lady, be careful."

"I'm trying."

"Try harder." He smiled.

"Why?"

"Because we're still in the middle of some crazy game that can have some pretty damn mean implications, that's why."

"Can we get out of it?"

Mako shook his head. "No way. We're in this to the end and it's not just us. We have a big, silent crowd on our islands who don't know what's happening at all, but if we don't do something to control it, their lifestyles are going to come apart. They own land and they have a government of sorts, but the one thing they don't have is money. They deal in fish and crabs and conchs and spend their wages on nets and engine parts. They're poor as dirt, but happy as hell, and knowingly they wouldn't give up their way of living for anything."

"But what can we do?" Judy asked him.

A few seconds passed, then Mako said, "We stay in the game and win it, kiddo."

Their eyes met, searching the other's thoughts, Judy's asking, Mako already knowing the answer.

Mako said, "You can direct any operation on *Lotusland,* can't you?"

After a moment's hesitation, Judy bobbed her head. "Most likely. There could be objections, but nothing that I couldn't handle."

"Good. That's going to be a major point here."

"But where does *Lotusland* come in?"

"That ship is the Trojan horse."

"I remember the story, but it doesn't fit."

"It will, doll, it will." He ran his fingers through her hair and gave her a squeeze. "Let's go back to the party, okay?"

In the shadows beside the nested forms of two inflatables, Chana Sterling watched them leave. When Lee Colbert took the miniature receiver out of his ear she said, "Anything important?"

Colbert totally disliked surveillance of personnel on his own team and only went along with Chana's idea to keep her quiet. He switched off the microphone disguised as a camera, glad to remember that he had forgotten to drop a tape in to record the conversation. "You want to know what guys whisper in a girl's ear while they're in the dark on the stern of a ship?"

Chana almost snarled. "Forget it!"

Lee wanted to tell her that she never would know, either. But he didn't.

Chapter Fifteen

In the short time they had been on the stern of the ship, something had disrupted the festivities. There was no glaring change in the action that anyone could point to, but Mako felt it and all his senses suddenly became alert. There were four separate groups of men in earnest discussion, a younger man seeming to travel back and forth between them as if passing information. Each group was led by the type they called "elder statesman," and, in fact, two of them had been, in the United States Senate.

Every few minutes a uniformed middle-aged crew member would come out of the passageway and go directly to one of the groups, hand over an envelope, take what was apparently a written receipt, hand it to the bigger man in the blue suit who was accompanying him, then hurry back toward the dark recess of the passageway.

"What's happening?" Hooker asked.

Judy frowned and followed his gaze, then shook her head.

"Something's going on, kid," he told her. "They're having an office meeting."

"Oh, they always do that."

"Do what?"

"Their businesses all seem to interlock and when something happens on the market they hold their committee meetings right here. Apparently it's a pretty good arrangement."

"You see those messengers coming up to them?"

"Yes. They're from the computer room."

"Each one of those guys has a bodyguard and they're packing a pretty big piece under their jackets."

Slowly Judy looked up at him, then said, "How would you know that?"

"Because I'm in the business, baby. How would you know what the big boys over there are doing?"

A tight expression came over her face for a moment. "I've . . . seen it several times. Why, what's wrong with it?"

"Nothing, but I thought these guys were all retired. Hell, they have their millions, what more could they want?"

After a moment's thought, Judy asked flippantly, "Billions?"

Hooker nodded and said, "You may be right, doll."

It was the wind that gave him the answer. From the small gathering to his left he heard the same word twice. It wasn't a new word. It had been in the news for a year and openly debated in public forums for a long time, but bandying it about here gave it a new meaning. The gentle breeze across the deck had carried the word right to him and he said, "Euro currency."

"What?" Judy was staring at him, puzzled.

Hooker pulled Judy away from the passengers, got each one of them a soft drink at the bar, and when they were alone, he told her, "They've gotten some inside information on the European financial market . . . something to do with the new euro currency."

"Would that be important?"

"In the right hands it could be damn important . . . and all the right hands in the business world seem to be aboard your boat, Judy."

"Mako . . . they're on vacation! This is a pleasure trip for them."

"The hell it is. Who authorized a computer room like this on a pleasure ship?"

"Well, that was Marcus Grey's idea. This way the guests can keep up with their business affairs. It was one of his promotional projects."

"Have you seen the equipment?"

"Yes, but . . ."

"Describe it."

"Mako . . . I can't. All I know is . . ."

"That it's state-of-the-art," he finished for her.

"Yes. Very highly specialized. There are no duplicates in the world."

"How many units?"

Mako slipped his hand around her waist and she moved close against him. It gave him a warm feeling and he said, "Let's get out of here. Crowds aren't my thing at all. Can you order up an inflatable to get us over to the *Sentilla*?"

Her smile said it wouldn't be any trouble at all.

But she didn't have to bother. One of the cruise

ship's waiters brought her word that Captain Watts had sent a launch over to pick them up. No, he didn't say what for, but it was an important matter.

Don Watts was waiting at the top of the boarding ladder when they got there. His face was serious when he nodded hello; he escorted them both to the wheelhouse, where they could surround themselves with the darkness of the ocean and the lights of the cruise ship and *Lotusland*. *Tellig* was there too, an even darker smudge on the ocean, her presence not reflecting any light at all.

There was another visitor there too and Hooker grinned at her.

Kim Sebring stood up and shook hands with both of them. "You guys really made them jump in the home office, you know that?"

Judy's eyebrows went up. "Why? We're pretty far from your home base."

"It was a double whammy," Kim said. "Your father was a big money donor to our cause at Woods Hole."

Judy simply shook her head. "My father was interested in anything about the ocean."

When Kim looked at Mako she grinned again. "My boss was in the service with you, Mr. Hooker. He got a medical discharge after the helicopter you two were in got shot down. He was all busted up and you had a piece of tubing stuck in your butt. He hopes you can still sit in a straight chair."

"I'll be damned. Old Bambi Hill. I thought he'd go back to his farm on Long Island."

"He did, but between tourists and traffic he got

run out and the only place he could go where there still was some privacy was the ocean. Woods Hole was a perfect spot for him."

"You two sound like cousins," Captain Watts interrupted. He got everybody seated, passed around cups of fresh coffee and said, "Mako, pursuant to your original problem, I have some new information."

"The eater?"

"Possibly." Watts tilted back in his chair, his fingers laced across his stomach. "We've picked up some radio traffic from boats between Peolle and here. It was pretty frenzied and sometimes garbled, but I have a good guy on the horn who can make sense out of anything. What he heard was all on CB, and friend, we were lucky it carried this far. Those old fishing boats aren't noted for having any sophisticated equipment."

"You're right," Hooker said. "Most likely inexpensive Radio Shack models, good, but old. Everything they have is out of date, including their outboard engines."

"They had two sightings of that *thing* you called the eater."

Judy leaned forward quickly. "What did they say it was?" Her voice had a breathless touch to it.

"They didn't say everything in English."

"Damn!" Hooker exploded.

Captain Watts held up his hand. "Don't sweat it. We recorded the conversation. I contacted Chana on the *Tellig* and they took off for the area immediately."

"Damn, she never let me know!"

"Was she supposed to?"

"This is my call, not hers." Suddenly he shook his head, angry at himself. "No, she did right. It was an emergency action. How long have they been gone?"

"*Tellig* left twenty minutes ago."

Hooker felt his breath ease out slowly in relief. "Send somebody over to the *Clamdip* and get Billy Bright. He'll be able to decipher what they said."

Watts reached for the phone, gave the order and hung up the receiver. "We have a fix on the position of the incident. I suppose you'll want to go there."

"Right. How far is it?"

"You should make it in a couple of hours."

Hooker nodded at Kim Sebring. "Where do you come in?"

Kim leaned on the edge of the desk and said to Hooker, "We finished our little ocean bottom experiment. It was very interesting."

Mako frowned, wondering what she was getting at.

"Captain Watts was good enough to contribute some of his findings too," she said. "Neither of us were doing any secret work, but we have both come to some oddball conclusions."

"The face of the earth is changing," Watts put in. "There are plate movements where we never suspected them to be."

"Like the San Andreas Fault?"

"At this point, not so severe. There are *indications*."

"I don't like the way you say that," Mako told him.

"Nothing may happen in our lifetime," Watts said softly.

"Oh boy," Judy whispered, the sense of it getting to her.

Kim leaned forward again, her hands poised to describe what she had found. "There are currents below that weren't there a hundred years ago. Scara Island was clean then, a breeding ground for seabirds."

"How do you know?" Judy asked.

It was Hooker who said, "Old charts. The captains of the old sailing ships did a lot of topographical work too."

Kim nodded in acknowledgment. "We've known a lot about Scara Island, but when we found out that the *Sentilla* was going to do some experimental sounding nearby, we coordinated with the navy to carry out our own investigation too. The navy was glad to cooperate."

"So," Captain Watts said, "why don't we have some more coffee until Mr. Billy Bright comes aboard." He called for the mess boy to bring what was needed and had the radio room deliver up a tape of the CB transmission, and they made small talk until the ship's launch bumped against the ramp of the *Sentilla*.

There was wariness in Billy's eyes when he came aboard. Nobody had briefed him, and until he saw Mako sitting there comfortably with Judy beside him, he was as tensed up as a tight spring. His eyes caught Hooker's and he said, "Sar . . . it is all right?"

Hooker pushed a chair toward him and nodded. "Everything's okay, Billy. We need an interpreter and you're our man."

Billy's face stayed blank.

Mako explained, "The eater's out there again. Our guys are on the CB, but we can't understand what they're saying." He motioned for Billy to sit down and flicked on the tape recorder. Captain Watts turned on another to record Billy Bright's rendition of the radio chatter.

Billy recognized the first voice immediately. "That's Poca . . . and Lule Malli . . . their boat, she got hit again!"

"They sinking, Billy?"

The Carib shook his head. "No, sar . . . the pump, she is holding."

Other voices came in, fainter but frantic. All their heads were turned toward Billy, waiting to see what had happened. Suddenly there was a pitched screaming and the sound of engines suddenly being revved up past the redline almost blanked out the voices. Billy's voice was shaking as he said, "They saw it . . . the eater . . . it was right behind them."

"They get hit again?"

Billy shook his head hard. "No, sar, they got away." He turned and stared at Hooker. "They all saw it, sar. They heard it breathe."

"They describe it?"

The tape had gone quiet. That was description enough. With death so close nobody had time to describe it. It was there. That was enough.

But Billy knew what was happening. "They see another ship to the west and Lule think it be the *Tellig*. They be helping in Poca and Lule, you think?" Suddenly his face wore a dark scowl. "They won't leave them, will they?" he asked anxiously. "Lule and Poca, they be good friends, them."

Judy finished it for him when she got to her feet. "So are we, Billy."

Billy grinned, the relief plain on his face. Hooker said, "We'll take any boat and tow them back. I'll stay in touch on VHF. Channel nineteen okay?"

"No problem," Captain Watts told him. "You need anything?"

"What I need is on the *Lotusland*." He glanced at Judy and said, "You have a handheld camera aboard, haven't you?"

"We have anything you can think of."

"Good. Get the newest digital camera you can! Get the smallest you have and the simplest to operate."

"Can do." She beamed.

"Any weaponry?" Watts asked.

"No, that rocket launcher I got before is enough. I have a few other pieces aboard. Strictly legal in these waters."

"Don't start a war, buddy."

"Hell, it started a long time ago."

"Something eating ships is hardly a war."

Mako grinned at him. "It's a good way to keep one going." He looked over at Kim Sebring and added, "I think Woods Hole will enjoy this expedition."

The *Sentilla*'s launch was the quickest way to get to *Lotusland*, then back to the *Clamdip*. Judy went up the boarding ladder of her company ship and in ten minutes she was back with a canvas bag she lowered over the side before going down herself.

As soon as her feet touched the deck and Hooker steadied her, the engines roared and the launch pulled away, turning sharply behind the stern of the *Lotusland* and heading south to where the *Clamdip* was anchored.

Hooker lowered his mouth to her ear and shouted, "You get everything?"

She nodded brusquely, then shouted back, "Tony Pell was gone, Mako. He had come from the party, got into slickers, and then he and Gary left in the big inflatable. They had a lot of camera equipment with them."

Mako felt a wave of impatience close over him like a cold fog. He knew what had happened. Somebody on the cruise ship had picked up the frantic call from Poca and Lule and relayed it to Pell. Now there was no way they could get to the area in the *Clamdip* before them. Damn!

The transfer took less than a minute and the launch went back to its mother ship. Billy had the engines going and the anchor raised, and *Clamdip* went into gear, picking up knots until it was at full speed. Every few seconds Hooker would flick on the bow searchlight, scan the water for any floating debris the radar didn't pick up, then cut it off. Ahead, there still were no lights of any other boats.

Billy waved his hand and pointed to the barometer. Mako pulled away from Judy and glanced at it. It had barely gone down a half point, but it had moved. "A good night for the eater, Billy?"

"Only he knows," Billy said. There was no inflection in his voice at all. His hand was tight on the throttles, holding them at maximum revs but ready to cut back if there was any discordant sound from the heavy engine rumbling below.

Mako found his night glasses and fastened them on the sea ahead. He checked his watch one more time, then swept the horizon again. He almost missed it, then came back thirty degrees and stayed focused on one tiny light. In four minutes the light became two and he said, "Steady on, Billy, they're ahead of us."

But Billy was ahead of him, having steered into position before Mako had spoken. With one hand Billy snapped on the CB radio, dialed it to channel sixteen and turned the volume up. Ahead there was the sudden pencil thickness of the beam of a flashlight touching the hull of a sixty-year-old converted sportfisherman that listed to port. Mako picked up the CB microphone and said, "Poca and Lule . . . this is Mako . . . are you all right?"

The reception was scratchy, but a voice came back, "Mr. Hooker, sar, the pumps, she hold good. We not taking water now."

"Good. We'll be alongside in ten minutes and take you in tow. Who's that in the other boat?"

"She be a big rubber one. She got outboard, but not enough engine to tow."

"Who is it?"

The reply came back slowly. "That mister be a bad one. He just sits and waits for something. He don' wanna help none at all."

So it was Pell, all right. Another sudden burst of light came from the strange inflatable illuminating the crippled fishing boat. It played around the hull, taking ghostly night pictures, a lens change probably bringing the anxious faces of the crew into view. When the *Clamdip* was almost in range for clear identification, the inflatable's engine revved up, and the boat spun and darted out of sight. Mako didn't bother trying to pick him up with his own spotlight. He knew what he was going to do, but right now he had to get a towline on the Malli brothers' boat.

When he had completed the lash-up and had the two hulls snuggled together he waved to Billy, and the *Clamdip* went into a low power setting for the trip back to Peolle.

"Is this the way you tow a boat?" Judy asked.

"How would you do it?"

"This way."

"Then why did you ask?"

"Just to see if you knew."

Mako grinned and shook his head. "Dames," he said softly.

Off to starboard he saw a red light and a higher white one. The lights moved, then a green one came into view. It passed to their stern for a mile, then turned again until the boat was running parallel to the *Clamdip*. Judy was frowning at the light until Mako said, "That's the *Tellig* out there."

"What are they doing?"

"Looking for the eater."

"How?"

"They have instrumentation coming out their ears. Go tell Billy to hand you my portable VHF. I want to speak to them."

A minute later she handed him the unit and he pulled up the miniature antennas and punched in channel sixteen. "*Tellig* from *Clamdip*, over."

It was Lee Colbert who came on. "Go ahead, *Clamdip*."

"How come you didn't make contact with the fishing boat, Lee?"

"She wasn't that bad off. We got her on the night-vision glasses . . . the real vision kind, if you remember, and their pumps had the leak in check. Those two guys had gotten something down in that broken plank and didn't seem worried about it."

"Hell no, Lee, those two had all the worry scared out of them. They got hit by the eater."

"That's what they said. You believe that?"

"Damn right, and so do you. What are you looking for out there?"

"The eater," Lee said calmly. "So far there's not a trace of it."

"It's here, pal. It's still out there looking."

"Who is in the inflatable? We picked it up on radar coming from the naval operation. Either he won't answer our VHF transmission or doesn't have a unit aboard."

"Don't sweat him, Lee, we have the fishing boat

tucked in tight and heading for Peolle. We'll probably be getting in around daybreak."

"What happens if you run into our maritime horror?"

"The eater?"

"Roger."

"You'll know it as fast as I do."

There was a pause before Lee transmitted again and said, "You want us to stay with you?"

Mako grinned and thumbed the transmit button. "And spoil Chana's fun? She'd rather wait to scour the wreckage and find what was left of us."

"She isn't *that* bad, Hooker."

"Wait till she puts a bullet in you, pal. Over and out." Hooker fingered the off button and told Judy and Billy, "Keep your eyes open for that inflatable. They'll have a VHF with them and if anything happens they'll be ready to zero in on us."

"Who's 'they,' Mako?"

"Our boy Pell, kid. He's on a money trip now. He's getting film clips of everything that happens for that picture of his and right now he's hanging around for the big bomb, the only shot that will put that movie at the top of the list . . . the eater, seen for the first time, hitting something real, something that can't be faked."

Judy understood what he meant and nodded gravely. "But . . . he'd have to . . . kill it somehow, wouldn't he?"

"Don't worry, he's prepared, all right. He's got Gary Foster with him and they'll have equipment that can knock out any kind of terror."

"Mako . . ."

"What?"

"If the *Tellig* has all that electronic equipment, why haven't they been able to locate it?"

"They're not a ballistic submarine, Judy. Their equipment probably isn't cut out for long-range surveillance underwater. This thing, whatever it is, doesn't follow any patterns. Everything it strikes seems to be a random hit, like a dog attacking intruders inside its own fence. Right now we're on top of a possible feeding site. It took the bait on Poca and Lule's boat and might be hanging around looking for another bite.

"The eater left a history, honey. It comes at you, but it comes slowly and quietly. It's been seen and heard, but it never made a rushing attack. That inflatable would be damn well aware of anything that surfaces, especially if it has a small radar unit aboard." He turned his head and looked at Judy quizzically.

Quietly she said, "*Lotusland* has several on board. They used them at night when they were out among the ice floes in the Arctic shooting documentaries." Her tongue wet her lips in a nervous gesture. "It's Pell for sure, isn't it?"

"Whatever he's doing is legitimate. In a way, he's still working for you. Even not responding to a disabled boat's need isn't a crime. He could have seen that they could make way unassisted and he left when he saw us coming up. We would have been able to offer a lot more help."

"Sar . . ."

"What, Billy?"

"The glass, she has dropped another point."

"Still in the normal range?"

"Yes, sar." At the wheel, Billy glanced around, his eyes probing the open water as far as he could see. His hand rubbed the throttle levers but there was no way he could add extra speed. On the other boat Poca and Lule were shoulder to shoulder, continually searching, continually listening for any sounds that didn't belong. When a manta ray leaped and came crashing down on the water a hundred yards to starboard, everybody jumped, then felt foolish when they realized what it was.

Judy tapped Hooker on the shoulder and said anxiously, "Where's the *Tellig*?"

No light penetrated the night from *Tellig's* last position. The sea was black. Nothing seemed to move against the bank of low-hanging stars. Even Mako's binoculars couldn't pick up anything in their limited scope.

"What's happened, Mako?"

"They're running dark."

"Why?"

"Nothing unusual. Their radar will be making a full sweep." He picked up the VHF and thumbed the send button. "*Tellig*, this is *Clamdip*. Over." There was no answer and he repeated his call once more before hanging up.

Judy waited quietly.

Finally Mako said, "That's a government ship on official business. They don't have to answer anybody unless it's a dire emergency, which this isn't. Hell, they know we're here. They can see us on radar. But believe me, if they were even touched by the eater, we would have heard about it on radio. Nothing's going to close in on them either, not with all the electronics they have on board."

"You sure?"

Mako waited a few seconds before he told her, "Pretty sure."

"That's not good enough."

"Doll, that's about as good as I can do. Here we are, lashed up to a crippled boat, we can turn a slow couple of degrees at a time, got minimum speed at best and are just plain sitting ducks for anything that wants to take a crack at us."

"That's a refreshing thought," she answered. "What can I do?"

"You can get me a beer out of the cooler. Some Miller Lite should still be there."

Mako was pulling the tab on the beer when Billy said, "Sar . . . he's here."

Both Mako and Judy felt the cold chill run down their backs and Billy switched on the portable spotlight. In its brilliant beam the mako shark, even blacker than the water, paced the *Clamdip* twenty feet off the side. It rolled, dove slowly without dipping the full length of its dorsal fin, then rose until its eye was above the surface and Mako knew it was staring straight at him. Then, almost laughingly, it slid below without leaving a trace behind it.

"He be looking for you, sar."

"Billy, there are a lot of mako sharks out there."

"Yes, sar," Billy agreed.

"You see any notches in his tail?"

"No, sar."

"See?"

"He didn't show his tail, sar."

Frustration mixed with annoyance. There was no way he could beat Billy's logic. That was *his* mako shark down there and that blooming fish was looking for him to get this name back. One great bite would settle that argument for all time and there would only be one real mako left.

What was really strange was that Mako knew there was something between him and those jaws. Something was going to be settled for sure sooner or later when brother met brother face-to-face. If he had that mako on the end of a hundred-twenty-pound nylon line, he could win. If they met in the sea with a one-on-one confrontation the result would be one bloody mess of blood and flesh.

His.

Mako said, "Damn!" He shook his head and went back to watching the sea. *Something* was still down there.

Chapter Sixteen

Anybody who lived on Peolle and could be there was there. Somebody had intercepted the faint CB transmission from the Mallis and the word spread like a ground fire. They lined the bank and were spaced down the dockside to help berth the damaged vessel when Hooker and Billy untethered it from the *Clamdip*. The smiles of the people seemed louder than a cheer, but those smiles hid the anxious minutes they had faced before they saw the two boats edging toward home. Now voices were low as they patted their friends, happy to have them back, and in their eyes you could read their thoughts, that a great story would be forthcoming soon, of being hit twice by the eater and still being alive.

Hooker held Judy's hand and nodded toward the crowd. "Remember this, honey," he said. "Put their faces in your mind. Look at Poca and Lule and grab the anticipation in their expressions. They're going to be the big wheels when showtime comes around a campfire."

"I'll never forget it, Mako."

"Then grab your camera and get some quick shots. It's something Pell's never going to see."

The camera lens was the latest technology could offer. The light wouldn't have suited a Hollywood cameraman but was perfect for this scene. Judy panned the area very slowly, pausing for critical actions, taking in the subdued motions of people as they crouched over the planking of the dock to see where the eater had bitten. Each face seemed to mirror a different emotion, bewilderment, consternation and always a suppressed fear of the unknown.

When she had finished, she packed everything in the camera case and passed it to Billy to be stored away. Only then did Hooker see Berger emerge from the back of the crowd and wave to him, indicating that he wanted to see him.

There was no way Charlie Berger was going to set foot on the dock and endanger his outfit, so Hooker said, "Wait here. I'll be back after I see what the fat man wants. And tell the brothers I want to see them both in a half hour."

"You want any more film shot, Mako?"

Hooker grinned at Judy. "Only if it looks good."

On the beach Hooker walked over to Charlie Berger, wondering what the fat man had for him now. He had long been aware of Charlie's knowledgeability and wasn't at all surprised to see his connection with Chana Sterling. He had figured himself to be out of that business now, but "now" hadn't lasted very long at all. He almost had it made, retirement in a lush area, his own boat and suddenly a lovely woman.

And in one shot the meteor had landed on his head and he was back in the jumbled mass of intrigue that kept this old-world system seemingly turned upside down.

Charlie waited until they were out of earshot of anyone and said, "A message came through for you from an Agency Electronics."

How the hell did they locate this channel, Hooker thought.

Berger anticipated his reaction. He said, "The Company works in odd ways."

"Not this odd."

"Apparently whatever you do seems to require an immediate response." He paused and stared at Hooker a moment. "And the Company doesn't need to go into any explanations, either."

"What about this call?"

"You are to contact this caller as soon as possible. They said you'd know how and didn't go into any details."

"Does Chana know about this?"

"I don't think so. The *Tellig* was out at sea and you were en route to Peolle. I'd be their nearest source. I was informed that you could use our facilities if you wished."

"I appreciate it, Charlie, but I'll make out okay."

In the short time he had been gone, a horde of helping hands had gotten the Mallis' boat up on the dolly that ran up the ramp on the old rusted iron railroad tracks. This night they'd have it settled on the beach for inspection and repair, and whatever they found would be part of the folklore of the island. The story would go out, photographs would document the incident, and the bigger magazines would send their teams again to enhance the news that would add to the mystique of Peolle, creating another tourist attraction.

Hooker spit down in the sand, disgusted.

Tomorrow he'd look over the bottom of the boat himself. He'd be able to see what had hit that ancient hull that had a thousand feet of water under it. Briefly, he remembered what Kim Sebring had said about the movements of the plates in the earth below, but had there been an aberration like that it would have shown with an epochal destructive force picked up on every instrument around the world. No, there was no sudden rising of a new mountain from the subterranean belly of the underworld.

Billy stood at the wheel of the *Clamdip*, crossing the placid waters that gave off heat and a smell of a world apart. A round oval of a school of bait fish suddenly erupted on the surface, and out of seemingly nowhere the gulls and other seabirds appeared, descending on the rolling mass, gulping their fill until the bait fish disappeared as quickly as they had come— and the birds left too, squalling their satisfaction.

Judy said softly, "Are we going where I hope we're going?"

"This time you can see how I live."

"I know how you live."

A frown touched Hooker's eyes and he glanced at her.

"Billy told me." She smiled.

"Am I a slob?"

"He said you take many medicines."

"He's wrong. I have them, but I don't take them."

"What are they for?" she asked.

"Painkillers, mainly. They're all legal."

"Do you hurt?"

He let out a small laugh. "Only when it rains. Down here it doesn't rain much."

The way he said it sent a sharp pang of sadness through her body. He was alone, but he wasn't lonely. He would hurt, but he wouldn't complain. He had a shell about him you couldn't see yet knew was there, an invisible armor he didn't want but had to have to protect others from becoming like him. Then she remembered his kiss and the way he had touched her and wondered for a moment if it was she who had the shell about her.

When she was in Mako's quarters she understood Billy's description of him living like a soldier. There were no luxuries. Everything was essential and everything was in its place. The building itself was a renovation of an earlier structure, obviously erected from the timbers and woodwork of old ships that had been storm-wrecked on the shores of the island. A stout wooden barrel under the eaves collected rainwater for an improvised shower while a hand pump brought groundwater up to the kitchen from a hand-driven pipe that went down thirty feet.

While she was on the porch listening to Billy telling her how his boss had successfully improvised to make his area a good base for his operation, she heard Mako rustling around inside, then begin speaking to someone in a muted tone. She motioned to Billy and they both moved out into the sand, watching the *Clamdip* riding alongside the dock.

Inside, Mako said to his old friend, "Man, I thought I had some security here."

"Come on, pal, that's my business too. I was with the Company myself, remember?"

"That was the old days. The Company's changed their tricks."

"The Company's government. I'm business. Regulations don't stand in the way of making a buck, kid, you know that. I still have my contacts too."

Mako let out a short laugh and said, "I should have known. So, what have you got?"

There was the sound of rustling papers on the other end and his buddy said, "I hope you don't want the details of all this . . ."

"I don't."

"Your subject, Anthony Pell, doesn't like to leave tracks. He left his Hollywood address at eight in the morning, and there ended the Anthony Pell identity. At LAX he boarded a plane to Miami—and this is an assumption, understand—using the name Arthur Peters, the same initials. Most likely he had those stamped on his luggage. When he arrived in Miami, a limousine driver picked him up and took him to the Olivera Hotel, a small but very expensive place whose clientele seems to be heads of businesses who like to stay unseen."

"That would be Tony Pallatzo, all right."

"It figures."

"He likes his first-class accommodations," Mako said, "but don't tell me he stayed with the limousine."

This time the voice at the other end chuckled back. "Hell, he went back to his old days on this one, Mako. They have those Rent-A-Wreck car places in Miami too. We checked every one of them before we located the AP initials again. This time it was Alfred Palmer, and like the airline deal, there was a credit card in that name too. We checked the addresses on the credit cards and they were commercial drops you could route mail through to another address. His was a post office box in West Los Angeles. He took a ten-year-old Ford, put thirty-eight miles on the odometer before turning it in again the next day. That one trip was just about all it took to go from the car rental place to the area you designated and back."

"Beautiful, buddy. You did a great job."

"You want confirmation?"

"Look, I got a few other goodies on this guy. He's bad, real bad."

"How many good guys do we know anyway?" Mako asked.

"Not too many, pal," his old friend told him before he broke the connection.

Pell had played it cool, all right, Hooker thought. He wasn't about to trust the job in this country to any underling. This was just too damn big to let anyone get a hold on it. And he would have covered himself with *his* bosses and they would have okayed the deal because Anthony Pell was a totally reformed hood, years from his origins, independently wealthy and absorbed in the big businesses of reputable men. But old Tony Pallatzo had made one big mistake. He had reverted to carrying out a hit in the only way he knew, with all the stupid supposed simplicity of a plain old street hood.

He did have one advantage. When he made the deal with the Becker Bank he must have sensed the possibility of the deal getting quashed before it was consummated. He could have had that strange intuition of the crooked, knowing that the committee of finance was affable, but the headman had a secret reservation about this new client. The mob had their own connections overseas too. Everything was in place and Becker was easy to drop. Even now there would be no uproar because the loan had already been repaid with interest.

"Cute," Mako said to himself. "Very cute."

When he slipped his hand into Judy's she jumped, startled, then squeezed his fingers. "You walk like Billy."

"Like I have sand in my feet?"

"Yes."

"Where'd Billy go?"

"To make up his bed on the *Clamdip*."

"You know, you two are trying to get me into trouble."

"How is that?" Judy asked impishly.

"Because he busted his chops to get us to meet and I'm beginning to think you had a part in planning all that. He did everything he could to keep us together and did it so cleverly that nobody could catch the act going on."

"You . . . don't approve?" she said.

"I wasn't planning on letting Billy go back to the boat."

This time she slipped her arm through his and edged him into a walk along the sandy path. "Aren't we a little big for a chaperone?"

"No. Hell, I don't mean . . ."

"Yes you do," she said, laughing, "and I'm glad you feel that way." His questioning look made her add, "I always wondered what it would be like to be seduced."

"You?" Her words surprised him.

"The thing is, I wouldn't want to be seduced by a seducer."

Mako stopped, let out a grunt and shook his head. "Now what kind of an idea is that? What other kinds are there?"

"Ones like you," she said simply.

"Damn, I'm not going to seduce you!"

"Why not?"

Only for a moment was he angry. It showed in his face very briefly, then his teeth flashed in a tight smile when he saw how neatly he had fallen into the net. In that single instant he reviewed every minute of his life; the door was wide open and he could step through it and be in a place where he really wanted to be.

He said, "Because someplace en route, kid, I went and fell in love with you."

"Is that bad?"

"You answer that," he told her.

"I think it's grand, my Mako man, because I feel the same way."

"But you're still not going to get seduced, kiddo."

"I know," she said. "My time will come."

"Tonight you can sleep in my bed. I'll take the couch."

"You have clean sheets?"

"All soldiers have clean sheets on base."

At first light the people of Peolle had gathered around the Mallis' boat, standing back with a strange awe of fearsome expectations, knowing the eater had touched this hull and left its mark on it. Beneath the keel Lule and Poca were crawling closer to the rent bottom, finally feeling the slash in the thick planking. Nobody spoke. Nobody ventured an opinion. All they could do was look and wait.

Mako told Judy to stay at the edge of the crowd and got under the boat with the two brothers. He didn't remain at arm's length from the gash in the wood; he went right to it, throwing the beam of his flashlight directly on the spot the eater had hit.

He felt a cold chill touch him when he saw the tooth marks. One had gone right through two inches of solid oak, nipping out a gouge a foot and a half long. The other three hadn't penetrated the way the other had, but they tore into the planking a good inch in one raking blow.

But what really chilled him was the shape of the bite, a huge curve of a mighty bite from a creature that was simply nibbling at its victim, rather than satisfying an unnatural hunger.

Mako hadn't noticed that Billy Bright had joined him, his eyes following his hands tracing out the arc of the teeth marks. His face was filled with wonder and curiosity and Mako knew what he was thinking. Before, the teeth marks had been odd or indistinct. The unbelievers could have reason to believe the damage was caused by flotsam that had metal edges that could rip and scar, like what drifted up on Scara Island.

But now here was the proof, not only the destructive rending of the teeth but the deadly, huge semi-circle of its gaping mouth. This incontrovertible proof was not something that would be spoken of yet. None of the islanders would go under the hull for any further inspections. They would accept the tight expressions on the faces of Lule and Poca and watch closely the actions of Billy Bright and Mako Hooker.

As he and Billy were sliding out, Mako saw Judy taking angle shots of the crowd, then coming back to the two of them. Very quickly she handed the Minicam to Mako and he went back under the hull, panned the bottom to show the nature of the damage, then went in for close-ups that showed the oval configuration of the tooth marks. When he finished he snapped the film cartridge out and tucked it inside his shirt.

Poca and Lule were waiting patiently for Mako's judgment call. He said, "That's an expensive hole in your bottom, friends."

"Yes, we can see that," Poca said. "But we have not much money."

"You want it fixed up for free?"

Lule shook his head. "That is impossible, sar. It would have to be replanked . . ."

"I didn't ask *how* it would be done. I just said would you like it done for free?"

"But how . . ."

"Okay, do this," Mako stated. "One of you always stay here. Don't let anybody go under your boat. Don't let anybody take pictures. If you see anybody with a camera sneaking around, you get help and get them the hell out of here. Think you can manage that?"

"And we get our boat fixed for free?"

Mako nodded. "Free."

The brothers grinned at each other, then turned their grins on Mako. "We do that, sar."

"And don't call me 'sar,'" he said.

"Yes, sar," they said together.

On the way to the *Clamdip* Judy asked, "Why keep a guard on their boat?"

Mako took the film pack out of his shirt. "I don't want this duplicated. Together, all these little film clips are going to be parlayed into the biggest scene you've ever come across. When this movie is made it will bury everything on the market."

Judy's brows came together in a grim expression. "That is," she said to him, "if the eater is destroyed."

Billy Bright licked his lips and caught Mako's eyes. "Is it . . . the *Carcharodon megalodon*?"

Billy waited for his answer.

Mako said, "No, Billy, it's not that monstrous great white shark. It's a lot bigger than that."

"How much bigger?"

"Like a barracuda to a bait fish."

"Then nobody can kill it."

"Somebody will have to, Billy."

When they boarded the *Clamdip* and Mako put his film in the concealed safe box, Billy called to him. "Sar," he said, "that movie boat, she is coming in to dock."

Judy went topside to see *Lotusland* tying up at the far end of the government pier. "Now what are they doing here?"

"Anthony Pell wants to make a movie for you, honey. He's following the action."

"Why are you smiling like that?" She was watching him strangely.

"Because one day he's going to catch up with it." His tone was low and had a dangerous edge.

Billy Bright was watching him from a corner of the cabin and for one brief second he saw Mako the way people who died had seen him, a dealer in death itself, the winning hand in every battle, bloodied often but always alive, someone to be avoided, someone terrible. Yet he knew that was exactly what Hooker had given up a long time ago.

But this was another time.

Judy said, "I'm going to meet them when they dock."

"Why?"

"I want to speak to Tony."

"He'll lie."

"I'll know."

Mako shook his head. "No you won't. He's an expert at it. Nobody will know that inflatable was in the water. He'll have every base covered."

"He'll have to get that film developed. That's something he can't do himself."

"No, but he'll stick by the process and get it right out of the machine. Who is there to countermand his orders?"

"I can."

"Hell, you're *here*."

"So?"

"By now he'd have that clip buried somewhere you couldn't find it."

"Mako . . . there aren't that many hiding places on *Lotusland*. There are people there I can trust and believe me, we'll get to it."

He knew there was no use trying to dissuade her. She was in this as deep as he was and she wasn't going to be talked out of making her own judgment calls. He said, "You be damn careful, you hear?"

Judy smiled gently. "I'm a pretty good actress," she said, "among other things."

"What other things?"

"Maybe I'll show you one day."

Billy said, "Sar . . . the *Tellig* ship, she is maybe four miles out. She coming to Peolle too."

"Maybe somebody's giving a party," Mako suggested.

Chana stepped to the dock, her eyes on the *Lotusland* tied up ahead. "What are they doing here?"

"Don't make waves," Lee Colbert told her.

"This is a government-owned docking station, damn it!"

"We lease the facility, Chana."

"And this bunch is legally obligated to enforce its responsibility."

Lee Colbert's voice turned cold when he spun around and accosted Chana. "You know, it's people like you who get us in hot water in these outposts. We're different cultures and even though we have an agreement with them, we're in their backyard and sure as hell we're going to go along with their way of doing things. Nobody's getting hurt here. We both represent American interests and we're going to let them tie up here, you understand that? First come, first served."

"Lee," Chana started harshly.

"Don't say it, lady, or I'll have your tail tied to a whipping post when we get back to the States. You may have some rank, baby, but I have a lot of combat time which you don't and the brass will see it my way!"

The female side of Chana Sterling suddenly emerged with a sweet smile and she said, "Why, of course, Lee. You're right. I certainly didn't mean to disrupt things."

In a low tone, Lee Colbert said, *"Women!"*

But Chana didn't hear him at all. She had just seen the figure of Mako Hooker in the dimming light at the end of the pier. He was finishing a can of beer, then threw the empty in a wire bin and walked in the direction where he had moored the *Clamdip*.

He was her own personal spoiler, she thought. He would come along at exactly the right time to fire a shot across her bow and ruin her well thought out plans completely. He was always bigger, always better. Now he was here and leading the parade again. The Company should have kept him retired. They should have ignored him completely. He was a legend, let him stay one, damn it! With a tight smile of satisfaction she remembered one vivid thing. She had fired a shot across *his* bow once and hers had landed square and punched a hole in him.

Then her tight smile faded as she remembered . . . and she felt like a stupid turd.

She said to Lee, "Why don't you and the crew go and see Charlie Berger. That bartender, Alley, will be glad to hear all the news. I'll do guard duty this time."

Lee wanted to tell her she didn't want to take a chance on running into Hooker again, but he didn't. He agreed curtly and told her, "Sure, the boys could use a few cold ones about now. Just don't forget your side arm."

Before the men left the ship she had checked the clip in the .45 automatic she preferred over the newer issue, dropped it in the holster and fastened the webbed belt around her waist. Then she went out to the bow, pulled up a deck chair and sat down.

Three boats left that night, their owners having no choice but to get to the fishing areas where the *mulako* would be gathered over the high rise in the bottom. There they would stay for the week of the full moon, then disperse to another quadrant of the ocean man hadn't discovered yet. But for this one week the *mulako* would offer up a season's supply of food that was nutritious, plentiful and easy to take. The natives of the islands had depended on this dietary staple for generations, ignoring weather conditions or total reliability of their boats.

Now the eater was the enemy.

They drew lots to see who would crew the three largest boats and those chosen went without complaint, but dread made their insides loose. The attack on the Mallis' boats was positive evidence that a wild menace was still at loose, unharnessed, deadly . . . and waiting.

At sunset they were waved away from the beach, starting a full night's sail to the *mulako*'s feeding grounds by dawn. For six hours they would run their nets, then pick up a compass heading back to Peolle. This time they wouldn't joke or laugh because, if they had gotten this far, they knew they might actually go all the way and be home safely. So they would watch the surface for any break, fearfully alert to any sign of an unnatural presence, aware that the lives of a whole island depended on them.

Without knowing it, all three boats passed directly over the bulk of the eater. They had no fish finders aboard so they never knew that death was only a hundred fifty feet below their keels. But at this time nothing disturbed that menace. After the boats had passed, it lifted its ugly snout a brief moment, rose gently until it was barely beneath the surface, then placidly settled down to its previous depth.

This night there was no celebration on the beach. Quietly the crowd drifted back to their small houses to wait, every person uncertain but hoping for the best.

The crew of the *Tellig* made a small group at the bar, sipping at their beers, listening to Alley's jokes and avoiding any talk of the eater. They were military personnel and they didn't accept unrealistic theories about the eater. If it even existed, it could be eliminated.

At nine-fifteen, Mako came in with Charlie Berger and ordered two beers at Charlie's table. Charlie downed the first one in a few gulps and had Alley bring him another. When that was half gone he said to Mako, "Are you making a report on how the Malli boat got hit?"

"I don't know how it happened, Charlie. I told you about the pierced planking. Why don't you go look for yourself?"

"I won't fit under there, you know that."

"So don't say anything."

"Why not?"

"Because it isn't over. If a report has to go through, let Chana send it. If something has to come down on somebody, let her be the target."

"Target? You know where she is right now?"

Hooker said no.

"She's guarding the *Tellig* while the crew gets a night off."

"Smart dame."

Berger took another pull at his beer and asked, "Where's yours?"

"Who?"

"Come on, Hooker, everybody on the island knows you two have the hots for each other."

"Easy, pal." Hooker's voice was suddenly threatening.

"Sorry, but you know what I mean. No offense."

"She's taking a nap."

"At your place?"

"Where else?" Hooker got up, tired of where the conversation was going, and said good night to the fat man. He got a grunt in return and left the place, waving so long to the bar crowd. Tomorrow he'd give Alley all the details about the night's events and he'd sell more beer to the customers.

He headed south along the beach to where Billy was readying the *Clamdip* for the next day's run. He'd make sure everything was in order, then get back to his digs to check on Judy and make certain the mosquito netting was in place.

When he got to the boat he saw the soft glow of the small light at the wheel, but there was no sound of radio music from Billy's shortwave set. He stopped before going over the side but heard no sounds at all. That wasn't like Billy. Leaving the boat unattended in times like these would be unthinkable to the Carib.

And suddenly Hooker realized that he was tired. He had let his guard down and filled his mind with other thoughts, and before he could make his next move, he felt the cold nose of a gun barrel touch his neck and knew it was being held at arm's length by somebody who knew what he was doing. This guy wasn't leaving room for his victim to spin and hit him.

The stacked pile of crab traps had hidden the waiting figure, and stupidly Hooker had unconsciously walked close. The sand had muffled any footsteps, but the metal of a gun against his skin made everything very real.

The voice behind him said, "Put your hands on your head."

Mako knew who it was. He remembered it from the first time he heard it. The little slob who had planted the bomb on his boat earlier now was planting one on him. Without using any names Hooker said, "Where's Billy?"

Gary Foster said, "You'll see him soon enough." The gun pressed harder against his skin. "Just keep going south. Try anything funny and you die right on the spot. Stay right along the waterline until I tell you to stop."

He was back in the real game now. The guns were out and his run was for keeps. The new dog had just nailed the old mutt but hadn't put his teeth into him yet. This kill was something the young pup was going to savor and he was going to do it right, not letting the big, shaggy mongrel who was stumbling along in front of him get one chance to make a surprise move and capture the fatal edge. There comes a time when old dogs have to die and let the new slashers lead the pack.

In the darkness Gary Foster couldn't read Mako's face at all, but Mako knew that he was thinking. The advantage was all his because he had the gun on Mako's neck. But it was an unnatural stance to take, his forearm stretched out, not realizing that the intended victim was thinking too, and the old dog wasn't new to this situation either. He'd play it cool, not letting Foster generate any sudden hatred and start blasting before he had had his turn at bat.

So he played the intimidated old dog, a little scared and feeling very stupid for letting himself be nailed like this. His feet were hesitant and he let his chest heave as though the exertion was almost too much for him, nearly stopping once, fatigued, until a nudge of the gun barrel urged him forward.

It was a game he didn't like, but it was taking him closer to Billy, wherever that was, and to the final end of things. And there was where it all would really stop.

He saw the inflatable from *Lotusland* before Foster told him to hold it. Another nudge and he was at the side of the boat, and when Gary Foster clicked the switch on the small flashlight he had two seconds to see Billy sprawled on the floor of the boat, his head a bloody mess, swelling his features. For a second he thought Billy was dead, then he saw the tiny bubbles foaming at his mouth and knew he was still alive.

A cold rage came to Mako, but it wasn't blind. It was cool and very calculating. He knew what was coming next, and when Foster told him to put his hands behind his back he didn't wait for the gun to smash him into obedience but put his hands there, his wrists crossed, his head drooping humbly, and felt Foster slap the duct tape around them twice before ripping the tape off the spool.

Gary said, "Get in there," and let the light hit the boat briefly. Mako stepped over the huge bulbous side of the inflatable, caught his toe on the safety rope that ran around the side and fell on his back right across Billy's legs.

He went to shift himself into an upright position and Gary snarled, "You stay there. You're not going to hurt your friend any. Hell, he might even die before we get where we're going."

So Hooker stayed put, exactly where he wanted to be. His hands were out of sight and Foster never knew he had positioned his wrists to give him enough slack to get free without too much trouble. Then Foster stepped past him and sat down beside the outboard engine and by then Mako was loose without anyone knowing about it.

While Foster was starting the big Japanese motor, Mako's hands made a quick exploratory move and touched Billy's ankle. The slob Foster was a typical city-bred foreigner. Billy, like all fishermen, always had a sheath knife on his belt. Foster would have snagged that one away before he clobbered the Carib. But Billy had another one. He kept it on his ankle, a reserve line cutter in case he was dragged over the side by a marlin.

Now Mako had it in his hand.

The big Japanese motor had a soft sound, not like

the roar Americans seemed to relish. Gary Foster sat at the wheel, glancing at the instrument panel until he was set on course. The light was dim, but Mako was beginning to get his night vision back and he could see the gun still in Gary's hand.

Now was when he had to initiate a conversation: Foster would want to brag about the conquest. The world wouldn't ever know of it, but Mako would hear his gloating and that would be enough.

It sounded trite when he said, "Where are you taking us?"

Foster's giggle had a childish quality to it. "Like the man said in the movies, for a long, quiet ride."

Mako brought his knees up as if he were going to stand and Gary waved the gun at him. "Stay put, smart guy. I could shoot you and put all the holes I wanted to in the sides of this boat. This isn't air-filled. It's a rigid baby and everything's packed with flotation."

"They're gonna miss us, Foster."

Again, that giggle. "Man, they're never going to find you. Hell, you think I'm an idiot or something?"

"Why you doing this, anyway?" Mako demanded helplessly.

Gary checked his instruments before answering, then said, "Because me and Pell are gonna be partners, that's why. I missed taking you two out once before, but not this time, buddy, not this time. Now you'll just disappear like smoke."

Underneath Mako Billy let out a low moan and said something in his own language. Foster grunted,

"He sure got a hard head, that one. I thought I had him down for good."

"What've you got against him? He's just a native fisherman."

"He works for you and that's enough."

"You just can't kill us and . . ."

"That's just what I'm going to do. And let me tell you something. I could kill you here and now or let you sweat a little while. It don't matter. The sharks will be waiting when we get there and no parts of you will be floating back to shore."

"What sharks?"

"I got a sealed barrel floating out there loaded with fish guts and blood and an explosive timer. When I touch the detonator button here, that place will be alive with sharks minutes later and you two can have a good swim."

Mako knew Foster was grinning at him. He couldn't see his face, but he knew it and said, "What's so damn funny?"

"I'm trying to think how I'm going to shoot you. I don't want the whole boat all bloody, but you got to be still while I throw you over."

"How're you going to explain the holes in the canvas?"

"Who cares? This hull has a mess of patches on it now. Besides, when it gets back it'll be scuttled."

Under him Billy was moving and Mako heard him groan. "Let me get off this guy."

"Sure," Gary said sneeringly, "but move slow and easy. You're gonna die and damn well know it, but I hold all the cards and you don't want to die too soon. So, play it cool, man, play it cool."

Very easily, Mako squirmed off the form of Billy and heard a sigh of relief bubble through his lips. Then he felt a tap on his leg. Billy had been out, all right, but not out that much, and he didn't want Gary to know it.

Mako turned his head toward Foster. "Throw some water on his face, will you? The guy can hardly breathe."

With a lighthearted grunt Foster picked up a bailing bucket, held it over the side until it was half filled, then tossed the contents into Billy's face. The Carib let out a gasp, spit out some salt water and groaned again. Only Mako knew that groan was a fake.

"Can you do that again for him?"

"Why, what would he care? He won't be around long enough to enjoy it." Then the idea suddenly appealed to him. So he let the Carib know what it was really like to swim with the fishes. He'd have a bullet hole in him first to keep him a little quiet while one of those big gray babies took the first bite.

Once more he dipped the pail over and threw its contents at Billy's face. This time his eyes partially opened. The stars were out, and with the limited light, night vision was sharp and clear, though sharply restricted. A flurry of motion over the surface of the ocean brought a couple dozen flying fish in a frenzied formation passing over the inflatable, and something else touched the bottom; Billy moaned and pushed himself partially erect on his elbows.

"Easy, there, man. You lie down again."

Billy nodded dreamily, took two long breaths of air, turned his head to one side momentarily and flopped down again.

Once more something touched the bottom of the boat. Gary Foster had his feet up on the rail around the small wheel box and never felt it.

From the bottom, Billy Bright said, "You be one lousy piece of crab bait, you."

Gary Foster's teeth clamped together and he looked for something to throw at Billy. He grabbed the pail and reached over the side to scoop it full and smash it into Billy's face, when the sea erupted into a monstrous terror of bulk and teeth that grabbed Foster's arm above the elbow and hauled him over the side; the scream he let out was so brief that it was hardly any sound at all.

Mako stood up, the little knife still in his hand. Billy grinned when Mako slipped it back in the holster on his leg. "Sar . . . what would you do with that small blade?"

"You wouldn't want me to tell you, my friend."

Very seriously Billy said, "Yes, sar, I really would."

Mako nodded. "I would have flipped the blade into his eyeball and he would have died a second later."

"Sar . . . you can . . . throw a knife . . . like that?"

Mako just smiled his answer back and Billy knew.

"Your Mr. Mako Shark got there first, he did."

"What?"

"That was your shark, sar."

"Look . . ."

"Twice, he touched the bottom of the boat, sar. He was telling you he was coming."

"Billy, damn it . . . "

"I could smell he, sar. I saw his tail with the cuts on it."

There was no sense arguing. Mako went and sat down where Gary had been so recently. On the slanted instrument board he saw the detonator and picked it up. If the boat was still on course that barrel should be straight ahead. He touched the detonate button and a full mile ahead the flare of an orange explosion made a small blossom before the darkness closed in again. Now the sharks out there could revel in their soup of blood and guts.

"Your shark, sar. He be happy," Billy told him. Mako waited for the rest of the explanation. "You give him his name back now. For sure you be real brothers like we be. He save you, so he be ver' happy."

Mako let out a little laugh and hoped Billy was right. Then he spun the inflatable around and headed back to Peolle.

Chapter Seventeen

Two hours before sunup, Hooker and Billy paddled the inflatable up to the stern of the *Lotusland*. Nobody heard them. Nobody saw them. Hooker tied off the bowline to the landing platform, then they slipped into the water soundlessly, and without making a single splash they breaststroked their way to the shore. When Hooker was sure the area was totally deserted he stood up, motioning for Billy to follow him. They angled southward, heading for the *Clamdip*, stopping often so that Billy could rest.

The left side of Billy's face was grotesquely swollen and even the salt water couldn't dissolve the clotted blood that tangled his hair. A cut behind one ear was still bleeding and every few minutes Billy would hold up his hand to stop and spit out a crimson mess from his split gums.

"You want to stop here?" Mako asked him.

Billy's head shook adamantly. "No. I be better soon, sar."

"You need a doctor, pal."

"Doctor not on Peolle." He paused and eased himself into a squat. "For a little while we rest, okay?"

"Sure, okay, Billy. Just tell me when you're ready to walk." He dropped to his knees in the sand. He never was able to go into that almost double-jointed squat the natives felt so comfortable in. "Think you want to talk about it now?"

"Yes. I can talk."

"What happened?"

"I was sleeping on the big deck chair. He was very quiet but I heard him and tried to get up." Billy took a deep breath and his face contorted with a fresh pain. "He hit me with something. I was . . . on the deck . . . there was that tape on my mouth and around my feet and hands."

"Where was he, Billy?"

"Below, sar. I heard him . . . tearing things apart. I must have made some sounds because . . . he came up and wanted to know where it was. I made like . . . my head was all dizzy and didn't know what he meant." Once more he paused, wiped the blood from his lips and went on. "Film, sar. He wanted the tape."

"He was going to make a big hit with his boss," Mako muttered.

"I didn't tell, sar," Billy said simply.

"He could have killed you, pal."

Billy nodded gravely. "I think, sar, he tried. He took the fire extinguisher and hit me with it. Twice, I remember. I woke up on the inflatable and he hit me again, with the gun this time."

"He probably thought you were dead then, but he had to get rid of you. And me," Hooker added.

Billy was ready to get up, but before he did he asked Mako, "Sar, were you . . . scared?"

"No, that little pissant didn't scare me. But I was afraid, buddy. I didn't know what had happened to you, and Judy was by herself in my hooch, and I had to play it right down to the wire."

Billy didn't fully understand, but he got the sense of it. "What do we do now, sar?"

"We let the pot boil."

"What means that?"

"We do nothing for a while and let them sweat. When the time comes, our friend Pell will make his move. He'll have to. He's going to see that tied-up inflatable, wonder what the hell happened to Gary Foster and what Marcus Grey and Judy will do, but most of all he'll be terrified of what his real bosses in the grand offices where the money mob do their business now will say. He'll go right on their hit list for sure."

"Sar . . . but in between . . ."

"He has to dump me, Billy. I don't want anything from him except his hide. Anything else he can wiggle out of. His bosses will let him off the hook if he comes up with a great money deal, figuring that everybody can hit a foul ball sometimes. He has paperwork and cash to insure his position with the movie company, and if he gets one big show out of this deal he's in the big time."

"Except for you," Billy said.

Mako's teeth showed a brief flash of white in his grin. "Right. Except for me."

With a serious tone Billy said, "Miss Durant . . . she doesn't like these terrible things."

"Billy . . . if I don't reach Pell first, she'll be the next one he'll kill. He can't let her stay alive. She knows too much now and she has enough clout to go after him. Trouble is, what law can she use here in these islands? Even the *Tellig* will be out of here. So will the *Sentilla*."

"Sar . . . *you* are here."

"Sure. And let's say I take Pell out." Mako nodded thoughtfully. "Let's go see Judy. We'll take one of the old boats off the beach. Nobody's going to be leaving here until those fishing rigs get back."

Mako let Billy rest while he recovered the film from the *Clamdip*. He stowed the canisters in large self-sealing sandwich bags, dropped them into a larger white garbage bag and headed back down the beach.

A hundred yards down the curved dunes, four dories were upside down. They lifted the first two up and found only paddles, but under the third was another antique Johnson outboard. Billy assured him that it was very reliable, old Mogo kept it in good shape and even had a two-and-a-half-gallon can of gasoline stashed there too.

The craft was light and they dragged it down to the water. Mako carried the engine down, filled up the small tank and stowed the can in the bow. They pushed off, paddled out a quarter of a mile, then Mako pulled the engine over. It started on the first yank and he headed for his own island a mile away.

Judy had been sleeping with a nervous intensity. Mako had lit a kerosene lamp, and the second the soft light touched her eyes she sat up abruptly, her eyes wide, alert, the cords in her neck stretching tautly.

"It's me," Mako said.

The relief she felt on hearing his voice was evident. She jumped up, the old sweatshirt barely covering her, and threw her arms around his neck. "Oh, I'm glad you're here right now. I don't like to be away from you at all." She threw her head back, looking up at him, then she frowned. "What's happened, Mako?"

"Billy's been hurt," he told her. "He's pretty well banged up, but nothing serious."

"Who did it?"

"One of your crew. Gary Foster."

"Why . . . he's a nobody. He's . . ."

"He's an explosives expert. He tried to plant a bomb on the *Clamdip* after your party and he came damn near killing Billy and me."

"Where is he now?" There was alarm in her voice now.

"He was going to treat us to a burial at sea. That idiot city boy gave himself one instead."

"Does . . . anyone else know about this?" she asked anxiously.

"No. And who will find out? He died accidentally during the commission of a major crime, if it makes anybody's conscience feel better; he invited a shark attack and one of those predators snatched him right over the side. I think he pulled this last stunt on his own. Somehow he had the idea Tony Pell was going to make him a full partner in the movie that's being planned."

"But Tony wouldn't do that!"

"Gary didn't know that. He wanted the film we shot and us out of the way."

"All this trouble for a movie . . . that isn't even written yet?"

"Judy, these key sequences can't be faked. Those faces in the background when they see the teeth marks . . ."

"But you said it all depends on the eater . . . being destroyed. How will that happen?"

Mako's hands were tight on her arms. He said, "I don't know, Judy. Whatever the eater is, it started slow, then made itself known more frequently. It traverses this quadrant of the ocean more than any other and we know it's still out there. Sooner or later it's going to be spotted when we're in a position to hit on it."

"Mako . . . we have no big guns here. No depth charges . . . nothing capable of killing off that creature."

"We'll think of something, kiddo," he said, then tightened his arms around her again. "Now look, I'm going to leave Billy here with you. Get him cleaned up and don't gag at the mess his face is in."

"Where are you going?"

"Back to find Pell. I'll take the dory back and you call your place and have somebody run your small boat over here so you'll have transportation. Billy knows where my equipment is."

"The film . . ."

"I've already stashed it where it'll be safe."

"Mako . . . be careful." Her hands invited his mouth down to meet hers. It was a long kiss, sensuous, not one of good-bye but of anticipation.

Hooker said, "Take good care of Billy," and when she nodded he went back into the night, which was about to lose itself to the faint glow of sunup.

Mako spent the early morning hours cleaning up the *Clamdip*. Foster had pulled open drawers, turned over furniture and had even opened the panel behind the instruments where he had planted the bomb earlier. The security box was too cleverly constructed to be found in a hurried search and Foster had missed that completely. Even the rocket launcher, stored up on the racks that held a half dozen deep-sea trolling poles, had escaped his attention. So did the mini camera that had been shoved aside in the frenzied search for the tape pack.

Tony Pallatzo studied his face in the mirror of the well-appointed bathroom in his quarters aboard the *Lotusland*. He was always pleasantly surprised at how well he had transformed into a reputable businessman in one of the most competitive, lucrative industries in the world. He saw this next film the way Bugsy Siegel saw the Flamingo Hotel opening up Las Vegas, a plum that would drop right into the hands of the Big Men in New York.

Now he was going to do the same thing, but his would be a successful venture, done surreptitiously but legally. The elder Durant was out of the picture now, his daughter only a minor irritant that he could remove the same way he had removed her father if necessary. Luckily she didn't have a great desire to own and run a motion picture company.

He looked at his image and frowned. The only problem was Mako Hooker, and when he thought of him there was a tug at his memory that he couldn't put in its place. The streets of Brooklyn were years away, years he didn't like to remember, and for some reason, when he thought of Hooker he thought of those streets again and the Gallo bunch he had run with.

There was a knock on the door and a cameraman stuck his head in and said, "You seen Gary Foster, Mr. Pell?"

"No. Why should I?"

"Benny said he took the inflatable out last night."

"I didn't authorize that!"

"Well, it didn't get lost. It's tied up alongside, but Gary isn't anyplace around."

"You look in his room?"

"Sure. It's empty."

"Very well," Pell told him, "I'll check it out."

He finished brushing his hair in place, annoyed because that stupid Gary Foster had gotten out of hand again. If he was chasing down one of the island girls he was going to get his behind kicked. Ever since he had recruited him to take Hooker's boat out of action, Foster had been taking too many liberties.

On deck, he went down the ladder to the ramp and looked at the inflatable. Ordinarily, it would have been tethered and cleaned out before anyone left it. Nothing would be in disarray. This time the boat was a lousy mess, nothing in place at all, and what was worse, the floorboard was stained with a brown substance that was drawing flies to its edges. Nobody had to draw him a picture to tell him what it was. Somebody had bled all over the place. Damn that Foster, Pell thought.

There was something else there that shouldn't have been there. It sat on the lip of the small instrument panel. Its placement wasn't accidental. Somebody had put it there to be seen. This time Pell stepped into the boat, looked up to see if anyone was at the rail and when it was all clear, he picked up the small black box and knew immediately what it was. The ignite button was still down and he realized that the detonator had been triggered. Something had been blown to hell. Pretty soon Gary Foster was going to join whatever it was.

He got one of the hands to come down with a hose and soap to clean up the inflatable. He told him somebody went fishing and let the catch bleed all over the floor. It was logical. The guy got busy with the hose and brush.

Then Pell went looking for Gary Foster.

On the deck he stopped and wiped the beads of perspiration from his upper lip. It wasn't hot enough to sweat yet and this bothered him. He was getting that anxious feeling again and he wished he had a gun in his hand, because he sensed some noiseless thing was stalking him and he felt an odd rumbling in his bowels. He went back to his room and took out his .38 revolver, made sure the chambers were full and screwed the silencer on the barrel so that all he had to do was thumb the hammer back. He tucked it in his belt and buttoned his jacket over it.

This time he made a thorough search of the ship, starting from the hold, working his way upward. A couple of crew members gave him a curious glance, but he was the boss and had a right to go wherever he wanted to on board. When he reached the upper level the radio operator came out of his cramped quarters, saw Pell and stopped short.

"This just came in, Mr. Pell. Message from the cruise ship." He handed Pell a typewritten form. It was from Marcus Grey. All it said was that they were leaving within the hour at the suggestion of the passengers.

Pell nodded, said there was no answer and crumpled the message into a ball and tossed it over the side. Suggestion of the passengers, he thought. Weren't cruise ships regulated better than that? They weren't on a deep-sea fishing trip. Idly, he speculated on whether the government could use this peculiarity to put a dent in their intended operations. Let the lawyers figure it out, he reasoned, and went on with his attempt to locate Gary Foster.

Behind the *Lotusland* Chana Sterling leaned against the side of the pilothouse and steadied her binoculars on the ship tied up ahead of them. Something was not right up there. She had seen Pell come on the deck and stare at the inflatable tied up below, and she watched the consternation on his face as he scrutinized the area hidden from her by the inflatable's bilious sides, then saw the deckhand go down to scrub it out. Twice Pell had peered over the deck rail to make sure the job was being done thoroughly, then continued his stalking routine, lifting the canvas covers off the two lifeboats to inspect what was there.

When he turned, not realizing he was being seen through high-powered glasses, Chana got a full view of his face. Anthony Pell was in a violent but subdued rage. Tiny muscles in his neck stood out, his jaw was clenched and his eyes mirrored some powerful emotion churning behind them. He unbuttoned his jacket and reached into his back pocket for a handkerchief to wipe off his face, and she saw the butt of the pistol stuck in his belt. He spun around, opened a door and disappeared inside.

Something is going to happen, Chana thought. Things were building up. There was nervousness dancing around everything now and she couldn't quite fathom it all.

"Hell," she said aloud, but to herself, "that's an emotional reaction and this is a military exercise. Knock it off, girl." She put the glasses back in their case and little by little that combatant expression she always wore came back on her face.

Lee Colbert pushed the door open and came in. "We just got a CB radio call from those fishing boats.

Those *mulako* schools have just been located. Looks like they're going to corner the market on this run."

"Great if you like fish."

"You can get used to it, I guess."

"They're staying out longer than they expected to," he mentioned soberly.

"So they're scared," Chana said. "That eater business has them wetting their pants."

Lee grinned at her remark, made a clucking sound with his tongue and said, "What do you think it is, Chana?"

She turned slowly and gave him a piercing look. "You know what it is, Lee. You *know* you've seen the physical proof of it."

"Proof of what, lady?"

"Those mines, that's what it is! Old, still partially and fully active mines from another generation. Some wound up on Scara Island and others are still almost floating around right under the surface to knock off whatever they touch."

"Then why do we see teeth marks?"

"Baloney, that's what you can do with your teeth marks."

Lee grinned and shook his head. It was rare to see confusion get the better of Chana and he was enjoying the moment. He said, "They're staying until their holds are full. They expect to start back at dusk."

"I hope they don't want an escort."

"These people are pretty damn independent."

"They're pretty shook up too."

"I can't blame them. They've had enough trouble

so far. Right now a year's supply of chow is riding on this fishing trip."

"Come on, Lee, this place is loaded with seafood. They go fishing every day here. They're always having beach parties with shellfish and crabs and everything we consider delicacies."

"You'd like ice cream for every meal?"

"Don't be silly. You know what I mean."

Lee waited a moment before he said, "Chana, these fish are staples. It's a main course item. They're items they need, not want. Quit knocking their lifestyle because they're not devoted to steak and eggs."

Chana stifled her annoyance by saying, "That cruise ship has pulled out."

"Smart," Lee answered, "they're getting out of the eater's waters."

Chana said something very unmilitary under her breath and was glad when Lee went back outside. She picked up her glasses again. Pell wasn't in sight, but she saw the natives begin to drift back to the dock area. They had hours to wait before the fishing boats returned, but they had to be here, patiently waiting and hoping that nothing would happen, that the eater would be moving in faraway currents, maybe champing at sargassum or manta rays or those things that made the monstrous splashes in the night.

The three fishing boats out of Peolle were well within sight of each other. The *mulako* schools were like balls of flashing lights, packed closely together in one twenty-foot rolling mass in constant motion, a single living entity big enough to deceive predators into thinking it was too dangerous to attack. The fishermen knew this prey was actually made up of much smaller fish constantly swimming to get to the center of the ball, only to be spun out to the outside of the ball again. Nature had this strange way of protecting its own, but the *mulako* were defenseless against man's determination.

While every man of the crew worked at the netting and the loading, everyone constantly searched the ocean for the real enemy, the one that could eat boats. None of them knew what to look for or what to expect, but they knew it could be silent and wouldn't smell until it was right on them, and by then it would be too late. But it was still daylight and the eater liked to eat at night, and by nightfall they would be under way back to Peolle, where they would be safe.

Willie Pender had volunteered to captain the biggest of the three boats. He had already survived an encounter with the eater and the men wanted to stay with someone smart enough to outwit and almost snag this *thing* that had been terrorizing them. Manning the net hoist, Willie wasn't as certain that he had luck riding with him at all. He knew the eater for the killer that it was, but was glad the others felt more at ease with him leading the way. Nevertheless, even he kept his eyes peeled. His head was constantly in motion, searching for any disturbance at all, any sign of the enemy's presence. The sea was getting flatter with every hour and any motion at all would be very noticeable.

The holds were nearly full and the sun was going down in the west; Willie Pender squinted up at the sky and sniffed several times. He had checked the barometer twice, but it was stuck, and he remembered that this was not his boat and the instrument before him was an old one reclaimed from another age-demolished vessel. He tapped it vigorously. The brass needle under the glass jumped to a new position. This one wasn't favorable at all. On the deck he ran up the "quit fishing" flag and pulled in his nets. They were done. He hoped the eater was too.

But the eater wasn't done yet. His somnolence had been disturbed. Something had changed, something unseen yet felt, and it had awakened the eater from inanimate motionless to gentle, mean alertness. It coursed through its mass, striving for the motion this disturbance had instilled. Very gently the sea began to flow around it, giving the eater fresh life, and very gently it began its noiseless trek toward the surface, not hurrying at all.

Judy had taken Billy back to Peolle in her runabout. She got him on the *Clamdip* and set out to find Miss Helen, an elderly native who had some nurse's training long ago during World War II, and who she asked to attend to Billy's face. When she was satisfied that there was nothing broken and no infection had set in, she left Miss Helen with him and walked to the *Lotusland*, gradually quieting herself down as though nothing had happened at all.

Chana had given the crew another night out on the island, preferring to sit in her deck chair and watch the action through her night glasses. Nobody interfered with her, knowing she had odd behavior patterns, and the crew was glad to get time off to mingle with the lusty ladies around a beachside campfire or hit Alley's bar. Beside her was a portable CB radio set to the fishing boats' channel and she had caught the message that the *mulako* boats were homeward-bound. Lee went ashore to spread the news in case the report wasn't received by the few active sets onshore. They were still hours away, but the fact that the three ships were filled with their catch and en route to Peolle was an excuse to light the fires on the beach and sing happy songs in a strange language.

There was no sign of Pell on the *Lotusland*. One of the crew thought he had seen him walking the dockway but it had been too dark to be sure. He told Judy something had been bothering Pell all day. He was furious at everybody and exploded when something annoyed him. He ordered a deckhand to clean out the inflatable to please him and he made the guy do it again before he was satisfied.

Judy thanked the crewman and when he walked off she went to Pell's room. On her key ring was one key that was a master to every compartment on the ship. She opened Pell's door and stepped inside. She had been there often enough and in five minutes was certain there was no place he tried to hide anything. He'd be too smart to secrete something on his own premises anyway, but it was a starting point. One thing she did notice. The drawer in his desk where he kept that gun, the drawer that was always locked, was slightly open and there was no gun in there at all. The slightly oily fleece rag he had had it wrapped in was there, but no gun.

She ignored the private quarters of the other crewmen. Pell would have wanted an area he could have gone to quietly that had total privacy and a good place to hide a few film packs. Everything he shot would have been on tape anyway, so the packs wouldn't be hard to hide at all. For an hour she picked through out-of-the-way places in the ship. She found nothing at all. At the end of the corridor was one last door she had almost ignored. It was a small lavatory for the crew who worked belowdecks. The EMPTY sign was in the slot over the knob and she opened the door. The toilet was a tiny place, but well equipped like that on a passenger plane. She locked herself in and looked over the area. This would be a valuable hiding place. It was in plain sight, simple to service, and there was a slot for a box of facial tissues very few of the crew would use when there was a container for large paper towels next to it. She pulled out the tissue box. It was a quarter empty, but much heavier than it should have been. Down at the bottom was the four-by-seven-and-a-half-inch tape pack that Pell had used to capture the scene of the damaged boat of the Malli brothers, and with the camera equipment he had at his disposal, he probably had great close-ups too.

On the way to the private quarters that were always reserved for her, she went by a half-open door of a small office and smiled at the sound of an old-fashioned manual typewriter going at full speed. She pushed the door open with her forefinger and said, "Hello there. Working late?"

The young guy at the old Smith-Corona glanced up with a lopsided grin, then stood up quickly when he saw who it was. "Miss Durant. I didn't expect, expect . . ."

He was one of the writers who had scripted the last two pictures, and here he was hard at work on another. "No apologies, young man. Why aren't you enjoying yourself on the beach?"

"Gee, Miss Durant, I'm having more fun here. You know what I have?"

"No. What?"

"One hell of a picture, that's what. This thing has everything. Man, the action . . . and what damn suspense. All we need now is that eater thing. It's as exciting trying to write this yarn as it will be to see it on the screen, Miss Durant, that . . . that eater out there had better be something really out of this world. Nothing else will do. It's got to be the monster of monsters but how the hell anybody can capture it I can't figure. Damn, I have just about everything sketched out . . . except that ending." The guy paused and sucked in his breath. "It had better be good."

Where the confidence came from she didn't know, but Judy said, "It will be."

He didn't really believe her, but he smiled anyway. "Maybe I shouldn't mention this, but there's a leading lady in here I modeled after you."

"Hey," she laughed, "you barely know me."

"I don't have to. Hell, I'm a writer, not a biographer."

"Oh?"

"I've even worked in a guy like Mako Hooker."

She felt a blush color her face, but the young guy didn't notice.

"He was some kind of a cop, you know," he told her.

She said "Oh" again, asking an unspoken question.

"Being just a plain old writer makes you pretty observant. That guy has all the earmarks of a pro."

"Who can tell?" Judy shrugged.

"If you get any ideas about the eater, tell me, will you?"

"Can't you dream something up?"

"Not this big, I can't. This one has got to be absolutely wild and totally believable. No outer-space junk. Just something we all might face."

"How about *Carcharodon megalodon*?" Judy suggested.

His eyes went wide open. "The great *great* white shark!" Judy simply nodded, her face bland.

"Damn!" he softly exploded.

"You swear too much," she said, and closed the door.

In her compartment she tucked the tape in the stack of others she had collected, put a sticker on it dated two years ago and left it in plain sight.

Outside she stood on the deck and looked up at the sky. There was no moon out now and the blackness was deep with thousands of star eyes peering out of it. These tiny luminaries would be guiding those fishing boats home and she hoped it would be a fast and safe journey. By now they should be a third of the way to port . . . but that still left a long way to go. Quickly, she turned and went to the radio room and walked in. The operator knew what she wanted before she said it and told her, "Willie Pender called in fifteen minutes ago. Everything's going okay."

But not everything was going okay with Willie Pender. The ocean was flat, calmer than he had ever seen it. The wind was a gentle breeze, not enough to stir up a ripple on the water, yet a slow rolling wave had just lifted his boat up on a rise and slid it down the other side. A lesser one followed, then it was quiet again. On the other two boats he could see the sudden activity. Beams of spotlights reached out over the surface, mingled with Willie's light, but nothing was there at all. None of the boats slowed down, their old engines throbbing along normally. If one were to quit, the other two would race to assist, but their minds would be filled with dread.

What did the big sailors call the thing the ocean just did, Willie thought. Rogue waves. Yes, that was it. He thought again and knew he was wrong. Rogue waves were huge devastating things that suddenly came up out of nowhere and went back to nowhere after tearing up everything in front of them. No, that was just a very *strange* wave. It didn't belong here at all. It had no explanation.

This time he knew *he* was wrong. Everything had to have an explanation, and he didn't even want to *think* about this one.

Anthony Pell suddenly remembered where he had seen Mako Hooker a long time ago. He had seen him slap the crap out of Bull Shultz and handcuff him around a streetlight. He nailed Louie Factor at a distance of a hundred feet with a .45 caliber automatic, then turned the small truck that was carrying six million dollars' worth of cocaine into a blazing inferno when his slugs penetrated the tank and the lethal gasoline poured onto a hot exhaust pipe.

He had dragged Tony Pallatzo out from behind that garbage can where he had been hiding, beat the hell out of him because he was not worth killing, then kicked him in the butt so hard there was still a painful crack in his tailbone.

Mako Hooker hadn't changed any. He was just here, that was all. He was what the writers called a nemesis, a *something* that's out to destroy you. They were back on the streets of Brooklyn again, only this time Tony Pallatzo was Anthony Pell, bigger, stronger, filled with the expertise of killing, and the nemesis was well past his prime. Tony could taste his revenge. It was his time now.

The gun in his belt was new and unused. It had been stolen in shipment from a factory and only had one purpose. It could kill, then be discarded. The piece could rot out at the bottom of the lagoon with all the rest of the junk down there.

All he had to do was find Mako Hooker. That wouldn't be too much trouble. There weren't many places to hide on Peolle Island.

Chapter Eighteen

Charlie Berger was seeing Hooker in a new light now. There was an affinity between them that hadn't been there before and Charlie knew it was because previously he had only known Mako as a retired mainlander. Even new knowledge was speculative, but he had done things that weren't just rumors anymore. And on these islands rumors could be taken with a good deal of fact backing them up. Even the passing asides from Chana and the obvious relationships between professional agency personnel made a lot of sense, and when Hooker had caught him away from his big chair in Alley's bar he silently acknowledged the meeting and stayed off the beaten path and in the shadows to Charlie's cottage.

On the porch Mako handed him a single letter-sized envelope and he put it in his inside pocket without reading it. There were no lights on in the house, so the porch was in almost total blackout. Mako said, "This isn't a will, Charlie. It's just a record of events as I see them. In case I get 'disappeared' or wind up dead, get this to the Company. Bypass Chana and go through emergency channels. I coded it so you won't get chewed out for going around the chain of command."

Berger nodded thoughtfully. "You want me to read it?"

"It makes no difference if I'm dead."

"What about the Durant lady?" The way he said it made Mako understand that he and Judy had been a well-discussed topic among the gossipers.

"I've got to keep her alive," Mako said.

For a few seconds it was quiet, then Charlie said, "It's that bad, huh." It wasn't a question.

"It could be," Mako said.

"What're you going to do?"

"Look for a guy named Tony Pell," Mako said.

"Alley saw him two hours ago. He thought he was looking for somebody too."

"Where?"

"Down by the *Clamdip*. Alley was at a beach party not far off. The light from the bonfire was enough to make him out."

"Come on, Charlie, how would he recognize Pell? He hardly knew him."

"The guy had on city clothes. You know anybody else who wears them around here?"

"No." He frowned at Charlie. "How do *you* know about that?"

"I know about everything. Just like Sydney Greenstreet." He gave a familiar, low, guttural laugh.

"Yeah."

"Be careful," Charlie warned.

"Yeah," Hooker told him, and disappeared into the night.

By accident, Anthony Pell learned that Judy was on the *Lotusland*. The deckhand whom he had made clean up the inflatable almost bumped into him as he came around the corner of a building. He started to blurt out an "excuse me" but Pell cut him off with, "Is everything all right on *Lotusland*?"

There was no anger in his voice at all and the hand gulped with relief and said, "All's fine, sir. Miss Durant, she came back to the ship, but that is all that happened."

"Good," Pell told him pleasantly. "I think I'll go back myself." With that he nodded curtly and strode off. The deckhand made his way into the night just as quickly. Anthony Pell was no mate of his and was better off out of sight and mind.

The bait itself had set the trap, Pell was thinking. Judy was on the *Lotusland* and Mako Hooker wouldn't be far behind her. Whatever they had going for themselves was going to be the end for them both. If he got Hooker alone his death could be concealed easily and quickly. Judy's demise could look very accidental. All sorts of terrible things could happen to anyone careless enough to get too close to whirling propellers and electrical outlets or tangles of wire rope or hemp line.

Chana had gotten restless. She had intercepted Willie Pender's radio call describing the errant wave he had encountered, but there were no follow-ups and no calls for help. Ten minutes later somebody at a CB station on the beach asked if the boats were all right and Willie had said they were. There had been no other strange waves. In her mind Chana was trying to picture what Willie had felt. The wave wasn't big enough to be dangerous, but there was no indication of its origin. What she knew of ocean topography was that some waves could race across the ocean with the speed of an airplane. At some point they would turn into a tsunami, a tidal wave of gigantic proportions. Other waves could be activated, then diminish as they traveled from their propulsive source.

Never, out here, had she ever heard of either kind of wave.

Except now. Except Willie Pender's wave. Whatever initiated that one could have come from a long way off.

She got up, told the sailor in the wheelhouse she was going for a walk and headed for the gangplank. The stars were bright in the sky but didn't illuminate the ground at all. So Chana treaded carefully, passed the *Lotusland* and walked onto the beach. She stood there wondering which way to go.

Anthony Pell didn't do any wondering, though. He saw the silhouettes of the three men walking through the sand. One carried a railroad-style lantern and the other had two empty ice buckets. Between them was Mako Hooker, and none of them had seen Pell. The trio stopped, the two islanders moved off to the icehouse, where the old refrigerator spit out ice cubes when it was working, and Mako headed straight ahead toward Alley's bar.

Pell's feet made no sound at all in the sand and the light was in front of his kill. Behind Hooker he was invisible in the dark. He hastened his pace, careful not to trip over anything and make a sound that would alert his quarry. Out here there would be no witnesses. There would be no sound of him dragging a body to the water's edge until he could get to the inflatable again. It was a nice night for a midnight spin.

Chana didn't have far to go to Alley's bar. At least she'd have Charlie to talk to, to help her shrug off the restless feeling she had. Chana hated premonitions. There was a basis of reality for some of them, some faint knowledge, not enough to draw conclusions but enough to make her expect danger. Something was going on, she could feel it. She knew it.

Up ahead was Alley's bar and walking into its light she saw Mako Hooker. She slowed her walk so that she wouldn't intercept him, then she saw the other figure behind him, walking strangely, with knees bent and arms pointed forward, and at the end of the arms was an elongated outline of an illegal weapon that was about to smash Hooker's head into pieces.

She couldn't yell a warning, she could only do the military thing she had trained so hard for: she snatched her gun from its holster, took a fraction of a second to aim and her finger touched the trigger. The bullet tore into Anthony Pallatzo's skull and knocked him completely off his feet into the sand.

Almost simultaneously Hooker hit the ground, and

Chana thought the assailant had fired too and made his hit. But Hooker had rolled and got to his feet, and swung around, taking in the action that had happened behind him. He saw the body on the ground, then the uniformed figure walked up to it but wasn't looking down at the target. The uniform was looking at him.

"Chana," he muttered incredulously.

"He was just about to kill you," she told him.

"You sure waited until the last second, but thanks. Can I ask you a question?"

"No. I was aiming at him this time. Not you."

"Thanks."

"No trouble."

Chana went to the body and turned the head over with her toe. The gaping wound made him almost unrecognizable. "Anthony Pell," she said. "He doesn't hate you anymore."

"There'll be an inquiry into all this," Hooker suggested.

Chana was seeing her hopes of promotion going right down the drain. She nodded and let out a muttered curse.

"But you're in luck this time, kid."

"How? This guy was a big shot."

"First, you have a reputable witness," Mako said. "Me." He bent down and took the weapon from Pell's flaccid fingers and held it up. "Second, an illegal weapon being used by a felon."

"What!"

"Later I'll give you the rest of the picture. There's

a third part . . . we're both military personnel on active duty and Uncle Sam will take care of this minor disturbance."

"Damn, but you're unscrupulous."

"Realistic, baby. Now let's get back to the *Lotusland*. We need some camera work done. Stills and some taped filming. Move it."

Up ahead the doors of the bar swung open and a small group gathered on the porch. They knew what they had heard and their curiosity had gotten the better part of their trepidation.

Mako heard Alley call out, "Who's that out there?"

"It's me, fireman, Hooker."

"Was that a shot we heard?"

"You'd better believe it."

"Who got it, Mako?"

"Just one of the bad guys pal. You want to take a look?"

It was Judy who brought the cameras down. Her face had paled and her tongue constantly tugged at her lips to keep them wet. There was a strained look on her face and Mako kept his arms around her shoulder to keep her from shaking. She had heard the shot and was immediately overcome with horror for the man she loved so much. She could see him as a deliberate killer, and her relief when she learned the shooter was Chana was like having ice put on a burn. A violent world had never been hers and to view it firsthand was a shock to her.

Lee Colbert made up the official report, then the body was wrapped in a plastic body bag and brought onto the *Tellig*, where it would be delivered for an official inquiry.

Charlie Berger nudged Mako and said, "There's more to this than meets the eye, isn't there?"

"Much more," Mako said.

"Which we probably will never hear about, I imagine."

"Oh, you might get wind of it, Charlie, but I don't think many others will."

"Mind telling me why . . . since we all seem to be in this together?"

"It's got international overtones with very heavy domestic intrigue. Like murder, corruption and all that stuff."

"And all that stuff," Charlie repeated. "Please forget that I ever asked."

It was Alley who grabbed Hooker's arm and said, "Buddy, get on the CB."

Mako almost knew what was wrong. "Those boats get hit?" His voice was low and anxious.

"No, but they got the thing spotted. They just came on the air yelling their heads off."

"You get the message?"

"Not all of it. The set in the bar barely picked it up."

The *Lotusland* was closest and Judy said, "Use the ship's radio, Mako. We can pick up their signal with no trouble."

"Good." They got outside the crowd and raced

down the planked walk. Once aboard Hooker got to the ship's CB unit and sent out a call. He repeated it four times before Willie Pender came on and said, "She is out there! She is right out in front of us!"

"Willie, this is Mako Hooker."

The sound of his voice seemed to calm Willie right down. He said, "Yes, sar, she be right close. I see she myself when she came right out of the sea, sar."

"How far away?"

"I do not know how far. Maybe not far enough. What do we do?"

"What's your fuel supply, Willie?"

There was a silence while Willie checked his gauges, then he said, "We got better than half full."

"Good enough. Now here's what you do. Turn ninety degrees to starboard for fifteen minutes, then pick up a new course directly back to Peolle."

"But . . . the eater . . ."

"It doesn't chase you, Willie. You have to come to it. Right now you can run your way out, so get moving. We have your position and I'm going to take the *Clamdip* out and escort you in. I can have miles under my keel before they can unberth these ships here."

"You're not foolin', Mr. Hooker?"

"No fooling, Willie. Now get moving."

Alley glanced at Judy and frowned, then to Mako he said, "Why are you going out?"

"How does a trapped fireman feel on a flaming rooftop when he sees a ladder and help coming his way?"

Alley's mouth parted in a smile. "He feels great, but you don't have a ladder, buddy. No torpedoes, no depth charges . . ."

"Moral support, pal. And right now they need all of that they can get."

Judy laid her hand on Mako's shoulder. He knew what she was going to ask and he shook his head. "You stay here and look after Billy, Judy. This is a solo trip and I won't have time to look after anybody else. Please . . . do it my way."

Her fingers squeezed her accord and she said, "Right, Mako man."

Chapter Nineteen

Miles away in the west was the mild orange glow of a lightning strike. It was the front line of a weather system, but it wouldn't be reaching Hooker's area until a good twenty-four hours later. The darkness was so complete that only the cold light of the stars indicated which way was up. There was no discernible horizon and no indication of the islands that were just beyond the curvature of the earth.

Automatically Hooker glanced down at his instruments. His compass told him he was right on course and his loran confirmed his position. But something was still not right. There was a knot in his stomach and he could feel a prickly sensation in his skin, and he knew the little hairs on his forearms were sticking straight up.

Crazy, he thought. Mad. He was beginning to know what Billy Bright felt when he was out here at night, and Billy Bright was one smart cookie. He could *sense* things that couldn't be seen and draw conclusions from events that had no meaning at all to anybody else. Like when there were no flying fish around when there should have been.

The surface of the ocean was unnaturally flat and Hooker eased the throttle back to dead slow, then cut the engines off completely. For a minute the only sound was that of the bow edging through the water until the momentum ceased, then there was the total stillness of the night. No slapping of the waves against the hull. No splash of the fish making runs on the surface. There was nothing at all, just a horrible stillness.

Hooker just stood there, fingers tight around the wheel, trying to hear, and he finally realized that there was nothing to listen to. He wanted to yell, not because he feared something, but just to break the unnatural silence. His eyes reached out into the blackness and he wondered just what he was doing, standing unmoving in the middle of a noiseless ocean.

Then he suddenly realized what he was doing. It was what the rest of the sea and its creatures were doing. He was waiting. And he knew that something had been waiting for him too.

Billy had been right. He should have taken his advice. Whatever *it* was, who could face it down? Hell, it ate ships. It owned the damn ocean and wasn't accountable to anybody. No human hand ran it and no living thing chose its destination. Nor its dinner, he thought sarcastically.

Hooker let his hands slide off the wheel and he walked to the stern of the *Clamdip*. The soft gleam of the binnacle light made the polished transom glisten, and when he turned and scanned the blackness around him there was not a single other light to be seen. The field of death had been chosen. The combatants were here. They had been waiting for each other and there was going to be a mighty struggle, and only one would leave this place.

For a long moment Hooker thought about the foreign unreality of it all. It was almost mystic, as if he were in an alien world in which he had no control at all, and for a brief interval of time he almost let his mind go defenseless. Then his training took over and he responded to a noiseless *alert* signal because he sensed something had changed, and that there was a presence he could challenge, engage and possibly beat. Possibly.

He heard the breathing first, a steady, rumbling, bubbling breathing that couldn't be located, seeming to come from all around him. It wasn't loud and it wasn't distant. It was someplace near and it was watching him. Whatever it was, it moved and the hull of the *Clamdip* rolled very gently. Momentarily the breathing stopped, then started again, louder this time.

The eater was coming in closer.

Then Hooker got the smell of it. It had the odor of deep death: vile, disgusting, so nauseating you knew it could be only one thing, the gut-wrenching smell of human decay.

It was closer now and he could hear it. The boat was moving closer to *it*, so *IT* was coming to get him, slowly, silently and invisibly. And for some reason he looked up at the sky and saw that the lower stars had been blanked out by some great shadow that kept rising until it would be crouching over him for the final bite that would wipe any trace of him and the *Clamdip* from existence, and there was nothing that he could do, nothing at all. And then, in that same glow of the binnacle light, he saw its eye, a pale, whitish semiround thing looking down on him, and he backed up, startled, his hand hitting the camera he had left on the seat. And with a blinding beam the flash went off for a fraction of a second and Hooker saw the eater. He saw the teeth. He had looked death right in the eye and laughed!

The weaponry was right beside him. He grabbed the rocket launcher, slammed it into firing mode, turned toward the stern and pulled the trigger. The projectile didn't travel far at all before it slammed into the gigantic bulk of the enemy, tearing through its skin to erupt into an inferno in its guts.

Even before the screaming, wrenching sounds started, Hooker had the mini camera in his hand, its powerful light brightening up the area so the whole world would be able to see the eater dying, hear its wild, bubbling noise, an enormous death rattle, and see its slow roll as the ocean filled its cavernous insides. The eye agonized and twisted out of sight as the death rattle turned into a frightening bellow, and as it appeared, the eater slowly slid back into the depth of the ocean and the stars came back into view again. The *Clamdip* rolled in the water's disturbance, then settled into a proud stance as Hooker looked at his loran, jotted down his position and switched on the engines.

The sea stayed flat until he was two miles from Pe-olle, then a soft chop began slapping at the sides of the *Clamdip*. Billy Bright was waiting at the dock when he berthed. He was happy and laughing, but there was still something on his face that said he had done a lot of worrying about his friend out there, alone with the eater. All his instincts, all his native intuition had told him that this night the eater would be hunting for prey, and all the signs said it would be in the area Hooker would be sailing across.

Billy had to ask. It wasn't like him, but he had to. Quietly he said, "Sar . . . you see she at all?"

"Judy didn't come with me," he told him solemnly.

Annoyance at the flip remark made Billy shake his head. "I mean . . . the *other* she."

Hooker let a slow grin crease his face. It was the kind of grin that was the last thing a lot of enemies had ever seen. Behind it was the memory of the battle and the outcome, and it only lasted a second. Hooker said, "I killed it, Billy."

"Sar . . . !"

"It's dead. I know where it is. We can recover the remains and show it to the world. It did its share of damage but now we'll use it to keep these islands, where nobody can mess them up at all."

"But sar . . . why we get . . . the remains? If you killed it . . ."

"Tonight you'll know why, Billy." Hooker let out a little laugh. "You ought to be waking your buddies up with the good news. They can go night fishing again."

They processed the tape on the *Lotusland* with

only the technician in the lab with Hooker. Two copies were made from the original and Mako kept all three. Despite the unprofessional circumstances, the photography was perfect, clear and sharply in focus, with nothing to distract the viewer from the vividly shocking scene he was watching. The utter blackness made an ideal background for the subject, which looked even blacker, yet the form and shape of that monstrous thing left no uncertainty as to what it was.

Very distinctly Hooker remembered the look on the technician's face while he viewed the tape, the absolute look of horror, the throbbing of the vein in his neck as he saw what was happening and recognized the monstrosity for what it was; then his held-in breath escaped from his chest like a burst balloon and his shock-widened eyes had looked over at Hooker, filled with unbelieving amazement.

The natives believed. Billy Bright had told them, so they believed. Judy believed because Mako had told her and Mako was to be believed. She could see it in his face and knew it was true, even if she didn't know all the facts yet. Alley believed because old firemen and old agents don't lie to each other. Berger believed because Hooker scared the hell out of him somehow and he knew he could do it.

Chana wouldn't let herself believe it at all. Lee Colbert would wait for all the facts before he would decide, but he knew he was going to believe it.

No notice went out where the showing would be, no time announced, but just before the night came the islanders had all arrived and gathered in front of the big building Charlie Berger shared with Alley. A large portable screen from the *Lotusland* had been set up and silent eyes watched it uncertainly. The crew from the *Tellig* sat on the floor with the rest, and when the doors finally closed Mako Hooker took Judy's hand and they both walked up to the screen.

The silence was complete.

Nobody blinked.

Hooker held the thumb activator that would turn on the projector and the audience waited.

He said, "There has been a terror out there in the ocean. It has taken ships and lives and disrupted these islands like nothing ever has before. It was silent, it was unpredictable, and it was deadly. There was nothing specific in its moves . . . it just came and went whenever it wanted to. It seemed haphazard, an enemy whose movements couldn't be determined. Even our technology couldn't locate it." He paused for a long moment, then added, "But everybody knew it was there."

His words generated a gentle rustling from the natives, hoping his next ones would be more comforting. They knew what Hooker had said and what Billy Bright had said, but only when they had seen the death of the eater would they truly believe it.

"Most of you here weren't alive in the year 1914. There was a war on and Germany was running submarines in this area." There was a subtle nodding of heads as a few remembered. "Some were destroyed off Reboka Island, as you know, either sunk by Allied gunfire or scuttled by their crews." Again there was the nodding of heads. Those events were all part of their history.

"One wasn't shelled by our side and it wasn't scuttled," Hooker said. "It went down and sat on the bottom to hide from our destroyers on the surface. Our detecting devices were crude then and nobody was able to locate it. When the enemy ships left and the way was clear, the captain gave orders to surface."

The audience waited. They knew something critical was coming.

"At that time the flotation of submarines was activated by a Kingston valve that allowed water to flood the tanks when the air was compressed back in small cylinders in order to submerge, then blow out the water ballast to fill the tanks with air again to surface."

Hooker let a picture of the operation set in their minds, and when he knew they all had it, he told them, "The valve had jammed. Nothing happened. They sat on that seabed, rationing the air until they were gasping for breath, until they died and that old submarine simply nestled down further in its own grave, the bottom filling in around it, creating a suction effect that was nearly permanent. The U-903 was, for all purposes, almost a dead thing.

Heads bobbed in silent acknowledgment this time.

"*Almost,*" Hooker said.

The heads stopped bobbing and waited.

"Like all dead things, the submarine started to

decay. It wasn't flesh as we are; so many years had to pass before a tiny hole showed in its steel skin. Now oil, its lifeblood, could leak out in tiny little blobs, but with all the oil discharges in the ocean now, nobody noticed those tiny spots with the sheen of oil.

"Oh, that ship was dying, yet it was coming alive too. Time had worked its power on that Kingston valve, and over the years a hardly noticeable leak had taken place there too and the compressed air had seeped out, and bit by bit the pressure had forced the seawater out of the flotation tanks, let the air in so the hull regained its buoyancy. A small, gentle buoyancy that would barely lift a matchstick, but it *was* a buoyancy, a positive effect, and every day it grew a little bit stronger, knowing that when the right time came, the buoyancy would take effect.

"Many years could have passed, or that tiny pinhole of decay could have let in more seawater than the lifting effect could handle, but it was mankind itself that caused the balance to change. Out on station was the naval ship *Sentilla,* engaged in a scientific investigation. When her electronic equipment had a breakdown the personnel resorted to using blasting charges to record echo soundings in the strata below the bottom."

The audience seemed to sense what was coming next. There was no movement, no sound from the crowd, just an intense excitement, one that made them taut with anticipation.

"One by one, the shock effect of those blasts made the bottom tremor. Little by little the suction that held the U-903 in place began to erode away . . . until one day the positive buoyancy inside that steel hull was enough to let her rise slowly, maybe an inch at a time, from that sandy, mucky grave site until it hovered an inch or so above the seafloor like a wounded, baffled fish who has fought himself off a barbed hook, free finally, but in a strange, unknown place.

"We don't know what the water temperature was, nor the air pressure above the surface, but we do know that the balance of the ship was so delicate that it would respond to every change in condition. It had no propulsion, so it would flow where the current took it. Pressure changes could force it to the bottom . . . or allow it to rise slowly, very slowly, causing no disturbance at all until it . . . and some other object met. How many times must it have appeared on the surface and stayed for hours without ever having been seen at all?"

Hooker saw the questioning in their eyes and answered it before they could ask it. "It didn't look for boats to hit. Of all the hundreds of times you were out there, how many times was there a contact? That ocean is big and deep. The old hulk was subject to many variables . . . pressure changes in front of storms, temperature drops, current movements all determined where she could be, and when a ship and that hardened body collided, there was destruction."

Someone from the native audience said, "The teeth. We know it had teeth! Even *you* saw the teeth."

Hooker held up his hand and shook his head. "I saw what you *said* teeth could do." He let his eyes drift over their heads and in the rear of the room he saw the puzzled look on Chana's face. Burger didn't get it either. "This was a World War One submarine. On its bow it had a device naval submarine warfare has long since abandoned. It was called a net cutter, an angled steel support of a row of sharpened tooth-like cutters that could shear metal cables that were slightly underwater, used to snare submarines. Those were your teeth. But whatever they hit, even that slight pressure would sink the hulk down under again to come up somewhere else when the pressures and temperature were just right."

That skeptical voice again. "But it breathed!"

"That small, pitted hole in the bow that decay caused was letting out pressured air. It stopped when the water covered it, then came back when the hole was exposed again."

"Why didn't it sink?"

"Because that Kingston valve was still letting compressed air seep out. The buoyancy was nearly neutral."

There was a new voice now, tinged with a trace of disbelief. "You said . . . you killed it."

Hooker found the person, stared at him a second and grinned. "I did," he told him.

There was more curiosity in the voice this time. He simply said, "How?"

This time Hooker didn't answer. He simply looked over to where Alley was sitting and nodded. Alley reached up and turned off the lights.

It was black again. It was almost like being out on the sea in total darkness. The sudden change from light to darkness made it blacker still, and no matter what they knew or had heard the smell of fear seemed to come into the room. They all were about to see something they had dreaded and even now didn't want to see at all. Yet they had to. They had to see it die, positively, irrevocably die a death that could never arise again to terrorize them. They had to be sure. The air was alive with their tension.

And Mako Hooker pushed the button in his hand and the screen boomed into a blank, silvery flower of nearly blinding light. There was a sharp gasp when nothing was there, but before any mutter of discontent was heard, night came again with the suddenness of a blink, then the form appeared, black against even greater blackness, but the camera light gave it stark substance and depth, an eerie monstrous shape giving birth to itself as it thrust up from the water with deliberate slowness. On its nose the deadly form of the huge teethlike wire cutters made it grimace like an unleashed horror, and as the rattle of its ghastly breath came through the sound system, there was the white streak as the projectile from the rocket launcher tore through the night, blasted a hole in the rust-weakened outer shell, erupted into a great twisted hole of mangled metal and let the ocean in to give it a final and complete burial. The hulk began to heel, and then the eye came into view. Hooker stopped the tape and they saw what it was. The 0 on the conning tower had faded. Only the top part was left, like an arched eyebrow. An encrustation below it gave a pupil-like appearance.

Hooker touched the button again. The sound got wilder, a metallic gurgle as the hulk turned, and as slowly as it had appeared it went down.

The light on the screen went blank and everyone sat in the darkness again. There was no sound for a second, then you heard everybody letting his breath out. To himself Mako smiled. He knew how an audience would react. He didn't need any further proof. He said, "Alley . . . ," and the lights went on.

The hum of conversation was quiet at first while the thrill of satisfaction held the people of Peolle in its grip. It was dead. The eater was dead and it would eat no more. They knew it for what it was, but to all of them it would always be the *eater* and great stories would be wound around it, truth and imagination merging to make wonderful things to tell around nighttime fires, and the name of Mako Hooker would be a living thing in everybody's memory for generations to come.

Now the building was loud with voices. Nobody would be going home until the sun came up, and to one side Billy Bright was trying to be grave about the whole affair, yet he was enjoying the role of hero helper to his boss. He saw Mako grinning at him and shrugged a resignation. Then he was happy too. He saw Judy slip her hand through Mako's arm, and squeeze a little; then Mako lowered his head and kissed her gently.

Billy Bright didn't see them leave, but suddenly they were gone.

The mystery never ends.

The biggest names in crime fiction from Pocket Books.

DENISE HAMILTON
Sugar Skull
With murders marked by intricate
Sugar Skulls, the Mexican Day of the Dead celebration
takes on a horrifying new significance.

MICHAEL MCCLELLAND
Oyster Blues
Shell' em. Shuck' em. Shoot' em.

S.W. HUBBARD
Swallow the Hook
In a small Adirondacks town, a big-time scam can be lethal.

ETHAN BLACK
Dead for Life
A tragic mistake from the past holds the key
to stopping a killer bent on revenge.

ERIN HART
Haunted Ground
The truth never rests in peace…

M.G. KINCAID
Last Seen in Aberdeen
In a Scottish village, murder is just the beginning.

Wherever books are sold.

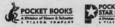